DOCTOR WHO

BLUE BOX

KATE ORMAN

DOCTOR WHO: BLUE BOX

Commissioning Editor: Ben Dunn
Editor & Creative Consultant:
Justin Richards
Project Editor: Sarah Lavelle

Published by BBC Worldwide Ltd
Woodlands, 80 Wood Lane
London W12 0TT

First published 2003

ISBN 0 563 53859 7
Cover imaging by Black Sheep, copyright © BBC 2003

Printed and bound in Great Britain by
Mackays of Chatham
Cover printed by Belmont Press Ltd, Northampton

In memory of Jack Warren Orman ('Papa')
1916–2001

Journalist Chick Peters has written for *Infodump*, *Computers Now!*, *Phreakphest* and *Newstime*. This is his first book. The narrative that follows is based on interviews, reconstructions and Chick's own witnessing of events.

REM

Once upon a time there was a young princess who lived by the seashore. One day she and some of the court's ladies were gathering flowers in a field, when they were approached by a huge bull. It was pure white, from its glittering horns to its tail. At first the young women were badly frightened, but the bull moved so slowly and gently, meandering harmlessly through the many-coloured flowers, that they soon lost their fear.

The princess was charmed by the bull. She held out flowers to him, and he slowly chewed and swallowed them, to everyone's amusement. She made a garland of flowers and laid it over his neck while her friends giggled. He let all of the young women pat his head and stroke his shoulders, but the princess was his favourite.

Finally the bull lay down in the grass amongst the flowers. Laughing, the princess clambered onto his broad back, sitting there as though he was a horse.

In an instant, the bull had leapt up, the princess holding onto him in surprise, trying not to tumble to the ground. The bull began to run, heavy hooves pounding the grass, and then the damp sand as it rushed onto the beach. The princess's friends ran after it, calling out in alarm, but they couldn't catch up with the bolting animal.

The princess cried out as the bull plunged into the ocean, his skin the colour of the foaming surf that surged around him. She was terrified he would drag her beneath the waves. But instead the bull swam in powerful strokes, further and further from the shore, deeper and deeper into the ocean. Soon the shore behind was just a shape, then a line, and then it was lost to her.

All she could do was cling to the neck of the bull, and pray that one day it might take her home again.

10

One

I want to describe the Bainbridge Hospital for you. But they don't let journalists in. In fact, they don't let anybody in. Just the patients, their carers, and sometimes the men in black suits. CIA? Probably, with the headquarters at Langley so close.

All I can describe is what you can see from the outside. Take a trip south from DC, then south-east along I-64; one of those antique Virginia farmhouses in the distance is actually the hospital. Whichever way you approach, you're always separated from the tidy white building by a field of waving crops.

In late 1982, I drove around for a couple of hours trying to find a road that would lead to the building itself. I never found one, not even one barricaded and marked KEEP OUT. In my passenger seat, Sally tried to stay patient as we meandered back and forth, the white building always tantalisingly visible in the distance. At last she said, 'If even a reporter can't find the way in, how do the CIA get there?'

I pulled over into the gravel and shut off the engine. The country silence rang in our ears. 'Maybe they walk in,' I said, exasperated. 'Or maybe they've got underground tunnels.'

'How about helicopters?' said Sally. 'You seen any helicopters?'

I shook my head. But for all I knew, she was right.

Bainbridge was supposed to be where the government kept mental patients who knew too much. A loony bin for spies whose cookies had crumbled under the pressure. Rumour had it they weren't the only patients: defectors recovering from brainwashing, soldiers who'd been dosed with LSD in secret trials, commandos undergoing intensive mental programming to turn them into fearless super-soldiers. And civilians who had, one way or another, been caught up in the hidden machinations that lay under the surface of life in the free world and had been spat back out again.

We got out of the car to stretch our legs. I got my camera bag out of the trunk and pushed a brew into the pocket of my jacket. Sally sat on the bonnet, swinging her legs and reading her romance novel. I screwed the telephoto lens into place and stared through it at the house in the distance.

There were a few people out in the grounds. Without the lens, they were like white dots against the green lawn. Through the lens, I could see they were mostly in wheelchairs, pushed around by uniformed nurses, or parked under trees. I couldn't make out any faces from this distance. The afternoon sunshine was warm: they'd be out there for a little while.

'I wonder how close I can get?' I said. I slung the camera around my neck, and swung my legs over the low wire fence that bounded the cornfield.

'Aren't you gonna ask me to come with you?' said Sally, jumping down from the hood. Her cowboy boots crunched in the gravel. She put her head on one side, feathered blonde hair falling fetchingly around her oval face, and smiled.

'I'm working,' I told her, from the other side of the fence. 'Sorry, Sally. I can't stop to fool around in the corn.'

'Well, what am I supposed to do if someone comes along?'

'Tell 'em the car won't start and your boyfriend went to find a phone. Get a Bud out of the trunk if you want one.'

The rows of corn ran perpendicular to the road. I moved sideways through a few rows, so anyone who did stop to check on Sally wouldn't have a view straight down the row I was in. The ground was warm and a little moist from last night's rain. I wished I was wearing boots; my sneakers were getting covered in mud.

It took about a quarter of an hour to walk to the other side of the cornfield. The cold can kept me company. When I could see I was running out of cover, I ducked down and knelt in the dirt. Now I had a much better view of the patients. A couple of old guys played chess at a little stone table – they didn't have wheelchairs, and neither did a few others I saw walking around on gravel paths or sitting on benches in the sun. The wheelchairs were arranged in a horseshoe under a shady cluster of big oaks.

There. I focussed on one of the faces, a familiar one. A woman in her late thirties. Her platinum blonde hair had been trimmed back severely, like a soldier's haircut. Her eyes were a hot blue. She stared at a spot in the distance. Every so often, as I watched, she would raise her hand to bat away an insect buzzing around her face, but she never took her eyes off that spot.

Let's call her Sarah Swan. Her real name is on the government's files, of course: a casualty in the secret war to keep America safe. Not that Swan is an innocent bystander. But one year ago, she was one of the best-known hackers in the District – hacker in both senses of the word. Swan was not only an accomplished programmer and head of development at an innovative defence contractor. She was also a computer criminal, perpetrator of illicit electronic acts both great and small, respected and even feared by her fellow hackers, crackers, and phreaks.

That was last year. Now Swan sat in a wheelchair and stared at nothing.

After a while I got tired of kneeling in the mud, waiting for

Sarah Swan to do something. I zoomed out a little and looked around. I didn't like what I saw: the nurses had grouped together, talking about something, and a few shot glances off in my direction. Maybe they could see the glint off the camera lens, or maybe I had tripped some hidden sensor in the field. I stuffed the camera back in its bag.

Hurrying back through the corn, I got diagonal glimpses of the car through the rows. Soon I could see there were two cars: mine, and a black-and-white police car.

Shit burgers, I thought. I crouched down in the corn and whipped out the telephoto lens for a better look. Sally sat behind the wheel of my car, looking nervous as hell. There were two troopers, also sitting in their car, parked in front of mine.

I didn't know which way to jump. The troopers had a clear view up and down the road; there was no way I could walk out of the field without being spotted.

I waited in that ditch for an hour. I was sure that eventually they'd get bored, get out of their car, and start searching the cornfield. I was damned if I could think up a good story to tell them. But there was no film in my camera. I kept telling myself that, over and over. I was only using the lens, like it was a telescope. There's no film in the camera, so there's no way they can claim you were spying. It was bullshit, I know, but when you're stuck in a muddy ditch for an hour with your bladder bursting and your girlfriend looking pissed off enough to drive away and leave you there, you need to tell yourself something.

Finally, one of the policemen, a big guy with a big gut, got out and had a few words with Sally. I had no idea what he was saying or how she was reacting. But then Sally started up my car (after a couple of faked failed attempts, bless her) and pulled out onto the road. The cop car followed.

She came back again, alone, about half an hour later, just as I was deciding to get up and try and walk to the nearest town before it got dark. I threw my camera in the back and took over the steering wheel. 'Lemme take you away from all this,' I said, and we headed north, back to DC.

'I did just what you said,' Sally told me. 'I told them my boyfriend had walked up the road to find a phone. They offered to make the call for me, and when I said that it would be OK, they didn't have to, they offered to wait here with me. What was I supposed to do, tell them to get lost?'

'You did fine,' I said. 'You did the right thing.'

'Did you find out what you wanted to?' she said sullenly.

'Oh yeah. Last piece of the puzzle.'

'Well, I just hope they don't come after us. That fat cop was real polite, but his partner kept trying to look down my shirt.'

'Relax,' I told her. 'You weren't doing anything wrong.'

'What about you?'

'Trespassing, maybe. You know,' I said suddenly, 'I think I left a beer can out there in the field.'

Sally said, 'You better hope they can't get your fingerprints off it or something.'

The back of my neck tightened up like a twisted rubber band. She was joking, but actually my fingerprints have been on file since that little incident in Los Angeles in 1978, the reason I moved to the east coast.

We could turn around, try to find the spot where I pulled over, try to find that empty can out at the end of the cornfield. I thought about it, but in the end I just kept driving back into Washington. 'When the book comes out,' I said, 'they'll know all about it anyway.'

Two

The sad story of Sarah Swan ends in a wheelchair somewhere in Virginia. I could start the story in any one of about a dozen places. But let's begin in a kids' theme restaurant on Rockville Pike, Maryland, two days before Christmas 1981. Let's begin with a young lady we'll call Peri Smith.[1]

The right word for Peri is 'petite'. She's short and slender, with dark hair cut in a bob, deep-brown eyes, and a full mouth that curves into an impish smile. That night she was wearing jeans and a burgundy sweater. It's not the image that you get when you think of a computer criminal: the picture in your mind is some socially inept, grody teenage boy, either bloated on Doritos, or pale and skeletal like a forgotten potted plant.

It was Peri's parents who gave her the wanderlust. A mating pair of archaeologists (her mother had divorced and remarried when Peri was ten), they took her with them from one continent to another throughout most of her teenage years. Staying still for her first year of college, in a tidy dorm instead of a cheap hotel or a tent, had felt like being set in concrete. She joined her step-father in the Canary Islands for the summer vacation, looking for a way out. When she met a migratory English hacker-hippie who called himself 'the Doctor', she knew she'd found it.

They had an unusual relationship, these two travellers. For

---

[1] Not her real name

10

one thing, he had never shown a flicker of interest in her. The Doctor was twice Peri's age at least, but he didn't act like a father or an uncle – more like a big brother with a bad case of sibling rivalry. They spent a lot of their time in half-hearted bickering, usually when one of them made some stupid mistake. He burnt dinner, she got lost, he couldn't steer, she got attacked by some animal.

This time it was the Doctor's turn to screw up. They were supposed to be visiting her family, but the Doctor had got them there at the wrong time, messing up her reunion plans. So now she sat in a booth, looking at a cartoon pizza menu and picking over the contents of her plate. It seemed a little weird to be surrounded by familiar language, money and food. A little creepy, even, reminding her of those long months dragging around at college.

They'd had a fight about it, like always. Now the Doctor was off sulking, sitting in another booth and bugging some waiter who had more important things to do than talk to him. She glanced over. The lanky, bald-headed waiter had actually sat down at the table with him.

Usually, the Doctor dressed like a cross between a flower child and a character out of Dickens. For this trip – to stop her father panicking – she'd insisted he wear something more normal. He'd come up with a tailored black suit and a multicoloured tie. His curly yellow hair still stood out a mile.

The next time Peri looked up from her salad, he was gone. So was the waiter he'd been talking to. Peri shrugged and stabbed her fork into a lettuce leaf. He'd get over it eventually, and then they'd get out of this dump and go somewhere interesting.

After half an hour, with her plate long empty and the ice cubes in her Coke melted, she decided she'd better go and look for him. She wandered around the restaurant, dodging uniformed waiters and shrieking kids. There was a big video game section, and against one wall four robot dogs jerkily mimed to the Beatles. She hoped the Doctor hadn't brought her here because he thought she would *like* it.

Peri played a couple of games of Centipede and went back to the booth. It was empty: the dregs of her snack had been removed and the table wiped.

Where was he?

Peri hovered on the sidewalk, trying to pick the Doctor out of the last-minute Christmas crowds running in and out of the cluster of stores bordering the parking lot. She slumped back into the booth inside, clutching her handbag.

Wouldn't this be just the perfect opportunity for him to dump her, so close to home? A theatrical exit like this would be just his style. But on the other hand, what if someone had grabbed him? He was always getting thrown into jail for one thing or another.

What if whoever had got him was waiting to get her, too?

She had the restaurant call her a taxi, and dashed into it the moment it appeared. She had plenty of cash and a couple of credit cards the Doctor had given her. She told the driver to take her to the first hotel she could think of, the Marriott in Bethesda – she'd been there once for an aunt's wedding. The hotel's tourist shop was still open, so she bought some toiletries and an oversized T-shirt that said 'WASHINGTON DC' to wear as a nightshirt.

She took a long shower and collapsed into bed, going over her options in her mind. She could have gone back to their boat, maybe left a message for the Doctor. But she didn't want to lead any bad guys there, and what was worse, she realised she didn't even have a key. What about leaving a message at the theme restaurant? Same problem. What was she supposed to do?

She wasn't sure where in the world her parents were right now. Could she keep on travelling, by herself, until she was ready to go back to college? Were the Doctor's credit cards real or were they fakes? How long would they last? Where was he? Was he OK? Would she ever see him again?

She dozed off around midnight, held tight between clean sheets, exhausted by worry.

Peri has slept well in palace beds and badly in prison cells, and sometimes the other way around. She is a little vague about exactly where she has been with the Doctor. But it's obvious they've travelled the globe many times over, usually off the beaten path, more likely to stay in a hut than the Hilton.

The hardest place she ever slept was on a flat plain of ice in a screaming fifty-mile-an-hour blizzard. She and the Doctor were squeezed into a tube-shaped tent, hoping desperately that the wind didn't rip the fabric; the smallest hole and the whole thing would've torn apart like a punctured kite. What kept Peri awake was not the fear, not the rock-hard ice underneath her, but the jet-engine roar of the wind. The blizzard lasted forty-four pitch-black hours. Crawling out of the half-buried tent, their faces covered by breathing apparatus, was like being born again.

Peri's parents had taught her that you ask for what you want, and you make sure that you get it. In five-star hotels or fleapit boarding houses, they checked their rooms before booking in, making sure the locks and the plumbing were OK and that the linen was clean.

Peri had learnt for herself that you couldn't always get what you want. You might imagine that after surviving the tent in the snow, Peri would never care how soft her mattress was or whether there were clean towels. But instead, it taught her that getting your own way was a precious privilege never to be wasted. She would ask for what she wanted, and she would make sure she got it.

She'd expected something to happen during the night. Maybe the Doctor would track her down and show up at the hotel – she knew he could find her if he wanted to. Or maybe an intruder in her hotel room, come to kidnap her. But when she woke up, there was just the whirr of the air conditioning and pale, snowy light from behind the layers of curtain.

She made herself eat a full hotel breakfast. She had always loved filling in the little forms as a kid, ticking the boxes for toast and juice and eggs. She didn't have much appetite, but experience had taught her that sometimes it could be a long time between meals.

She decided to go look for the Doctor herself.

Peri took a cab to a hairdresser and had her dark bob bleached blonde. She bought a new outfit, black jeans and a grey sweatshirt, and a good black coat. A pair of sunglasses completed her disguise.

The first place to check would be last night's restaurant – the last place she had seen him. She played video games for an hour: Space Invaders, Tempest, Berserk. Real aliens and robots, she thought, would take more to kill than a tap of the fire button.

At last the waiter from last night showed up. He was easy to spot, with his cue-ball head and his sunglasses: the kids stared at him nervously as he took their orders.

Peri ambushed him as he headed for the kitchen. 'Excuse me,' she said. 'I'm looking for my friend, the Doctor. You spoke to him last night, remember?'

The guy looked at her for a moment. They were both wearing shades, reflecting one another's faces. 'Big guy?' she said, holding her hand over her head to give an idea of the

Doctor's height. 'Fair curly hair?' She hoped they weren't having a language problem; her high school Spanish had been a disaster. But that wasn't the problem. He was ignoring her. He actually turned away and was about to walk in the kitchen door when she put herself in his way.

'Excuse me,' she said loudly. 'I'm asking you a question here. Now you can either answer me, or you can get the manager, and maybe he'll have some answers.'

That got his attention. He looked at her over the top of his shades for a moment, and for a second, she could have sworn that his irises sparkled like red glitter.

'I can't help you, Ma'am,' he murmured. 'Ma'am, I think it's up to your friend whether he talks to you. Ma'am, I think you should wait for him to talk to you. Yes? No?'

She couldn't pick out his accent. It was more like he didn't have one. He spoke in a monotone, like the robots from the Berserk game. She tried to interpret the sudden tumble of words. 'I should wait?' she repeated.

'Ma'am, I think you should wait. I can't help you, Ma'am.'

Peri stared at the guy. Was it some kind of message from the Doctor? Or was he just telling her to take off? 'Please, can't you tell me anything else? I'm really worried about him.'

But the guy just looked at her blankly. She got out of his way. He slouched into the kitchen, looking relieved.

Peri ate a couple of slices of pizza and went back to the hotel.

The phone call came at 6 a.m. on Christmas Eve, jolting her out of bed. 'Doctor!' she almost screamed. 'What the hell is going on?!'

'Calm down,' he told her, 'and listen. There's a young man I want you to track down for me. His name is Robert Salmon.' Peri scribbled it down on the hotel stationery. 'He's about fifteen years old, and lives in McLean, Virginia. He's a computer expert.'

'A computer expert? Doctor, where are you? What's this all about?'

'Later, Peri,' he said. 'For now, just find him. Get him to this phone. This planet may be in considerable peril. And I need you to steal something for me. I'll call again.' And he hung up.

Peri put the phone down. She was still shaking a little from the rude awakening. It wasn't unusual for the Doctor to talk about the end of the world. In fact, given some of what she had been through at his side, there was a chance the fate of the human race might really depend on her finding Robert Salmon.

Peri let out a sigh. She wasn't sure what was going on, but she knew there was terrible danger. In other words, things were back to normal.

Three

Peri stood outside the door of the university's systems administrator, reading the Garfield cartoons. She knocked a second time. No answer.

'He's in there,' said a passing student. 'Just kick the door down.'

Peri pushed open the door to discover Bob Salmon stuffed into a sleeping bag underneath his desk, his snores mightily magnified by the cramped confines of the office. The walls were hidden behind shelves of computer manuals, boxes of components and floppy disks, old issues of *Scientific American*, dog-eared printouts, and several partly dismantled Rubik's Cubes. It looked like it was all about to crash down onto the floor at any moment.

Bob woke up when the light from the hallway outside hit his face. He blinked up at her for a moment, then scooted out from under his desk. 'Can I help you?' He wriggled like a caterpillar, trying to get loose from the sleeping bag.

'The Doctor asked me to come see you,' said Peri, watching with dismay as Bob fished his sneakers out of the trash can. The Doctor had told her to look for a teenage kid, but Bob looked like he was maybe twenty. His fine, pale hair stuck out around his face like a halo. He wore a T-shirt printed with the black and white image of a tuxedo, complete with bow tie.

Bob had one foot halfway into a sneaker. 'The Doctor?' he said. 'Are you talking about the tall blond British guy?'

'That's the one,' said Peri, relieved she had got the right man.

They got coffee in plastic cups from a machine in the staff room. Peri sat down on a bright orange sofa in front of a long white coffee table. Bob sat cross-legged on top of the table.

'I haven't seen the Doctor for five years,' he said. 'Did he tell you the story?' Peri shook her head. 'There was a programmer working for the navy who put a trapdoor in his own program, so that he could log on to their computers any time he wanted to. If they had ended up using Professor Xerxes' software, he could have completely taken over their network, or spied on them, or blackmailed the government.'

Peri was finding it a little weird the way Bob avoided eye contact. 'So you and the Doctor stopped him?' she prompted.

'You bet we did. You bet we did.'

'The Doctor said you should come back to my hotel room.' Her ears turned bright red, but Bob was looking around the room. 'We only got into Washington last night, and then he just disappeared. He called me and said to keep you by the phone in the room until he called again. And there was something else.' Bob sucked out the last of the coffee and balled up the cup, an enthusiastic look on his face. 'He said he wants us to steal something.' Bob's head bounced up and down in agreement.

The moment they got back to Peri's hotel room, Bob fell face-first onto the bed and started snoring again. He had brought a huge bag of supplies, ranging from an Atari 400 to a half-empty jar of instant coffee. He'd insisted they stop by a 7-Eleven so he could buy two two-gallon bottles of chocolate milk.

Peri sighed, hung up her coat, squeezed the milk into the hotel fridge and got room service to send up a mushroom and avocado sandwich on rye and a grape soda. She thought of asking Bob if he wanted something to eat. His mouth was slightly open, and he was drooling on the bedcover. She decided he needed his beauty sleep more than he needed his lunch.

Bob Salmon was, obviously, also used to sleeping in odd circumstances. The sleeping bag was a permanent feature of his office, in case a bout of programming stretched into the wee hours and he needed to snatch some shuteye before getting back to the keyboard. Once he had programmed for three days straight, chasing a bug in the university's electronic mail system, turning his monitor from green-on-black to black-on-green so that his burning eyes could go on reading the screen. An alarmed student found him unconscious in the sleeping bag after the marathon session, and almost called an ambulance before the janitor explained it was perfectly normal.

Bob had developed the ability to work for inhumanly long hours while still in high school, so he could study and still have time for computers (or the other way around). His father, a programmer for the military, encouraged his interest but didn't realise just how far it went. More than once Bob had hacked away half the night, and spent the other half cramming for a test.

Programming is not a spectator sport. Bob spent long hours of his teens alone, hunched in front of the monitor in his bedroom. But he also spent hours with his father by his side, thumbing through manuals while Bob hammered away at the keyboard. Mr Salmon was delighted at the prospect of Bob following in his footsteps, and knew it wasn't always the case that teenage boys had something cool to talk about with their fathers. Unusually, his mother would often sit with him as well. Mrs Salmon was no programmer, but she loved puzzles, especially crosswords and chess puzzles. She could often follow the steps Bob took to solve a particular programming problem, despite the arcane tongues of the machines: Unix, VMS, Pascal.

The high school had a TRS-80 connected by phone to a nearby college for a few hours of connect time each week. The keyboard was prone to doubling the letters you typed, producing meaningless syntax errors like NNEW and RUUN. It was Bob who solved the little mystery of why the machine seemed to freeze up altogether when someone inadvertently told the machine to LLIST; the command meant 'line list', BASIC-speak for 'print out my program'. Over at the college, the program got stuck in a lengthy print queue. Bob was able to cancel the unwanted printout and get the machine working again. After that the teachers let him stay back after class and work on the TRS-80.

Mr Salmon indulged his son with as much computer equipment as the family could reasonably afford. He even provided him with a limited dial-up account to his ARPAnet-connected machine at work – on the understanding that Bob would never try to break anything or break in anywhere.

The ARPAnet is the Advanced Research Projects Agency network. College, research, and military computers across the US are connected by this vast network: over two hundred individual computers, all talking to one another, swapping files and electronic 'mail'. ARPAnet has been around since the sixties, but now it's exploding, with another computer joining the network every three weeks. At the current rate, the net will have more than doubled in size by the year 2000.

Bob was the sort of kid who just didn't get into trouble much: the one time he had been sent to the principal's office for talking in class, he actually cried. Nonetheless, the temptation struck Bob many times: alone in the wee hours of the morning, desperately curious about some other machine he could see dangling out there in the imaginary blackness beyond his monitor. But he never dared.

Except once. Bob spent one hot summer at 'computer camp', staying at a college campus with six other whiz kids. Bob soon found himself providing technical support to the guys who ran the college machines. It was like high school all over again, but this time the teachers knew almost as much as he did.

The day before Bob went home, he broke into the account used by the sysops for most of their test work. A file was displayed every time someone logged in to the test account, showing the home phone numbers of the technical team. Bob located the file and quietly added his own name and phone number to the end of the list.

The sysadmins noticed the addition right away, and amusedly gave Bob a call at home to see if he could fix a bug that was troubling their system. He did it in less than an hour. 'But please, please don't tell my dad,' he pleaded.

A couple of weeks later Bob's father asked him for a very serious piece of help: locating a trapdoor maliciously planted in the software he was helping to develop. That was when Bob met the Doctor.

The phone rang. Bob fell off the bed. Peri snatched up the receiver. 'Doctor?'

'Were you able to locate young Mr Salmon?' said the Doctor.

'He's not so young any more,' retorted Peri, but Bob was already begging for the phone.

'Hey, Doctor?' he said, cradling the receiver in both hands. His face split into an excited grin. 'It's me. Uh-huh. I did get into college. But I spent so much time working in the compute centre that they made me sysop, so I'm taking a year off my studies. How about you? Uh-huh. Uh-huh.' Suddenly, he froze. 'You want us to do what?' There was a long pause while he listened. 'Are you sure about this? OK. OK.' He grabbed a pen.

Peri pushed the hotel stationery across the desk towards him, but he was already writing something on his skinny arm. 'OK. Talk to you later.'

Peri was reaching for the receiver when Bob hung it up. 'He did not want to stay on the line,' he said.

'Well, what did he tell you?'

'He wants us to find a computer component so we can steal it,' said Bob. 'You won't believe where he wants us to steal it from.'

'Where?' said Peri. 'The Russian Embassy? The Iranian Embassy? Do we even have those? NASA?'

'TLA²,' said Bob, in a hushed voice. 'He wants us to go to the TLA building and steal something from Sarah Swan.'

---

² Not its real acronym

Four

Sarah Swan's first love wasn't computers, but telephones. Her first ever phone crime was tapping her parents' line, using a broken-down old tape-deck and a pair of earphones. A dedicated 'phone phreak' by the age of twelve, she built her own blue box from scratch out of Radio Shack components: a palm-sized brick of black plastic studded with buttons, it generated tones which fooled the phone system into giving her free long-distance calls. She traded tips and technology with other phreaks, mostly blind teenagers she spoke to over improvised party lines.

Fishing in a telco trash can for phone system manuals, a teenage Sarah came across a list of phone numbers for the company's computers. With a few hints from her sightless friends, she broke in and looked up her own home number. She discovered she could trim back her phone bill, add services to her home phone, change her number, give herself an unlisted number – anything the telco could do, she could do. And if she could change her own phone service, why not other people's? Soon she was selling "free" calls to her friends, editing their phone bills for a percentage of the money they saved.

Sarah was gripped by the idea of borrowing the power of a machine that didn't just let you talk to other people – it let you change the way they lived their lives. She found ways into other people's phone records and school records, all from a four-hundred-dollar Altair 8800 in her bedroom. College gave her access to bigger and better computers. Finally, TLA unwittingly let her get her hands not just on a VAX mainframe, but to computers all over the country: as a defence contractor, TLA was eligible for connection to the ARPAnet.

You did not cross Swan. You did not argue with her on the computer bulletin boards where hackers discussed their adventures. You did not flame her on the new-born discussion networks, Usenet and BITnet. Because if you did, Swan would do something to your phone. She might change its listing in Ma Bell's database to a payphone, so that when you tried to make a call from your own living room your phone demanded a quarter. She might forward your home number to her own phone (and heap abuse on your callers), or to the weather recording, or to a pizza parlour. Or maybe she would break into your school's computer and change all your grades to an F. These were not the negative power trips of a mere vandal; Swan's bullying was calculated and precise, tit for tat. Just how many of these horror stories actually happened, and how many were awed speculation about Swan's magical powers, I'm still not sure. But:

A PDP-11 at a certain pharmaceuticals company was wrecked in 1978 by a simple program that created one subdirectory after another until it filled the entire disk drive, forcing every program, every researcher's work to grind to a halt. The wrench in the computer's machinery was a mindlessly simple three-line program – nothing any daring computer criminal would be proud of sneaking onto an enemy system. The punchline was that there was a second program, this one only two lines long, which had been disguised as the system's own "list files" command. When the technical staff tried to find out what had gone wrong with their computer, naturally they tried to list the files, setting off the second bomb. This one filled the computer's RAM, its working memory, with dozens of "background processes", programs all demanding a slice of the computer's memory; and each of those background processes started up more background processes of its own, and each of those...

Swan was widely credited with the attack, supposedly because a juicy job at the company had gone to someone else. I don't know if it was her work, but I was able to confirm that it really happened. Repeated attacks rendered the Unix machine useless for days, costing the company thousands of dollars in lost time. No-one was ever able to prove that Swan was behind anything. She never denied anything. The reputation of power, after all, is power. And in the computer world, no-one can know who you really are; your reputation is all you have.

Bob's car was a pea green '79 Pontiac Grand LeMans. The back seat was buried in junk, mostly books and empty plastic milk bottles. He and Peri sat in the car in a Crystal City parking lot across from the TLA building: a two-storey cube in brushed concrete and grey brick flanked by a public library and a small park. Somewhere inside was the component the Doctor wanted. The first step was to find out exactly where: was there a high-security lab, a top-secret office?

'Couldn't we just break into their computers and find out?' said Peri. 'You're an expert on that, right?'

Bob scrunched down in the driver's seat. 'No,' he said. 'We can forget about hacking their systems. Swan is poison. If we mess with her, we can forget about ever making a phone call again, unless we want to talk to an operator in Djibouti.'

'Reporters,' said Peri. 'We could pretend we're reporters. See if we can get a tour of the place.'

'Not bad,' said Bob. 'But they are not going to let reporters near sensitive technical stuff.'

'I guess you're right.'

'If they were a bigger company, we could bluff our way in as employees. We could make up a couple of fake badges.'

Peri said, 'They've basically got just one really big computer, right?' Bob nodded. 'Well, where do they keep that? Do they keep all their computer stuff in the same place?'

Bob squinted for a moment, and then broke into a grin. 'I have a nice idea,' he said. 'Let's buy the lady a present.'

'Do you do this sort of thing a lot?' said Peri.

'You should have seen what we got up to in '75.'

Peri had made her share of phoney phone calls as a kid. But this was not the same thing. She kept picking up the phone, getting out of breath, and putting it back down again. 'Remember, they don't know where the hell you're calling from,' said Bob. 'They can't see you, they don't know who you are.' Easy for him to say. All he'd done was dial up the college computer and spend fifteen minutes messing around before he unplugged his computer and handed her the receiver.

You've faced a lot worse than this, Peri told herself. But none of her adventures on the road seemed as real right now as ripping off a computer supplies company.

You ask for what you want, and you get it. She punched in the number. 'TLA,' announced a cheerful voice. 'This is Alice speaking.'

'Well hello,' said Peri. 'I'm calling from Gallifrey Computer Supplies. We're new in the area, and we were wondering if you'd be interested in trying out some of our new specials.'

'I'm afraid we already have a contract with a supplier,' said the receptionist smoothly.

'Oh – can I ask who that is?' Peri scribbled down the name: Keyworth Computers. 'Well, if you're ever shopping around for great prices, just give us a call.'

She put the phone down, grinning like a teenager on champagne. 'Piece of cake,' said Bob.

But now there was a much more difficult call to make. Peri chewed on her bottom lip while Bob flipped through the White Pages. 'They can't see you,' he reminded her.

'I'm OK,' said Peri, dialling. 'Hi,' she said faintly when a voice answered. She cleared her throat. 'Hi, Trina. This is Alice calling from TLA. We need a Lisp Machine right away. I mean, like five minutes ago.'

She put her hand over the mouthpiece. 'She's checking if they have one,' she hissed. 'What are we gonna do if they don't have one?' Bob just shook his head, waving his hands at the phone. 'Hello? You've got one in stock. Great. Look, can I send one of our technicians over to collect it? It's super urgent. The boss is really riding me on this one.'

Peri broke into a relieved smile. 'Yeah, that's what she's like, all right. I dunno what they do with all this stuff. They're probably playing video games up there.' Bob looked scandalised. 'OK. OK. You can call Robert Link in Projects to confirm the order.' She rattled off a number. 'I'll send a couple of guys over there as soon as you do. Thanks – I mean it. You've saved my life.'

She put the phone down and collapsed in the chair. 'Oh my God,' she said. 'Oh my God oh my God oh my God.'

'I told you,' said Bob. 'If you sound confident and friendly and in a hurry, people will do anything for you.' He stared at the ceiling as he thought out loud. 'Our next problem is making you look like a delivery guy.'

Peri looked at him blankly. 'I need you to help me move that computer,' said Bob. 'And once we get into the TLA building, I'll set it up while you look around. It's the perfect cover.'

'It's not really stealing, is it?' said Peri. 'We're not gonna keep the thing.'

The phone rang. Bob coolly reached over and picked it up. 'TLA,' he said, his voice suddenly, surprisingly deep. 'This is Robert Link, can I help you?'

Peri heard Trina's voice again, this time as a tinny murmur in Bob's ear. 'Yes. Yes, that's right. Can you expedite that for me? Yes. Yes, good. Thank you.' He hung up without saying goodbye.

'What just happened?' said Peri.

'The receptionist at Keyworth Computers called back to double-check the order. I forwarded Robert Link's phone to our phone.' He tapped the plastic of the hotel telephone. 'Now she'll be convinced we're legitimate. Let's get going.'

'Why do I have to dress up like a guy!?' said Peri.

'Oh come on,' said Bob.

'Oh come on, what?'

'A girl like you, delivering heavy computer equipment? No-one will believe that.'

'Well, what are we supposed to do? Stick a moustache on me?' The grin was on Bob's face just long enough for her to notice. 'Oh my God,' Peri said again.

They stuck a moustache on her.

Peri pushed her bleached hair up under a baseball cap and pulled on a pair of red overalls. Luckily for their ruse, her slight figure was convincingly boyish once they'd stuffed a couple of folded pillowslips down her front to pad out her belly. She wiped off her makeup and cut her long nails.

Their first stop was the university, where Bob swapped his car for a van no-one was using at the time. He found a pair of faded lime-green overalls which just about fit him, and added a baseball cap to match Peri's. On their way to the supply company, Bob pulled in at a party store. He emerged with a reddish-blonde stick-on moustache in a plastic bag. Peri attached it and stared at herself in the mirror on the back of her sunshade. With the cap pulled down over her face, she could possibly be mistaken for a teenage boy with unusually clear skin. Wish you could see me now, Doctor, she thought.

She spoke in the deepest, most gravelly voice she could manage. 'How do I sound?' Bob just stared at her. 'You better do the talking,' she said weakly.

It had been an hour since the call to Keyworth Computers. They ran into the lobby, looking panicked, Bob pushing an upright trolley. 'We are in deep trouble,' Bob told Trina. 'The boss wanted this new machine installed an hour ago, and we were out on another call.' Trina asked for the invoice. Smoothly, Bob said, 'Oh, no. Didn't the courier get here before us? I can't believe these guys. Do you mind if I use your phone?'

He spent a minute shouting down the phone at a non-existent secretary. Peri slouched, shoved her hands into her pockets, and kept her gaze on the floor. She could feel the woman's eyes on her. She had a sudden, itching urge to giggle. This was so ridiculous.

'She says she's only just handed it to the courier,' sighed Bob. 'The boss is going to barbecue us.'

Trina had dealt with Swan in person a couple of times; she knew these 'workers' could easily lose their jobs if they didn't keep her happy. 'Listen – if I can get your signature now, I can match it up with the invoice when it gets here.'

'You're sure? That'd be great.' Bob scrawled something illegible at the bottom of a form. Trina handed him their carbon and pointed them to a huge cardboard box.

Peri helped Bob load up the trolley. She could feel her 'belly' slipping inside the overalls, and the fake moustache was itching as though a spider was crawling around under her nose. At any moment, she was certain, the woman would expose them both for the con artists they were.

This was not, in short, her idea of glamorous, high-tech computer crime.

They loaded the new computer into the borrowed van, rolled up at the TLA building, and manhandled their purloined package up to the main doors. Bob tapped on the glass, and the receptionist buzzed them in. A security guard lounged next to the water cooler, leaning on the wall while he talked to the receptionist. Peri looked away from the gun hanging at his hip.

'We've got a work order to install this Lisp box,' Bob explained. 'Can you just sign at the bottom here? Thanks.' He showed her the invoice the Keyworth Computers woman had given them, now attached to a plastic clipboard. 'OK, where do you want it?'

'The compute centre is on the first floor,' said the receptionist. Peri coughed behind her hand, checking that her moustache was still in place.

She helped Bob lug the box to the computer room, both of them following the receptionist, who seemed perfectly comfortable with the whole thing. Thieves were hardly going to roll up and give the company free machines, were they? Peri wondered if they could have left out a step and just arrived with a cardboard box full of bricks. But then, they wouldn't have had the paperwork or the official company logo on the carton.

And then he and Peri were alone in the 'compute centre'.

It was quiet and noisy at the same time, full of the hum of air conditioning, and cold enough to make the tiny hairs on Peri's arms prickle. The room was white, spotless, filled with neat rows of big grey boxes.

'I'd better get working,' said Bob. They wheeled the wobbling trolley down a row of machines, until he found one he liked.

'What's gonna happen when someone comes along and discovers this brand-new machine they didn't order?' said Peri.

'We're doing them a favour,' said Bob, extracting an artist's knife from the pocket of his overalls. 'This baby is top of the range. Hi-res graphics display. Stereo sound. A mouse! Who's gonna complain?'

Peri sighed. It was all annoyingly familiar: being dragged into unlikely and hazardous situations by someone with too much confidence and not enough interest in explanations. It must be some Freudian thing she had. Or maybe all the Doctor's friends were like this.

While Bob worked, Peri paced the perimeter of the computer centre, hoping to find a locked door, a NO ENTRY sign, something suggesting secrecy. There was a closet full of big computer tapes in metal canisters, but it wasn't even locked. As she walked along the rows of boxes, Bob appeared and disappeared from her line of sight. From time to time she heard him banging and thumping, or muttering to himself.

The constant noise of the room whited out most sounds: Peri saw, but she didn't hear, the sliding doors swish open. She ducked behind one of the computers.

'What are you doing here?' said the woman's voice crisply. It wasn't the receptionist. Peri had a sinking feeling she knew exactly who it was. She heard a bang and crash as though Bob had dropped something.

'I understood this was an urgent order, ma'am.'

Peri peeked out from her hiding place for a moment. Swan was examining the invoice on the clipboard. This is it, Peri thought, there was never any way we could have got away with this, I'm wearing a fake moustache, for God's sake. She was tempted to rip the thing off right away so at least she wouldn't be arrested in drag.

But Swan didn't seem to find anything wrong with the invoice. She put the clipboard back down on top of the box where Bob had perched it.

And then she watched him set up the Lisp Machine. For the next forty minutes.

Peri thought of hiding behind the nearest door – a closet filled with huge plastic bottles that reeked of noxious chemicals. She decided to stay where she was, crouched behind the tall grey box.

Her mind flashed forward to the consequences: kicked out of college, shot by the security guard, having to tell her parents. Having to keep running forever, never being able to go home. Somehow it was more frightening than ravening carnivores or rivers of lava. It was more real.

She could make a break for it. After so long in the Doctor's company, she was an expert at the mad sprint to safety. She could be out that sliding door and out of the building before anyone could stop her. But that would leave Bob to be the fall guy.

'All done, ma'am,' she heard Bob say at last, rather too loudly. Swan replied, but Peri couldn't make out what she was saying. They spoke for a few moments; she got the impression Bob was stalling, not sure where the hell Peri was or what she was going to do. She had no choice but to stay hidden until she saw Bob wheel the empty carton out of the compute centre, a stony-faced Swan at his heels.

She waited five minutes and then sauntered out of the compute centre. She took the stairwell by the lifts down to the basement, and walked out a side door into the parking lot. Bob was waiting in the van across the street, craning his neck, looking for her. She forced herself to stroll across the road instead of bolting.

What she didn't know was:

Sarah Swan stood behind a venetian blind on the second floor of the TLA building, the lens of her camera wedged between two of the slats. She adjusted the zoom. There. The young man was getting into his car – and here came a second overalled figure, apparently out of the TLA building, crossing the street and joining him.

They exchanged a few words, and then took off. Sarah's camera clicked rapidly as she tried to grab an image of their numberplate. Any number would do – a phone number, a social security number. Once Sarah had it, she had your fingerprints. She could find you, find out anything she wanted to know about you.

Sarah waited a few minutes, but the young couple had had a good scare: they wouldn't be back. She went downstairs. 'Back in half an hour, Alice,' she told the receptionist. 'I just have to take some film to the lab.'

20

One

Trina told me all about it at the bar that night. She's an English girl with a fetching lisp and even more fetching hips. We had been dating on and off for a couple of years, ever since I wrote a report on data-diddling by one of Keyworth's employees. 'Hey, Chickpea,' she said on the phone, 'Buy me a couple of drinks to help celebrate not losing my job, and I'll tell you all about it. Could be a good story.'

I'd come to the States five years ago after a magazine job in Sydney went sour. Two years in LA, not so far from home. Then that little incident that sent me running for the east coast. I'd been in Washington DC ever since, and I liked it there.

Washington is a beautiful bad apple, pretty and fresh on the outside, but when you bite into it, rotten at the core. It's a cesspool of poverty, crime, and drugs surrounded by green suburbs in Virginia and Maryland, the two worlds separated by the giant loop of the Beltway. I've seen a grown man nearly panic when a wrong turn took us into a 'bad area' of town. When I first moved into a house in Virginia, my next-door neighbour confided that he kept a shotgun in case – pardon my language – niggers came from the city to steal his stuff.

I prefer the grid of streets at DC's core to the Disneyland of strip malls and bloated houses in the burbs. So did Trina, who had grown up in Cowgate. I fell in love with her the night I saw her wallop a Hell's Angel for making a mess of the bar she was tending. The guy was too dazed and embarrassed to do anything but stumble out to his bike. The next day, Trina applied for the receptionist's job at Keyworth. 'I'm getting too old for this shit,' she told me. She was twenty-two.

We got a couple of steaks and a lot of Fosters and she gave me the story. When the courier didn't arrive, Trina quickly realised something was wrong, and she called TLA to find out what was going on. Swan checked up on the mystery delivery right away – *and* insisted on paying for the delivered and installed equipment. TLA would investigate the matter, she said. Keyworth should forget it ever happened.

'The thing I can't work out,' said Trina, 'is that I called them right away to make sure the order was legit.'

'The fakes could have given you any number,' I said. 'Even a payphone number.'

She gave me a withering look. 'I checked the number against my own Rolodex,' she said. 'It was genuine. In fact, I remember calling it a couple of times before.'

'Are you going to finish those mashed potatoes?' Trina shrugged. I helped myself to a forkful. 'They must have re-routed the call. They probably broke into the company's PBX and forwarded that number to their own phone.'

'So what the hell were they trying to do?' said Trina. 'Swan thought they wanted to use the drive to hide a program on her systems. She went over it with a fine-tooth comb.'

'Once they got into the computer centre, they could have done just about anything. Stolen research. Slipped a doctored backup tape in amongst the real ones so the computer would write them some big fat checks.'

Trina shook her head. 'They checked all of that. They lost like a day's work making sure everything was the way it should be. Nothing got changed or stolen.'

'I guess Swan cottoned on to it before they could do

anything,' I said. 'Boy, would I like to talk to her.'

Trina laughed as I made puppy eyes at her. 'Come on, Chick.'

'Give me a present for your birthday, pretty lady.'

'My birthday isn't until tomorrow. And there's no way Swan wants this to get out.'

'It's already got out.'

'Yeah, but I'm deep background,' said Trina. 'I guess you could ask to interview Swan, though. She likes to talk about herself. Just don't get me involved.'

'Don't worry,' I said, eating the last of the potatoes. 'I know her reputation. I'll bet she knows mine.'

Not only had Swan heard of me, she'd read my stuff, and she knew right away I might be able to help solve her little mystery. She didn't ask how I'd heard about the intruders: she just ushered me into the plasticky little staff lounge at the centre of the TLA building. It was more like she was interviewing me than the other way around.

'Everything I tell you is strictly off the record.'

'Not a problem, Miss Swan.'

'If you use what I tell you in a story, TLA's identity will be deeply buried.'

'Yes, ma'am.'

Swan nodded. She sat back for a moment, looking me up and down with her X-ray vision. 'You've heard the whole story,' she said at last. 'Who do you know that might try something like that?'

'My first guess would be an ex-employee – someone with a grudge, or with a money-making plan. Maybe by blackmailing you after planting a logic bomb in your system, or maybe just by fooling with your payroll program.'

'We can forget about former employees,' said Swan. 'I've already checked.'

'What do you have that someone might want to steal?
Anything new or unusual?'

Swan made a chopping motion with one hand, cutting off
that line of conversation. 'The police were useless,' she said.
'They'd never heard of a crime like this one – they weren't even
sure it was a crime. I'm sorry, but I don't care about any of that.
I want these people. And I'm going to get them, never mind the
police.'

'It sounds like you have your own procedure in mind, Miss
Swan.'

Swan considered me. I could see that the two sides of her
hacker personality were at war in that instant: the cool and
businesslike side that knew better than to show off, and the
enthusiastic side that loved nothing better than boasting and
bragging.

'Strictly off the record,' Swan said.

We drove to Swan's house in McLean in her Ford LTD, a station
wagon with faux wood panelling. It was a lot of car for one
person; I guessed she ferried computer equipment to and fro in
the spacious back. We stopped en route for Japanese takeout.

The house was also big for one person. Swan explained she
was renting until she found something she really liked. The
neighbourhood was quiet and wooded, denuded trees reaching
into a grey sky. I got a glimpse of a big back-yard inch-deep in
new snow. The driveway was clear, thanks to neighbourhood
kids in need of video game quarters. Swan pressed the big
button for the door remote and parked the station wagon in the
empty garage.

Swan only seemed to live in three rooms of the house –
kitchen, living room, study. The other rooms were empty, or
contained boxes of electronic equipment. One room was a

jumble of phones of various vintages. There was an unzipped sleeping bag scrunched up on the sofa; I assume that's where she slept.

We sat at the table, balancing our takeaway on top of wires and papers. Swan had ordered for both of us: plastic bowls of soup with about two dozen baby octopuses floating amongst the noodles. I gingerly made a pile of them next to my plate. Swan stared at me as I ferried ex-octopuses with my chopsticks. 'I'm no good with sushi.'

'We're top of the food chain, Mr Peters,' she told me, slurping up one of the soft little balls. 'We eat everything, and nothing eats us. That's the way we're made.' It was more the thought of tiny octopus guts that had put me off, but I kept my mouth shut.

Swan sat down in front of a TRS-80 set up on the kitchen table. (One side of the room was an impassable jungle of cables.) I scraped a chair across the floor and sat down behind her.

What I saw made my scalp tighten. Swan had a line into the Department of Motor Vehicles. With a few taps of the Trash-80's keyboard, she was in their database. She had the same access to licence plates, home addresses, and phone numbers as if she was a DMV clerk sitting at a desk in their offices, rather than a hacker in jeans and sweatshirt sitting in a jumbled suburban kitchen.

Swan had jotted down her intruders' number plate. She typed it into the relevant field on the screen. After several long seconds, the computer blinked and disgorged a fresh screenful of information. The van was registered to the university. Swan scowled. 'I was hoping for a home address.'

But she had narrowed the field right down. The van hadn't been reported stolen; whoever was driving it had ready access to the college's vehicles. As well as the technical know-how to set up a Lisp Machine. There couldn't be a whole lot of people who fit that description.

Swan was looking for ways to impress me further. 'Want to see your own record?' For a moment I was tempted – as though to prove to myself that what I was seeing was real. I'd investigated a lot of fraudulent use of computers, but I'd never seen anyone with such simple and complete access to public records.

'Uh, no thanks.'

'I can look you up any time I want,' boasted Swan.

'I believe you.' I sure did.

Whoever had hoodwinked Swan, I reckoned they'd be better off in the hands of the police than subject to her tender mercies. In fact, the guy I called next had once tangled with her. That was why he never had the same phone number for more than a week at a time.

Ian Mond – known as 'Mondy' to the handful of people who did know him – lived a shadowy existence in motel rooms, warehouse corners, and other people's garages. He carried just a trunkful of equipment with him, often sleeping scrunched in the backseat of his second home, a midnight blue Ford Escort, after doing some 'fieldwork': conning information out of telco staff, making unauthorised adjustments to the phone system, and tip-toeing into Ma Bell's offices in the middle of the night. He made a modest living selling cheap calls, 'upgrades' to phone services, and computer equipment that had taken a tumble from a truck. The Mystery of the Lisp Machine was just his kind of gig. I figured if he hadn't done it, he knew who had.

I spoke to him in his mom's basement, a musty space filled with 'borrowed' phone equipment. Swan had an arcane set of personal ethics that stopped her from messing up the phones or credit ratings of innocents, including Mrs Mond, so Ian was safe as long as he stayed under her roof. We sat on a couple of upturned milk crates while I filled him in.

'Isn't it obvious?' he said. 'It's either one of the staff in the college computer department, or a trusted student. Or both. You go for a walk through their compute centre and see if you can't spot one of your suspects right away.'

'Already done,' I said. Mondy nodded, satisfied that I was trying to help myself. 'I'm pretty sure I know who at least one of Swan's visitors was. Robert Salmon, the sysadmin, didn't show up for work today. He's a twenty-year-old blond.'

'I've talked to that kid a couple of times. He's OK.' Mondy peered at me through his thick, square glasses. 'Don't hand him over to her, Chick P.'

'Relax. I'm a journalist. I'm supposed to observe, not get involved.'

He nodded, still peering at me worriedly. 'Good. Good. Find out what he wants. Find out what she's not telling you.'

'For that,' I said, 'I'll need your help.'

Mondy has a devilish smile. 'All right,' he said. 'Let me get a few things together.'

I listened in while Mondy coaxed the cable-and-pair number he needed out of an innocent worker somewhere in the telco. It was easy as pie: he picked a phone box at random (at least, I assume it was random), flipped open one of his collection of pocket-sized notebooks, and dialled up a number at the line assignment office. His voice became gruff. 'Hi. This is Danny Heap from Repairs. I'm up a pole...' A few moments later he had the info he needed. 'Thank you kindly, ma'am.'

The phriendly phone phreak made me wait in the car while

he did whatever he did to the bridging box outside Salmon's small house. It was for my own protection, he claimed, but I think he just didn't want me to get a look inside his little black bag of goodies. He dressed the part, with denim overalls, a well-stocked tool belt, and what looked suspiciously like a Ma Bell ID badge.

We'd parked where we could get a view through the study window. The venetian blinds were down, but half-open, giving me an occasional glimpse of silhouettes in the dull light of the computer screen. The glove box of the Escort was always well-supplied with junk foods, guaranteed kosher. I munched on a dark chocolate bar, my eyes scanning the suburban street. A couple of cars went by, but nothing suggested anyone had taken an interest in Mondy or his accomplice.

At last Mondy slid back into the driver's seat. He reached into the back and grabbed the handle of a large black tapedeck, hauling it into his lap. Up went the aerial. He fiddled with the dial until he heard the tone he wanted. 'Hear that? That means the phone's off the hook right now,' he said. He pushed in a cassette.

We sat in companionable silence for a long time. I stared at the little yellow spots on the back of his head. Mondy gave me a 'What?' glance. 'The embroidery around your yarmulkah,' I said. 'Is that Pac-Man?'

'Did it myself,' he murmured. 'Aha!'

The sound issuing from the tapedeck had changed. Ian thwunked down the 'record' button. My first ever wiretap had begun.

Two

Bob said, 'So what's the Doctor after?' Peri shrugged. 'Oh, come on. He told you, I know he did. I know he did.'

'No, really,' said Peri. 'If I knew, I'd tell you. You'd probably have a better chance of understanding it than me.'

Bob's apartment was small and spartan. Other than a few tidy bookshelves – Peri was sure the books were alphabetised – and another shelf for record albums, there wasn't much in the place. A single Dali print hung over the sofa. She couldn't see a TV anywhere. The kitchen was pristine, but Peri suspected that Bob never cooked.

You would have thought Bob's study would be just as much a disaster area as his office at work. You'd have been wrong. It was squeaky-clean – he even dusted behind the computer with a cloth before he sat down and switched it on. A home-made shelf over the desk held a row of computer manuals lined up like soldiers. They *were* alphabetised, Peri saw. Another shelf held a row of books on the occult. A mandala postcard hung from the bottom of the shelf by a yellowing square of Scotch tape.

Bob said, 'I wonder what it is... a satellite-based laser?'

'A stolen space shuttle computer.'

'A suitcase-sized nuclear bomb.'

'Whatever it is,' said Peri, 'it must be something pretty major for him to just vanish like that.'

'And stay vanished,' said Bob. 'I don't remember the Doctor

being so paranoid. He was more likely to charge in and make a bunch of noise. He didn't care what anybody thought.'

'Maybe it's not just him. Maybe there's somebody with him that he's got to protect.'

'Maybe he's in jail,' said Bob. 'Sneaking into the guard's offices to borrow the phone.' Peri had to smile.

Bob logged on to check his electronic mail while Peri flipped through a computer magazine. It was full of circuit diagrams and listings of programs, excited ads for a dozen brands of home computer, and pictures of barbarians rescuing damsels. She couldn't find anything about the new network Bob seemed to find so exciting.

'Why is the net such a big deal, anyway? It's just a bunch of scientists and generals sending each other computer messages, isn't it? Why don't they just phone one another up?'

'One day you'll be able to order a pizza over the net,' said Bob, his back to her. 'It won't just be businesses that have modems.'

'You've got one.'

'If they knew I had one, the telco would charge me business rates. But one day soon, owning a modem will be just as normal as owning a phone. This year some people did their Christmas shopping online. You don't just get information from computers now, you interact with other people. Email and Usenet are going to completely change the way human beings communicate.' Bob was getting so enthusiastic he was actually looking at her. 'The written word is far more precise than speech. Imagine conversation without the mumbling, the false starts, the half-chewed ideas. Imagine a world of people talking in sentences that they've actually thought about first. The net is gonna change how we *think*.'

Peri was impressed. 'Is that what it's really like online?'

'Ah, we're still getting the hang of it. It'll work as long as everyone in the world doesn't get a computer.'

'But isn't that kind of the idea? To make computers like TVs, or toasters?'

Bob looked miffed. 'It's not going to make the net a better place if everybody in the world climbs aboard. College professors and scientists talking to one another is one thing. But garbage collectors? Housewives?'

'College students?' snapped Peri.

Bob looked at her sideways. 'H.G. Wells used to talk about creating a World Brain. Bringing all the world's experts, all their knowledge, into one place. That's what the net is gonna be: a World Encyclopaedia. Pure information from the best minds on the planet.'

'And pizza.'

'Lemme show you something here,' said Bob. He fired up a brand-new IBM PC and pushed a diskette into the drive. 'Same technology as the *Columbia*. Why don't you have a look at the demo programs?'

What a way to spend Christmas Eve: watching a computer draw spirals. You would never have known the time of year from Bob's house: there was no tree, no cards. No matter where they had happened to be, her parents always arranged something. A bit of tinsel on a twig, carols in the tent. They could make Christmas out of virtually nothing. To Bob, it seemed, it *was* virtually nothing.

What a relief to be interrupted by the jarring ring of the phone. She snatched it up before Bob could get his hands on it. 'Hello?'

'Hello, Peri. I trust you're well.'

'Fine, Doctor. Are you OK?'

'Never better. How did things go with your little expedition?'

Peri sighed. 'All I know is that whatever you're looking for, it's not in their computer room. I got to check the whole place before Swan scared us off, and there aren't any locked rooms or secret labs that I could see.' Her voice grew small. 'I'm sorry we couldn't find out more.'

'Given the circumstances,' said the Doctor, 'you've done remarkably well.' Peri relaxed a little. Bob was practically jumping up and down, making 'give me the phone' gestures, but she held on. 'And you've confirmed something I suspected: Swan's project is a private one, not to be shared with her workmates. Even the government is not aware of what one of its contractors has hold of.'

'What is it?' Peri asked point-blank.

The Doctor hesitated. 'Not yet, Peri. Not yet.'

'Well,' Peri said helplessly, 'be careful.'

'One more thing,' said the Doctor. 'It's extremely rude to eavesdrop on other people's phone conversations.'

'Aw, *shoot*,' said Mondy. 'No way!'

He tossed the tape deck to me and scooted his seat forward, starting up the engine. 'What about your equipment?' I said, craning my neck. Bob's study was dark.

'Never mind that,' said the phreak. 'I swiped it from an FBI tap. They can have it back.'

'Wait,' I said, just as he pulled out. He slammed on the brakes and glared at me. 'I want to talk to them.'

'You've gotta be kidding,' he protested.

'Let me drive.'

'No!' He was already out of the driver's-side door.

'I'm serious!' I said, as we ran around the bonnet, changing sides.

'Not a chance!' he insisted, sliding into the passenger seat.

'It's gotta be done!' I said, grabbing the steering wheel.

Bob's Pontiac roared out of the little court like a rogue elephant. We followed, trying to hang back as they wound through a series of suburban streets. But we must have been pretty conspicuous: they kept speeding up and slowing down, and I could see Peri looking back at us. Once they took an obviously random turn, and came back down the side street a minute later to find us waiting for them.

Bob got the Pontiac onto 495 and shot away. 'Oh shit!' shouted Mondy, as I followed them onto the Beltway, flattening the accelerator. Compared to Bob's car, the Escort was like riding a lawnmower. 'If you wreck my car, Peters, I swear I'll swap your home number with a cathouse!'

'Relax,' I said. 'We're not Kojak and neither are they.'

'This had better be worth it.'

'Swan's got something even Uncle Sam doesn't know about. And these guys want it. It's the story of the century.'

'Oh, quit exaggerating,' grumbled Mondy.

'Think about it. It's got to be something she can use for hacking, that's all she's interested in. Maybe it's a program for breaking into military systems. Or some new protocol for connecting computers. Or a successful artificial intelligence! Isn't your curiosity piqued?'

'Maybe Swan is a Russian agent and it's a KGB supercomputer,' said Mondy sourly.

'Shit, we're losing them.'

'Will you slow down!'

'I will if they will. Relax, he won't get far before he gets stuck in the traffic like everyone else.'

It was only a few minutes later that we both wound up in the queue of cars creeping around DC, bumper to bumper. I smoked and thought while Mondy fidgeted. What if Bob and Peri were Russian agents, I thought? Come on, I told myself, they're just a couple of kids. But what about the Doctor? What if the English guy was working for a foreign power, conning a couple of unsuspecting hackers into feeding him secrets? Visions of Kim Philby danced in my head.

We crawled through Beltway traffic for half an hour, keeping Bob's car within sight, but never quite catching up with it. It must have been the slowest car chase in history.

In the end, we pursued them to Tyson's Corner, a giant mall in McLean. Bob and Peri wove through the Christmas Eve crowd in the parking lot, trying to lose us in the toing and froing of cars. Tyres squealed as cars braked, trying not to back out onto us as we continued our slow-motion pursuit.

They finally managed to shake us off after five dizzying minutes when we got stuck behind a dingle. 'It's no use,' said Mondy. 'They'll burn on out of here and we'll never see them again.'

'I think they came to Tyson's for a reason,' I insisted. 'I want to look for them inside the mall.'

'Have you *been* in there?' said Mondy.

Miraculously, we'd found a parking spot. 'I'll tell you what,' I said. 'You check the payphones. If you see them, gimme a page. Got the number?'

'Memorised,' he said.

We jumped out and hurried through the rows of cars into the vastness of Tyson's. Mondy obviously knew the mall better than I did – he immediately vanished into the crowds, heading for the payphones. He'd know where every phone was.

I looked for computer stores, jogging through the mobs of shoppers. I reckoned Bob would want to stock up on equipment after having to make a run for it. But maybe he just wanted to get thoroughly lost.

After ten minutes, Mondy paged me. 'I've got them,' he mumbled. 'I'm right near them.' He gave me directions to another row of payphones. And he gave me the number of a phone right next to them.

I wish I could have seen Bob and Peri's faces when the phone next to them rang. (Mondy did, of course – he was standing just a few feet away.) It rang several times before Bob picked it up.

'Hello?'

'Bob, please don't hang up. My name's Charles Peters. I'm a journalist. Your "little expedition" into the TLA building got me interested.'

'Jesus, does the whole world know about it?'

'Excuse me, but we have to leave now,' said Peri, tugging at his arm.

'It's OK. Swan doesn't know who you are. All I want is the story – I can guarantee your anonymity.'

Peri shook her head. Bob said, 'Over the phone I don't think I can tell a real journalist from an FBI agent. Bye.' He hung up. They both looked around, wondering where I was. I must be watching them, right? They couldn't know I was in a completely different section of the mall.

Mondy called me back. (Don't ask me how he knew what number to dial.) 'They're heading back to their car.'

I met them at the door to the parking lot. Our eyes met as I strode towards them. They knew at once I belonged to the voice they'd just heard. Bob actually said 'Yikes!' when he saw me coming. He froze, probably expecting me to pull a gun and order him to do just that. Peri instinctively ducked behind him.

I held up both hands, trying to look harmless: just an ordinary guy in jeans and a sweater, not too tall, not too muscular, not too threatening. 'I'm not the FBI. I just want to talk,' I said.

'How did you find us?' demanded Bob.

I grinned. 'I'll tell you all about it. Let me come along for the ride.'

Bob said, 'Mister, you've got to be joking.'

Peri put a hand on his arm. 'I think we'd better,' she said. 'Sounds like he already knows everything.'

Behind them, Mondy gave me a wink, and then joined the flow of late-night shoppers. His work here was done.

I kicked a bunch of crap off the back seat and squeezed into Bob's car, obliged to hold a spare disk drive on my lap to make room for myself. They murmured to one another in the front seat, watching me in the rear view mirror.

'The Doctor's gonna kill us,' Bob said.

Peri shook her head. 'The Doctor's gonna kill *him*.'

We headed back to Bob's apartment in an awkward silence. When we got inside, Bob lurked about like a spy, pulling down the blinds, running a fingertip behind the Magritte print. At last, apparently satisfied, he sat down on the sofa beside his touch-tone phone, plucked its cord from the wall, and replaced it with a battered old rotary-dial phone from his bottomless bag of goodies.

Despite all the secrecy, Bob couldn't resist explaining how they and the Doctor were going to make contact. 'We've each got one number from a looparound pair,' he told me. 'The phone company sets up these lines so they can run tests. You give the other person one number in the pair, and you dial the other one, and then you can talk to one another over the test line for free. At night, anyway, when the telco's not actually using them. It's convenient when you don't want to give out your phone number.'

He dialled the number and held the receiver up to my ear.

There was no sound of ringing, just a click; and then a high-pitched electronic beeeeeep which sounded like the Emergency Broadcasting System. After perhaps ten seconds, the tone cut out for a moment, then started again. 'That's the singing switch,' said Bob. 'When the tone stops, you know someone has dialled the other number in the pair.' He settled back on the sofa, arms folded behind his head, the receiver squashed against his ear by the inside of his elbow.

'What if Swan knows about the, uh, looparound pairs?' Peri said. Her voice became pinched and high when she was stressed, often sounding as though she was about to burst into tears. 'You made it sound like she knows everything.'

'Swan thinks the phone system is for kids,' said Bob.

The tone was loud enough that I heard it cut out from across the room. Bob sat up at once. 'Hello, Doctor, can you hear me all right?' Peri put her ear close to the receiver so she could overhear their conversation. 'We've got a little problem,' said Bob. He and Peri both looked up at me as Bob filled the Doctor in on my presence. 'Are you sure? All right – OK, I'll tell him.'

Bob handed the phone to Peri. 'Why can't we see you?' she said. 'Well, how's that going to make it any worse?'

Bob sat down on the arm of the easy-chair. 'The Doctor wants to see *you*,' he told me. 'Right now.' Behind him, Peri put the phone down with an exasperated sigh. 'Go to a payphone. If you're sure nobody's following you, call this number. It's another looparound pair.' He rolled up my sleeve while I was reaching for my notepad, and inscribed a number in ball-point on the skin of my arm. 'The Doctor will give you instructions on how to find him. OK?'

'I guess you're not coming along?' I said.

Peri, slumped on the sofa, said, 'I guess we're not.'

30

One

Sheer luck led Sarah Swan to discover the intruder on her system that Christmas Eve. With no family to visit, Swan routinely worked through the vacation; she liked to have the company's computer resources to herself. That evening, long after everyone else had gone home, Swan was still in her office on the third floor of the TLA building. A single strand of purple tinsel was taped to her office door in concession to the season.

Swan was about to send an electronic message to one of her co-workers elsewhere in the building, and so wanted to see if they were still logged on to the machine or had gone home for the holidays. She typed in a short command:

```
who
```

And the terminal responded:

```
sswan          pts/0   Dec 24 17:48
jsmith         pts/3   Dec 24 19:55
hostmast       pts/5   Nov 24 04:07
uucp           pts/2   Nov 24 04:05
root           pts/4   Dec 24 00:01
```

Swan stared at the list of users for a moment. Who the hell was `jsmith`? Only members of the research team had access to the mainframe. (The other 'users' were automated programs.)

Swan did some checking. No-one was dialled into the computer, so her intruder wasn't coming in via a modem. He must have logged in remotely, from another machine on the ARPAnet. Either he had set up an account on her machine, or someone had given him one. He had come from –

– Where had he come from? There was no entry for him in the file that automatically logged visitors to the machine.

Swan kicked `jsmith` off and deleted the account. She did a quick check of the computer's files, reassuring herself that the intruder had done no damage. He could only have been logged in for a short time before Swan spotted the illicit access.

Swan made it her policy to tolerate just a little joyriding in the TLA system. After all, she'd spent years doing exactly the same thing herself – seeing what was out there, making her own map of the net. She kicked hackers off her system, no negotiation and no second chances, but she generally didn't hand out punishments. The intruder hadn't expected anyone to be around on Christmas Eve. She smiled. She'd probably just given some college boy a good scare.

Still, she thought as she headed down the dimly lit hall to the vending machine, it was an unpleasant coincidence after yesterday. She'd have to keep an eye on things over the next few days.

By the time Swan returned to her chair with a plastic cup of coffee, the intruder was back.

The Doctor was not what I'd been expecting. He was staying in a pricey hotel in downtown Washington, all freshly cleaned carpets and bright lighting. I tapped on the door of his room. No answer. I double checked: this was the right place. I knocked again. Still nothing. It took me a minute with a credit card to persuade the door to open.

The room was pristine, as though it had just been made up.

For a moment I thought I'd been played for a sucker – nobody had been staying here at all. But then I saw there were clothes hanging in the closet, and a computer sitting on the table next to the free stationery and the Gideon's.

The cupboard contained one ordinary-looking black suit and one extraordinary coat, a patchwork of colours that made me think of the Pied Piper – "with a gipsy coat of red and yellow". It wasn't a clown's coat, all ragged patchwork, but a garment of substance, well-made and hefty, a gentleman's coat that just happened to be a kaleidoscope of hippie hues. It would have kept out the worst of the DC cold, but must have stood out like a stained-glass window in the snow. I dipped a hand into the nearest pocket of the coat, hoping for some ID, and instead fished out a dog-eared *Roget's Thesaurus*.

The computer was an Apple II Plus. It looked like a big, flattened plastic typewriter with a miniature television set sitting on top of it. Two chunky metal boxes were stacked next to it, one on top of the other: twin drives for five-and-a-half-inch floppy disks. A flat blue cord connected the internal modem through a fist-sized black box to the phone socket.

'You were expecting something more advanced.'

I jerked sideways, violently, at the unexpected voice, and fell over the bed. I found myself looking up at a tall, broad-shouldered man in his early forties, with an explosion of blonde curls like William Katt in *The Greatest American Hero*. He loomed, scrutinising me with blue eyes that managed to convey suspicion, humour and weariness all at once.

'Mr Peters, I presume,' he said.

I hauled myself to my feet with some dignity still intact. 'Guilty as charged.'

I'd had a mental picture of a cross between an Oxford professor and Sherlock Holmes, delicately sipping tea while he lounged in a tweed jacket. This guy looked more like a boxer or a *film noir* gangster in his tailored black suit. How the hell had he got into the room without making any noise? He wore a rainbow-coloured tie printed with dozens of little cats, interlocked like figures in an Escher picture.

The Doctor bent slightly so our eyes were almost level. 'Now, Mr Peters,' he said, looking down his long nose at me. 'It was your decision to involve yourself in our doings, rather than the other way around. I would rather not have my concentration disturbed by a scribbler asking a lot of questions.' He spoke in a crisp English accent, with relish, as though just pronouncing words was a pleasure in itself.

'I think I've got enough computer know-how under my belt to follow what you're doing.'

He gave me a curt nod and sat down at the writing desk. 'Observe.' With a flourish, the Doctor typed 'Sphinx of Black Quartz, Judge my Vow'. The letters popped up on the screen, white on black. When I didn't seem impressed, he explained, 'You oughtn't to be able to do that. Strictly upper-case only on this model.' He flipped open the lid of the machine. 'But with a few jumper wires here, run to the 80-column card there, a replacement ROM chip courtesy of my friends at the Apple Pi users group... hey presto, eighty columns of mixed case!'

'So,' I said. 'Now it can do everything my typewriter can.'

'Unlike your typewriter, Mr Peters,' said the Doctor dryly, 'this is a thing of beauty and a joy forever. Just look at this: 64K total address space for the processor chip. A mere scrap by the standards of those new-fangled IBM machines. How could this overmatched museum piece ever hope to compete?

'But the makers knew. They set aside a few locations in the address space, and constructed it so that accessing those memory locations directly affected the hardware. Read from this address here and – zap! – you swap your ROM space for an extra 12K of RAM. Read from this one over here, and – zap! – swap in a different 4K block. Read here, and – zap! – you've swapped in another bank and turned your 40-column display into an 80-column one. And fiddle with these locations, and you swap the whole blessed memory space, all those banks and sub-banks, and double your available RAM. One hundred twenty-eight kilobytes of memory for the taking.'

OK, this I was familiar with: the hacker's love songs for their machines. 'It sounds like a lot of trouble to go to.'

'Oh, it's hideously overcomplicated, compared to getting a 16-bit processor and just having vast acres of memory there at your command. But that's what makes it such a triumph. Anyone can do incredible things if they've got incredible resources. It takes an artist to make poetry out of bits of string and paper clips. Now, if only this heap of junk could connect at faster than 1200 baud.'

'While we're waiting for it, can I ask you a few questions?'

'You can ask,' pronounced the Doctor, without taking his eyes off the screen. I hesitated. 'That's a little joke.'

'How long have you known Miss Smith?'

'Peri and I stumbled into one another's company some time ago,' he said absently. 'Some months, at a guess. Though at times it definitely seems longer.'

The Doctor spread his hands on the beige plastic that flanked the keyboard, as though gathering his thoughts. Then he typed a short, sharp series of commands into the Apple, sat back, and hit 'return'.

I heard the modem swing into action. But instead of connecting to another machine, it hung up after maybe six rings, and immediately started dialling again. 'So exactly what are we up to here, Doc?' I said.

'What *I* am attempting to do,' he said, 'is to dial into the mainframe at the TLA building. My computer will continue to dial phone numbers until one of their computers answers.' He paused for emphasis. 'Oh, and it's Doc. *Tor*. The second syllable is as precious as the first.'

We sat there for maybe a quarter of an hour, listening to the modem dial and dial again and again. The Doctor explained that his program was set up to call numbers that he knew were allocated to TLA's headquarters. Presumably he'd poked around in Ma Bell's computers for a few hints, although he might have guessed the range of numbers from their phone book listing.

At last the modem emitted a squeal of static, the sound of two computers shaking hands.

The Doctor's hands landed on the keyboard at a run. 'I'm going to try a series of account names,' he said, 'typically left behind by programmers as back doors into the system for testing.' He could type almost as fast as the modem could send data, so I was able to watch his attempts to break and enter as they piled up on the screen. Each time, he just hit 'enter' instead of typing a password:

```
Login: guest
Password:

Username or password incorrect; please
try again

Login: public
Password:

Username or password incorrect; please
try again
```

```
Login: sys
Password:

Username or password incorrect; please
try again
```

At last he sat back with a sharp sigh, and disconnected the modem. 'It looks as though Swan has nailed shut the back doors into her system.'

'So how are you going to get a real password?' I said.

'With a little luck, I still won't need one. A friend of mine has set up a legitimate account for me. I can try to break into Swan's computer again from there.'

I watched as he logged in to the university's computer as doctor. 'Now,' he said. 'From here we use a program called telnet to jump to Swan's computer.'

```
telnet tla2 25
```

After a few moments, the TLA computer responded with a ready message.[3] The Doctor's mouth lengthened into a smile. 'You see?' he said. 'The computer's not even asking us to log in. Port 25 is its email connection, and it has to be left open at all times.' He was lecturing me, despite his earlier claim that he didn't want to have to explain things. 'Now, first we use the open port to send a message to ourselves.'

He typed rapidly, drumming his fingers on the pale plastic of the computer whenever he had to wait for the screen to catch up with him. Mail accepted, responded TLA's computer.

---

[3] I have omitted the details of some of the Doctor's methods to avoid encouraging would-be hackers – although this information is readily available if you know where to look.

And sure enough, a short while later, the email arrived at the `doctor` account. The Doctor explained, 'Now that the open port has seen us send a genuine email, it will assume anything else we do is also legitimate.' I nodded, not wanting to interrupt the flow of his genius. 'And that includes sending an email which will convince the TLA computer to open up a new account for us. One with all the privileges we need.'

He typed in a series of Unix commands, adding a special twist to the address of his 'message' so that the computer would be forced to execute those commands.

'Now then,' he said.

```
Login: jsmith
Password:

Ready
tla2#
```

We were in. The Doctor looked like the cat that had got the cream. 'Swan may be security-conscious,' he said, 'but even she hasn't patched every puncture in her mainframe.'

Before he did anything else, the Doctor located the files which kept a record of the ports and logins, and snipped out the lines showing our unauthorised arrival. Then he spent a leisurely half an hour poking around in the guts of the TLA mainframe. Normally each user is locked into their own section of the computer, like residents in an apartment building, each with the key to their own door alone. The Doctor had convinced the computer to hand him the master key to the building, an account with root privileges, just as powerful as Swan's own account. If he'd wanted to, he could have locked every user out of the computer, or have erased every file. A mistyped command could have catastrophic consequences for the system. Watching a hacker at work was always like watching a tightrope walker.

'You know, I'm rather enjoying myself,' the Doctor said. 'I haven't played with technology this simple for a very long time. It's rather like discovering your old toys at the back of the cupboard. I'm not having much luck with these files.' He tapped a fingernail against the glass of the display. 'I think it might be easier to read through some of Swan's email. Perhaps she's discussed what I need to know with some of her colleagues.'

Breaking and entering computers is still a grey area of the law. But the law aside, there was something a little itchy about reading other people's mail. But before the Doctor could start purloining any letters, we were suddenly and decisively kicked off the TLA system.

'Someone's noticed us,' said the Doctor.

I had spent a few minutes in a half-panic, expecting the police to descend on the hotel room. When someone knocked at the door, I just about dived under the bed. But it was room service, with a three-course meal and a bottle of champagne.

The Doctor knew that whoever had slammed the door in our face had no way of telling which direction we'd come from. So we did it all again: another genuine email message followed by a, uh, doctored one. The Doctor typed with one hand while he sampled his dinner with the other. I cracked open the champagne and had a badly needed half-glass. The system opened up to us again in less than five minutes. 'It will take them days to puzzle out how we're getting in.' This time his username was `jeoffrey`. 'For he can spraggle upon waggle at the word of command,' non-explained the Doctor.

He used the `who` command to see who else was online at

TLA. 'Sarah Swan herself,' he said. 'Undoubtedly it was she who invited us to leave.'

'How long before she notices we're back?'

'No time at all,' said the Doctor, already sitting forward in his seat and tapping intensely at the keys. 'So, turn about being fair play, I'm going to log her out before she can do the same to us. There.' A few more commands, and the Doctor's bit of magic was running in the background – a time bomb quietly ticking. While she puzzles over that, I'm going to download a copy of all her email. Then we can read it at our leisure.'

I've sat and watched a lot of hackers at work. Whether driven by curiosity or greed – or a little bit of each – they all treat their 'hobby' as a game. Hackers match wits with systems and system operators, dumb and smart. They pit their skills and know-how – and more often, their sheer bloody-minded determination – against the people who want to keep them out of their chosen playground.

The Doctor treated his hacking mission just the same way. He reminded me of the enthusiastic kids in my high-school chess club, taking a piece with a twist of the wrist, a clack of colliding wood, and a triumphant quip. The difference was that he gave me the overwhelming impression that this *was* just a game. Nothing as sophisticated as chess: more like an adult stooping to sit in the dirt and flick marbles with a pre-schooler. More like a human being deigning to throw a tennis ball again and again for a dog.

My guess is that the Doctor spends most of his time with computers far superior to the humble Apple II – presumably the multi-million-dollar mainframes that hackers itch to have illicit access to. And yet, I can't help but feel that if the Doctor were confronted with the latest Cray supercomputer, it would just be another half-chewed tennis ball to him.

* * *

When Swan saw that her intruder was back again, she slammed her coffee down on her desk and grabbed for the log files. She must have managed to back them up before the Doctor could erase our fingerprints, because her next step was to try to break into the university's computer. Swan was not the sort to waste time reporting burglars to system administrators who knew less about their machines than she did. Besides, to be fair, it was unlikely anyone would be in the office at that hour.

If there *had* been anyone in the office, of course, it would have been Bob Salmon. It was Bob's account Swan wanted – although she still had no idea he was the man who'd delivered her a Lisp Machine just the day before. She simply wanted the abilities of his root account so that she could find out who was sniffing around her mainframe.

Swan was halfway through a series of guesses at Bob's password when the system slowed to a crawl, and then abruptly and rudely tossed her out.

She let fly with a series of curses that would have made the Ayatollah blush, and immediately tried to log back in. The mainframe let her in for a moment – and then logged her right back out again. After trying this three times, and having the door slammed in her face each time by her own machine, Swan was ready to commit mayhem.

Robert Link also had root privileges on the system. She phoned him at home and demanded his password. Encouraged by Christmas cheer, he was happy to hand it over. She logged into his account, sagging with relief when the mainframe didn't boot her out again right away. But she was already hammering in commands, checking to see what was happening on the mainframe.

Someone was downloading her email. Swan froze, hands rigid on the keyboard, as though if she didn't keep control of her body, she was going to explode into a screaming cloud of blood.

The system itself was almost frozen, grinding along at a fraction of its normal speed. There was a process running that Swan didn't recognise. It had to be the monster that had taken over her machine. She killed it.

The system immediately sprang back up to normal speed. Again she called for a list of processes; a single command could stop the electronic theft. But the moment she typed in the command, the system logged her out again. She logged back in, this time tried listing the files on the system. Again, the machine's door slammed in her face. And all the time her private email messages were being sucked out of the mainframe by person or persons unknown.

What she didn't know was:

While Swan was glued to her terminal, struggling to defend her turf, Bob and Peri were quietly slipping through a back door of the TLA building.

Peri had been furious at being left out of the Doctor's doings yet again, while a mere interloper like me had been permitted to sit by his side and take notes. But a few moments after I left Bob's house, he called back with new instructions.

His hacking had two purposes: one, obviously, was to snatch Swan's email and scan it for information about the item the Doctor wanted. The other was to keep her distracted long enough for a couple of amateur thieves to try to snatch that item out from under Swan's nose.

Peri was doing her level best to enjoy their little adventure. Since Swan would recognise Bob's car, they were obliged to park in a near-empty strip mall lot a few blocks from the TLA building. They walked through echoing near-darkness, slipping behind the row of offices into trashcan land. Peri wore camo gear: a pair of black trousers and a dark sweater under her black coat. Bob had reminded her to wear sneakers instead of high heels. He had simply wrapped a black leather jacket around himself, skinny legs sticking out underneath in their faded jeans.

Peri was somehow unsurprised when Bob picked a lock at the back of the TLA building. His amateur locksmithing had begun as a way of getting a closer look at the university's mainframes when they were wastefully idle in the middle of the night.

In her travels Peri had navigated many a labyrinth, cave tunnel and corridor of power. She steadied herself with a hand against the wall and followed the tiny beam of Bob's torch. The building had the unnerving quietness of any place missing its usual crowds – like high school after the school day was over, thought Peri. At least if anyone else was around, they were sure to hear them coming. They tiptoed up the fire-stairs to the first floor, then opened doors until they found someone's office. Bob looked longingly at the terminal. 'Better not risk it,' Peri said. 'We don't want to mess up whatever the Doctor is doing.'

He nodded and reached for the phone, but Peri had already picked it up. No-one had deigned to tell her the numbers for the loop-around pair, so she'd simply watched Bob dial the number in his study.

The high tone stabbed into her ear. Peri sat down in the chair belonging to whoever worked in the cramped room. It was actually kind of hard to do. In real life, she thought, you'd never just go into someone's office and sit at their desk. Bob seemed pretty comfortable, running his flashlight along the shelves to check out the collection of computer manuals. 'Don't take anything!' Peri said, alarmed. Bob snapped off the light and sat down on the edge of the desk.

They sat there for a while. The only sound was the squeal-pause-squeal of the phone. 'Bob,' whispered Peri, 'have you ever been in jail?'

'No.'

'Have you ever been in trouble at all?'

'Worried about getting caught?' She wanted to grab him by the hair and shout, 'Of course I am, you moron!' but instead she just nodded. 'Don't be. What we really have to worry about is what Swan will do if she finds out who we are.'

'We're burglars! Can she really do worse things to us than put us in prison?'

'To the police, we've got things like rights and privacy,' said Bob. 'And they don't have enough manpower to spend all day making our lives hell. Swan's hobby is picking on people who've annoyed her.'

'Well, how?'

'Cancelling your driver's licence,' said Bob. 'Killing your phone and your computer. Wrecking your credit rating. Sending pizzas to your house. Or taxis. Or ambulances.'

'She can do all of that?'

'The right computers can do all of it. Get into them, and you can borrow their power for yourself. I'd much rather tangle with the Feds than Sarah Swan.'

Peri looked around the stranger's office. Tonight they'd be at home with their family. Maybe peeling potatoes for Christmas dinner. She wondered if they would realise someone had been in their space. That would be a creepy feeling. 'Have you actually ever done this before?'

Bob shook his head, flashing a grin in the near-darkness. 'Never in my life.'

The phone said, 'Are you there?'

Peri gripped it. 'We hear you, Doctor.'

'Good. Since you're calling, I assume by now you're somewhere inside the building.' Peri felt slightly deaf in one ear. She shifted the receiver to the other ear, but the Doctor's voice was still annoyingly quiet on the other side of the test line. (He was calling from a payphone in the hotel lobby, his computer still connected to Swan's.)

'We're here. What are we supposed to do now?'

'Swan will be busy for a little while. The item we're after is in a storeroom in the basement. I had assumed she would keep it close at hand, but apparently she's locked it away where no-one would think to look for it.'

'How do you know that?'

'Hackers have one weakness,' said the Doctor smugly. 'They always want someone to know what they're up to. They need an audience.'

'Uh, right, Doctor.'

'Now, off you go.'

Peri put down the phone. For a panicked moment she wondered if she'd left fingerprints on it, before she remembered that she was wearing gloves. I could never do this professionally, she thought.

Two floors above them, Sarah Swan was physically disconnecting the computer from the ARPAnet. It was the equivalent of tearing the phone cord out of the wall.

Bob and Peri snuck out of the office that had been their hideaway and went back to the fire-stairs.

Halfway down, Peri grabbed Bob's arm, rather harder than she'd meant to. They both froze. In the empty building, the sound of footsteps was hard and clear above them.

The only way to go was downwards. They rushed down the stairs, sneakers pattering, hoping to God the firedoor was enough to muffle the sound.

Peri was still holding Bob's arm. She steered him into a narrow side corridor which led to a bathroom. Bob killed his flashlight as the firedoor opened up above them.

There wasn't time to squash into the cubicle. Instead they stood stock-still in the lightless corridor, trying to be invisible. A fluorescent bulb flickered into life, but its pale light only reached a little way into their hiding place.

Swan walked right past them a moment later, in a hurry. She had a fire axe.

Peri crept to the end of the brick corridor and risked a look around the corner. Swan was unlocking a low steel cupboard against a nearby wall. She swung it open and crouched down to look inside. The beige metal door was covered in warning stickers about dangerous chemicals and explosives. My God, thought Peri, is the woman making a bomb?

But when Swan locked the cupboard again, she hadn't taken anything out of it. Peri crept back into the unlit end of the hall just as Swan stalked past. They heard her steps going up the stairs, and the groan and slam of the firedoor.

Bob was about to step out into the basement, but something made Peri stop him. They stood together in the dimness, trying not to breathe audibly.

Then the firedoor closed a second time. Peri risked a quick look, but the stairs were empty. Swan must have been standing at the top of the steps, listening, wondering whether anyone had been waiting for her to leave.

'She's so paranoid!' murmured Peri.

'We *are* out to get her,' Bob whispered.

They crept across the floor to the locker. 'Now, what do you suppose she might keep in here?' smiled Peri.

'*A Scandal in Bohemia*,' said Bob.

'What?' said Peri.

Bob gave her a 'don't you know anything?' look. 'Sherlock Holmes had Irene Adler show him where the letters were hidden by making her think her house was on fire.'

The stickers on the locker said HAZCHEM BIOHAZARD EXPLOSIVE CORROSIVE OXIDIZER CONTAINMENT ONE. Peri tugged gingerly on the cabinet's handle, but it was securely locked. 'You'd better see if you can open it.'

Bob stared at the lock in embarrassment. 'I can only do doors,' he said.

'Well, what are we going to do?' hissed Peri.

Bob put his hands on either side of the squat locker and tried shaking it. Peri jumped back. There was a distinct rattle as something slid around inside the metal box.

'Hey, it's light,' said Bob. 'Give me a hand here.'

Peri got her hands under one end of the cabinet while Bob hefted the other. Awkwardly, they stood, balancing the near-empty locker between them.

'Let's go,' said Bob.

They half-ran across the concrete floor, trying not to lose their grip on the box, and scuttled up the stairs like a pair of crabs.

Moments later they were outside, behind the building. 'Wait!' hissed Peri. 'There's no way we can lug this thing three blocks without somebody noticing!'

'You're right,' said Bob. They carefully lowered the box to the ground. 'You stay here, I'll get the car.'

He jogged off, leaving her standing behind their stolen goods.

Peri looked around. There was nowhere in particular to hide. She settled for squatting down beside the cabinet, her head sweeping from side to side as she checked again and again for cameras or guards or an axe-wielding hacker.

They stuffed the cabinet into the back seat of Bob's car and slowly, calmly drove behind the buildings until they got out onto the main road.

'I'm pretty sure no-one's following us,' said Bob, five minutes later. 'And no sirens. We've got away with it, scot-free.'

Peri burst into tears.

40

One

Peri apologised to Bob about fifteen times for her brief session of sobbing in his car. He reassured her about fifteen times that it was no big deal, they were all under a lot of stress. Bob was acutely aware that he didn't know what to do with a weeping woman. He concentrated on driving back to his house.

The Doctor was waiting for them on Bob's sofa with a copy of Kliban's *Cat* in his lap and a pair of bifocals perched on his nose. (I was sitting on a wooden chair, watching TV.) 'What have we here?' he asked, standing up.

'Oh, Doctor,' said Peri, enormously relieved. They exchanged a hug. She's about chest height on him, seems tiny standing beside him. So do I, really. He takes up a lot of space, not just because he's a big man: he moves around a lot, he fills the air with words and gestures. He's the focal point of any room he's in.

Bob stared at him for about thirty seconds. Before he could say anything, the Doctor said, 'Do you remember that thing I told you could happen?' Bob nodded mutely. 'Well, it happened.'

'No, man,' said Bob. 'I mean, your *suit*.'

Peri exploded. 'Where have you been all this time? Why all the secrecy? Why'd you rush off like that? I didn't know if you were alive or dead!'

'Desperate expediency, I'm afraid.'

'Oh, what's that supposed to mean?'

The Doctor said, 'I'm sure that even you noticed the

restaurant we visited was more than it seemed to be. It acts as a meeting place and message drop for... unusual people.'

'You could've at least left me a note,' whinged Peri.

'The people I'm working with barely gave me enough time to catch my breath!' retorted the Doctor. 'They've objected all along to my involving anyone else – even trusted friends.' That seemed to mollify Peri, and Bob grew in height by about two inches.

I had the persistent feeling, listening to the conversations between the three of them, that I was constantly being carefully shut out of certain areas. It wasn't just that I'm a journalist, or that they had shady dealings with shadier characters. I had a real sense that there were things that Man Was Not Meant To Know – at least, man outside their small group. It wasn't quite the same feeling I'd once had talking to a group of UFO enthusiasts, who were keen to impress upon me that they had secret knowledge that they couldn't risk sharing, and so constantly dropped hints and fragments of that arcane lore. It was more like the feeling I had during a conversation with two desperately shy gay friends who were out to each other, but not out to me, and were frantic not to let me know.

Bob quickly recovered his poise. 'We've got what you wanted right here,' he said, tapping the short cabinet with his foot. Peri looked nervous. Maybe Swan had been checking her blackmail photos or her Strawberry Shortcake collection.

'Pop it up on the table, there's a good chap,' said the Doctor.

Bob and Peri manhandled the cabinet onto his paper-strewn dining table while the Doctor took off his jacket. He extracted a small burglar's kit from the pocket and went to work on the cabinet's lock. A few more moments, and he quietly pulled the door open.

By now we were all standing around him, craning for a view. There was a thick envelope on the bottom shelf, and on the top shelf, a bulky, colourful object. The Doctor reached inside and pulled it out.

It looked like a toy or a puzzle. It was all orange, purple and green plastic loops, forming a misshapen, hollow ball. The Doctor slipped his hand inside the space, but it didn't fit well.

'What the heck is that thing?' asked Bob.

'This is an extraordinarily dangerous piece of technology,' pronounced the Doctor, turning it over in his hands. 'Fortunately, Sarah Swan has no way of discovering its secrets.'

While they were marvelling at this bit of nonsense, I reached into the cabinet and took out the fat envelope. It was packed with computer printouts and hand-written notes, an entire composition book full of what looked like phone numbers, net addresses, odd remarks like "Easy", "Back door", and "Test???". Every page had an assortment of random words. I was looking at computer passwords, dozens of them.

'If Swan couldn't do anything with that gizmo,' said Bob, 'why'd she bother hanging onto it?'

'Hope springs eternal,' said the Doctor. He took a wad of tissue paper out of his pocket, and started carefully wrapping the thing. 'Which means she must have some idea of its significance.'

'So now we've got it – I guess you hand it over to the, uh, people you're working with?' said Peri. The Doctor nodded. 'So we did it,' she said. 'The good guys win again.'

'Alas,' said the Doctor. 'I'm afraid we're not quite finished yet.' Peri didn't look at all surprised. 'There's one more of these... components out there somewhere. Swan doesn't have it; nor does she know where it is. Her email is full of exchanges with other collectors, her efforts to track it down. It was one of those collectors who informed my contacts that she had this.' He picked up the wrapped puzzle and put it into a shopping bag. 'There. I've already arranged a meeting with them. But I don't think I'll deliver this just yet.'

'What's the plan, Doctor?' said Bob.

'I want a little time to examine our strange device. This is my chance to learn something about it for myself... although I won't be able to stall them for long.'

'We're coming along to that meeting!' insisted Peri.

'Right on,' said Bob.

'I've already explained,' said the Doctor. 'They won't risk contact with anyone besides myself.'

'We risked a lot to get that for you!' said Peri. 'While you sat wherever you were and twiddled knobs, we were breaking the law!'

'Perpugilliam Smith,' he said severely, 'you have done far more dangerous and far more dubious things in your time. But few that have benefited your little planet more.'

'That's right, man,' said Bob. 'We're not scared.'

'Stop trying to protect us, Doctor,' Peri insisted. She planted her fists on her hips and looked up at his face. 'It's time you let us in on what's happening.'

It made me think of my pet, Stray Cat. She was in my lap once when another cat climbed onto the balcony. She hissed and spat and bristled and then she took a swipe at my face: she couldn't attack the enemy, so she attacked whoever was around instead.

The Doctor raised both hands, scowling. 'I knew this would happen if I showed my face.'

'Since when did you ever take a no from someone?' said Peri.

'True,' said Bob. 'If they want more help from us, they have to include us.'

'Don't go overboard, Bob,' said the Doctor. 'We are trying to save the world. All right, I'll see what I can arrange.'

'Hello, Mond,' said the voice on the other end of the phone. 'Guess who.'

'Aw shit,' said Mondy. He glanced at the tape recorder set up next to the phone in his mother's basement. The tape had automatically kicked in the moment it began to ring.

'Nice to hear your voice too,' said Swan.

'I thought you swore you would never so much as dial my mom's number.'

'I didn't dial her number,' said Swan, amused. 'Does she know you've got six other numbers forwarded to her phone?'

'You said you would never hassle my mom,' said Mondy.

'Why don't you run upstairs and see if I'm bothering your mom,' said Swan sourly. 'Or maybe you'd like to shut up and find out why I called.'

'Oh my God. What? I guess you've already done about everything you can think of to me.'

'New technology is always coming along,' said Swan lightly.

Some buffer in Mondy's brain overflowed. 'All I ever did was get in an argument with you. That was two years ago. And it was your fault anyway for being such a bitch!'

'Whereas you're such a smooth diplomat.'

'Why can't you just drop it, Sarah? Why've you got to try and make my life a mess? How many other people are you screwing up this way?'

He caught his breath, clutching the phone, waiting for her answer to come crackling through the silence. He half-expected to hear police sirens as she sicked yet another 911 call on him. He knew the answer, anyway: the technology is vulnerable, but human beings are the weakest links.

'That's not what this is about. I want a favour, Mond.'

He spluttered. 'You've got to be kidding.'

'If you give me what I want, I'll stop bugging you. Now and forever.'

Mondy was thunderstruck. 'You're full of it.'

'You know I keep my word,' she said. 'I never have bothered your mom, have I? Or your brother in Calvert County.'

'No,' he had to admit.

'Good. Then you know I mean it. No more trouble for you if you just do what I say.'

Mondy hesitated. Was this the real reason she had picked on him for so long – because she knew one day she'd want to use his skills?

He smacked the listening end of the receiver against his forehead a couple of times. 'Ah, shoot,' he said at last. 'What do you want me to do?'

The Doctor's black suit turned out to be Peri's idea. 'You're not wandering around Washington in your circus outfit,' she had insisted. He'd made a lengthy speech about the historical variability of costumes and fashions, but Peri had put her foot down for once. 'Maybe in Berkeley or something,' she said. 'Not here.'

Peri told me she'd been wearing more and more garish clothes herself, not to compete with him, but to try to make him realise just how outlandish his own outfit was. It hadn't worked. He was too comfortable to care.

It took me a while to notice that, hidden by the dapper black trousers, he was wearing fluorescent orange socks.

The amazing thing is, not only did the Doctor's 'contacts' say yes, they even let me come along – once I persuaded him and he persuaded them. I think the Doctor let me tag along for the same reason he let me sit in on his hacking session; he wanted me where he could see me, a controllable element.

As good as his word, the Doctor had Bob drive us to a small apartment in northwest DC, off Connecticut Avenue. The rooms were furnished – classy, but anonymous, modern wood and plastic reflecting the taste of no-one in particular. There were no books, no knick-knacks. The kitchen looked as though it was never used. It was another hotel room, not a home.

The man the Doctor wanted us to meet sat stiff-spined in an easy chair. He wore a black coat and hat, as though he was just about to go out. He had a blandly handsome face with a blandly pleasant expression. Behind him, there was a parrot in a cage, constantly chirping and clucking to itself. It was a weird breed: long stiff tail, oversized beak, eyes so small they were barely visible through the mix of lemon and lime feathers.

'Sit down,' murmured the Doctor. We arranged ourselves on a couple of pale sofas, and I flipped open my notebook. 'Allow me to introduce Mr Ghislain.' The man's eyes moved back and forth over us a couple of times. 'With the invaluable help of my friends here, I'm very close to finding one of the missing components,' he said smoothly. 'But they would like to know a bit more of the background to our job.'

He said, 'Allow me to tell you a story.' He spoke precisely, almost in a monotone; his voice had a trace of accent which I couldn't place – French? 'You may take or leave this story as you please.'

Once upon a time (Mr Ghislain told us) there was a space vehicle. It was not made by human beings. In fact, it had been travelling for centuries by the time human beings discovered radio.

The spacecraft was sent from a world circling Epsilon Eridani.[4] The people of Eridani could not make ships that could travel faster than light. But they were patient, and had established colony worlds gradually and quietly over a huge volume of space, communicating with one another with slow messages and slower parcels. This particular spacecraft contained a supercomputer, broken into five components for storage in the slow packet, a gift to a fledgling colony circling Van Maanen's Star.

The spacecraft's flight path took it through Earth's solar system, a slingshot around the sun that would boost its speed towards its destination. But the closer the ship came to Earth, the more saturated its systems became with radio transmissions. The Eridani had not anticipated this; they expected a long, patient voyage through silence.

Bewildered by the flood of signals, the slow packet concluded that it must have already reached its destination, and landed its precious cargo on the planet Earth.

When the Eridani realised what had happened – almost eleven years later – they took the unusual and expensive step of chartering a faster-than-light ship from a neighbouring civilisation, and sent two agents to retrieve the package. But during those eleven years, their parcel had already been discovered by human beings. It had passed through a succession of hands, the components becoming separated as owner after owner tried to discover their secrets.

---

[4] This is a real star: a class K orange dwarf about eleven light years from Earth. The Doctor mentioned that scientists on Earth had scanned Epsilon Eridani for radio signals in 1960; they might have detected the Eridani if they had checked a wider band of wavelengths. He also suggested that the Eridani probably hadn't evolved on a planet circling that star (too young, at only a billion years of age), but had colonised a world there, one of their many waystations across our section of the galaxy. I have to give him credit for working out the back-story in detail.

The Eridani have managed to find three of the components in the three years they have been on Earth. But then one of them was killed by a human being they had employed to help them in the search. The human was also killed.

It was at this point that the Doctor stepped in with his offer to help find the final two components. Human beings must not learn the secret of the Eridani supercomputer. The Doctor believes it would disrupt their society to gain this knowledge prematurely. The Eridani do not wish their primitive neighbours to become their technological rivals.

That is the whole of the story.

I hadn't stopped writing once while Mr Ghislain quietly related his tale, although I'd been tempted to flip the notebook shut and walk out. I wasn't interested in heading off into outer space, but only in voyages into the inner space of the world inside the computer. But if this was the way some of the hackers thought, I needed to know about it. Or was the ludicrous cover story a way of stopping the secret leaking out – because if someone spilled the beans, no-one would believe them?

Everyone was looking at me to see how I would react. 'Whatever you say, folks,' I declared. 'I'm just along for the ride.'

Like the man said, you can take or leave this story as you please. My take on it? The 'Eridani' are code for the Russians. The other aliens they're supposed to have borrowed a ship from? Maybe a submarine their agents hitched a ride on. And the slow packet? That part's straight: the components of a new generation of supercomputer. They lost control of it on American soil, and now they want it back.

If you accept the Doctor's earlier claim – that the US

government doesn't know anything about it – then the supercomputer's parts had got into the hands of private citizens. But lucky for the Ruskies, the parts had been split up. Swan got one, realised how important it was, and had set out to search for the other pieces.

What did she hope to do with the machine? Patent it as her own work? Sell it to the highest bidder? Whatever her plans, you have to wonder if she realised just what fire she was playing with. Bob and Peri did her a favour by stealing that thing out from under her nose before the other side could find it.

Or before our side could find it. What if I'd guessed wrong, and the Eridani were Americans? What if I'd guessed right, and the Doctor was working for the Russians? Or even just the British? Bob and Peri were just following the Doctor's lead, but what was his angle?

TWO

When we got back to Bob's house in the early evening, the first thing he did was go into the bedroom and emerge with a crowbar and a hex socket. 'Gotta check for wiretaps,' he muttered, giving me a look.

Peri picked up a phone and listened to the dial tone. 'It sounds normal to me,' she said.

'No clicks?' said Bob? 'No funny sounds at all?'

She listened for a few moments. 'No. Maybe I wouldn't know what to look for.'

'Well, I do,' said Bob.

The Doctor showed no interest at all in this. He knelt next to the coffee table, peering at the Eridani's plastic toy. He turned it over in his hands, examining the configuration of the coloured rings. He tried moving them; they slid over each other, forming new patterns. He took odd-looking tools from the pockets of his suit and poked and prodded the device. None of us had the slightest idea of what he was doing.

I followed Bob outside to the bridging box – the grey-green box squatting on the corner of the street. 'I'm kind of hoping we find something in here,' he said. 'I don't wanna have to climb the pole.' I hoped so too. I could already see a couple of Bob's neighbours peering out of their windows at us.

The box turned out to be unlocked. Bob put down his crowbar and used his socket wrench to persuade the door to open for him. A moment later we were peering at a panel of wires and terminals that routed phone calls to every house in the street.

Bob unlatched the panel and let it fall forwards. Tucked behind it was a linesman's test set: a phone receiver that could be attached to any line by wires and clips. 'They often hide them here,' he said. 'Since nobody's using this one, I'll just borrow it for now.'

He put the panel back in place, and ran a finger over the terminals until he found his own line. 'Oh, crap,' he said. 'There we go.' The wire pair for Bob's house was marked with thick red crayon. I'm no electrician, but even I could see there were a couple of wires attached to it that didn't appear anywhere else on the panel.

'That's not the same as the tap Mondy used,' I told Bob. 'He had a six-inch chunk of metal he said was stolen from the FBI.' And yet it was clumsy and obvious. If this was Mondy's work, he was trying to warn us that we were being watched.

Bob muttered something about skinning cats. He disconnected the offending wires from his home phone, and attached them to one of the other wire pairs in the box, apparently at random.

Back inside, Bob reported his find. Peri said, 'We can't stay here, can we? Somebody knows we're here.'

Bob sat cross-legged on the sofa, still clutching the crowbar, with one hand pressed to his fair hair. '*She* knows. She must have tracked us down.'

I said, 'How do you know it wasn't Ma Bell who tapped your phone? Or the police?' But no-one took any notice of me.

'But how?' said Peri.

Bob poked the crowbar at me. 'You talked to her.'

'That was before I tracked you down,' I reminded him. 'I'm not about to inform on you to anyone. I'm here to cover the story, not to make it.'

'I'm sure Miss Swan has many ways of garnering information,' said the Doctor. 'Whoever placed that tap, Peri is right. Pack your things, Bob.'

That night we drove to Baltimore, arriving close to midnight. We crowded into the single available room at the motel, the staff lugging a spare bed into the room for me. I unfolded it and sat down. There were two singles and a double bed. Bob spread his bags all over the double bed, marking it as his territory.

Peri lay down on hers without taking off her clothes. I don't think it was modesty; we were all terribly fatigued.

I'd peeked in the trunk of Bob's car. He didn't just have his bags of computer equipment; there were a collection of neatly labelled plastic boxes which looked as though they always lived in the trunk. Computer parts, or tools, I assumed.

He shook his head. 'In case of nukes,' he said. 'Computers will be worthless after a nuclear strike. It's water and freeze-dried food and stuff.'

'Stuff?'

'Oh, you know. Torch and candles. My tent. Some pots and pans. A camp stove. First aid kit. Tool kit. A chemical toilet. Things like that.' Bob went on munching, unaware that we were all staring at him.

I was reminded of Mondy's stash: he'd once confided to me that he kept a pack of supplies in a disused building somewhere near his mom's house, phone equipment, running shoes and more kosher snax. He had memorised a map of his neighbourhood. If he ever heard the heat en route on his police scanner, he could vanish for days.

Mondy. Swan had got to him. He knew most of what was going on in the hacker and phreak communities at any given time: he was the obvious person to contact and hassle for details. And she had plenty of leverage over him.

Maybe it was the only way Mondy could think of to warn me. He might even have called the cops and told them someone had been fooling with the bridging box in Bob's street – meaning himself.

I just wanted to believe the guy was still on my side.

Bob, as usual, had no trouble dropping off. The Doctor didn't seem as though he was planning to sleep; he sat cross-legged on top of his covers, apparently meditating. I closed my eyes, but didn't fall asleep just yet.

Peri tossed and turned. Understandably, she didn't seem too comfortable sharing a small room with three men. Finally, she whispered, 'Bob's really enjoying this, isn't he?'

The Doctor opened his eyes. 'Even as a young man he relished the thought of an emergency to deal with,' he said. 'As a child he probably played at being Robinson Crusoe.'

'This isn't a game,' said Peri. 'I've had about as much of this as I can take.'

'An entire world's safety may depend on our actions over the next few days. You're part of that work, Peri, and not for the first time.'

'This isn't an adventure,' she retorted. 'This is more like a nightmare. Like a screwed up version of normal life. I can't do this much longer. I mean, here we are back home – this is my big chance just to go back to living a normal life.'

'Peri,' said the Doctor softly, 'you're thinking of leaving?'

'Yes,' she said quietly.

He hesitated. 'You're tired,' he said. 'We're all a little fatigued.' Bob indicated his agreement with a wall-shaking snore. 'Let's talk again in the morning.'

Peri said, 'OK.' But from where I was lying, it sounded as though her mind was already made up.

We had driven past Swan without even realising. In her navy coat, she would have been an anonymous, dark figure walking in the snow. I don't think any of us even noticed her.

Swan watched us go. She waited until the police were finished cruising up and down Bob's street, looking for whoever had been tampering with the bridging box. She waited a little longer in case the telephone company sent someone to check things out. Then she walked up to Bob's front door and let herself in with the key Mondy had provided.

Inside, she snapped on the lights. She had brought a flashlight just in case, but it would look far more suspicious to the neighbours than a few lights around the house. Inside her mittens she was wearing black cotton gloves. Despite the burglar gear, she wasn't here to steal anything. Unless you count privacy as something that can be stolen.

Bob's study was Swan's first stop. She ran a gloved finger along the spines of the occult books. She had many of the titles at home herself. Magical systems are not unlike computer systems: both are attempts to change the structure of a world through the use of special languages. Hackers jokingly call their more abstruse bits of programming *incantations*. Swan was amused that computers ran on 'hex' code. And both are attempts to usurp power. The magician harnesses the powers of the elements or the spirits. The hacker borrows the power of the phone system, or the computer network.

Swan wasn't superstitious; she read number theory and genetics as well as alchemy and astrology, and saw them all as reflections of programming. But a lot of hackers took the occult seriously. They'd try to hack any system if they thought it would bring them a little power, or better, a little kudos. What was Bob's attitude?

Swan went through Bob's filing cabinet and the drawers of his desk, jotting down numbers and details in her little notebook. Soon she had his banking details, his driver's licence number, his credit card details, and plenty more. She could have got a lot of this through hacking, of course, but the simplest solution is often the best. She had stolen plenty of passwords just by looking over someone's shoulder as they typed.

Bob's bedroom was a mattress on the floor, a couple of toolboxes, and a collection of stuffed animals cluttering a chipped dresser. On Bob's bed she found a scrapbook open to a collection of newspaper cuttings. She sat down on the bed and turned the pages carefully with a gloved finger.

The military computer scandal had been all over the papers at the time. Despite his father's efforts to shield him, Bob's name and even his school photo turned up in print, one of a 'small group of civilians' who helped stop the navy's computers being cracked wide open by Xerxes' program. A foreign hacker named 'the Doctor' was mentioned as well, a man twice Bob's age. Nothing more was known about him, except that he'd been instrumental in uncovering the plot.

Swan had Mondy's cassette tape from our all too brief session of wiretapping. The Doctor was back, and alert to another danger to the world's computers. Swan smiled a sour smile. How much did he know?

Swan went into Bob's kitchen to make herself a cup of coffee. That was when she saw the metal cabinet sitting on the table.

Swan's mind went blank. She switched on the flashlight and pointed the dull circle of illumination at the beige cube. The door was still open.

She stepped up to the table, dropping the flashlight onto it, and grabbed the cabinet, as if trying to convince herself it was real. She read the familiar warning stickers on the door twice. The flashlight rolled off the table and bounced away across Bob's kitchen floor.

Swan reached down to grab it and found herself sitting on the linoleum, staring up at the violated cabinet. 'I'm gonna kill them,' she said. 'I'm gonna kill that kid and all of his stupid friends.'

Somehow, that promise seemed to clear her overloaded mind. Swan pulled herself to her feet, got the lights on, and made herself that cuppa. Her hands moved automatically as she considered what to do. The unique device she had gone to such great lengths to obtain was gone, stolen out from under her nose. (One slip! One! One hint of the device's location in an email!)

She could make this good. She could make it better than before. If we wanted the device, she figured, we might have the others as well, or know how to find them.

Swan rinsed out her coffee cup and laid it in the drainer by the sink. She picked up the flashlight and stuffed it back in her coat pocket. She went into Bob's study, took a clean sheet of paper out of the printer, and found a black felt-tip marker in the desk drawer.

She left her message stuck to the fridge with a smiley-face magnet. On her way out, she noticed the clock. It was Christmas Day.

50

One

The Doctor took us out for breakfast at a scary vegetarian café somewhere in downtown Baltimore. The other patrons gave us the kind of curious glances they were used to getting themselves. Picture the four of us: the Doctor in his black suit, tucking into a hill of eggs and mushrooms and baked beans and toast; Peri slumped over a stack of organic pancakes; Bob, chain-slurping chocolate milkshakes like an enthusiastic butterfly; and me. The little black-haired Aussie in the crumpled dark-grey suit, wrapped defensively around a bottomless mug of black coffee.

Ladies and germs, there is nothing in this world to compare to good old bad paint-stripper American coffee, trapped in a percolator jug and mercilessly boiled and reboiled into a thin black fluid of evil. Every gulp fills your nose with the aroma of nailpolish remover. You end up peeing the same smell. Add a few spoons of sugar to take the cruel edge off the stuff, and you have a confection equal parts foul and sweet. Mercifully, the hippie restaurant was selling the real thing instead of some pussy substitute. I had three cups and Peri had four. Bootstrapping our brains.

'Today,' announced the Doctor, 'we'll return to Washington, and deliver the device we have to the Eridani. My explorations have yielded as much information as they're going to. Then it's only a matter of locating the final component, and the Eridani can be on their way.'

'What about the wiretap?' said Peri. There were deep patches of dark under each of Peri's eyes; she wore no makeup, and her hair was still damp from the hotel shower. She dropped her voice. 'What if the police know what happened at TLA?'

'Perhaps it would be best to stay clear of Bob's home for a little while,' conceded the Doctor. 'Until we establish just how much the authorities know.'

Everybody looked at me. 'Don't be ridiculous,' I said, stirring more sugar into my coffee. 'Why would I wreck my own story?' Boy, did I want to talk to Mondy. It was never hard to get him on the phone – problem was, how did I make a call without the other three noticing? There was a payphone in back of the restaurant, but you could see it from our table.

'How do we find the final component?' said Peri.

Bob pointed a finger at her. 'Swan's email,' he said.

'That's right,' said the Doctor. 'She emailed a number of people, fishing for information about the Eridani components. Individually, the messages give away very little; she wasn't careless. But when you have the complete set, there's information which I believe can lead us to the final component.'

We finished up breakfast. (The Doctor paid in cash; no sense leaving a credit card trail behind us.) Outside the womb of the cafe it was a crisp, quiet Boxing Day. Growing up in Canberra, I'd seen snow fall just once – wet flakes that disintegrated as they touched the front lawn. If we wanted to go tobogganing, we had to drive up into the mountains. I still love what snow does to the air, making it dry and cold, smelling of clean water. Besides, Washington was built on a swamp, and winter there beats the *hell* out of summer.

'Ah, Peri,' said the Doctor, putting a hand on her shoulder. 'I have a mission for you.' She brightened up a little. 'Would you take Bob's car to the airport and leave it there? Rent another, and drive it back to the motel.'

'I think I can handle that.'

'Hmmm.' He didn't seem to notice her sour expression. 'Take Mr Peters with you.'

Peri glanced at me as I flicked my Bic. I couldn't read her face, but she didn't look too happy about her passenger. Bob didn't look exactly ecstatic either at the prospect of losing his wheels. 'Don't worry,' Peri tried to reassure him. 'We can leave it in the long-term parking lot – it should be safe. I guess it'll throw off anyone trying to find us, too.'

'Lemme get some of my stuff out of the trunk first.'

Moments later, Bob was babbling excitedly to the Doctor as they jumped into a taxi, already plotting their next move.

Peri and I looked at one another over the roof of Bob's car. 'Can you drive?'

'Of course I can drive. Even if you Yanks insist on using the wrong side of the road.'

'No,' she said, 'I meant, could you drive to the airport? I'm kind of out of practice.'

'Oh. Sure.'

We wove over slushy roads through morning traffic. 'Seems like the boys are leaving you out,' I commented, watching Peri out of the corner of my eye. She had put the passenger seat back a little and stretched her legs out. 'Forgetting about you while they play with their computers.'

'Oh, this is pretty standard,' said Peri, bitterly. 'The Doctor always knows more than I do about everything. He's a lot older than I am. He's travelled a lot more. He's even finished college. You should hear him lecture me on how there's so much I could learn from him! Could learn, if he ever bothered to tell me anything!'

'Seems like being the Doctor's sidekick is hard work,' I said.

'It sure is, sometimes. Sometimes it's great. You get to see things nobody else has ever seen.'

Peri seemed happy to have someone to talk to – though from time to time I noticed her catching herself before giving too much away. She didn't let it turn into a one-way interview: she wanted to know all about my American dad, why I'd decided to come back to the States when I grew up. 'I've had some bad fights with my stepdad,' she admitted. 'But we still talk. We're still friends. I guess I'm lucky.'

At the airport we tried to call the motel, just to check on the Doctor and Bob, but the phone line was busy. 'Figures,' said Peri.

'Guess I should call my dad anyway,' I said. 'Wish him merry Christmas and that.'

Peri looked stricken. 'It must be tough being away from your folks like this.'

'No... no, actually, it's OK. They won't be worrying about me. You go ahead and make that call.'

'See you at the newsagent in a few minutes.'

As soon as Peri was out of earshot, I called Mondy's beeper. It never failed: a few minutes later, he called the other end of the loop-around pair we always used.

No sense in wasting time. 'Did you talk to Swan?'

'Ah, shoot,' said Mondy. 'Like I had a big fat choice.'

'You little bugger,' I hissed.

'You know what she did?'

'I shudder to think.'

'She put everything back the way it was, Chick. My credit rating. My record. My *phones, mazel tov*. I have my life back. Wasn't that worth a teensy weensy bit of data?'

'Yeah, well, you chucked me in the deep end, mate.'

'Look, Swan doesn't have enough info to get Bob into real

trouble. Trust me. She's just trying to get you guys to panic, to make a mistake.'

'I don't think it's gonna happen. The Doctor's really careful.'

'So are you, man. Stay careful. Listen, you know you can't tell me anything now.'

'You bet I know!'

'I can't give away something I don't know. But she can still find things out, things you wouldn't believe.' We both knew what he meant. 'Try and stay out of it, Chick. Really don't get involved.'

It was already the middle of the night in Melbourne. If I had actually called my Dad, he would have slammed the phone down before I could contaminate it.

The Doctor and Bob were having a whale of a time. The Doctor set up his Apple II in the motel room, plugging the modem into the phone socket. They had a list of email addresses, people Swan had mentioned the Eridani device to. Judging by the content of the messages, they were fellow collectors, people she was hoping to swap goodies or bits of information with to increase her collection of legal and illegal technology. (What I had seen at her house was only a fraction of that collection.)

So while we were at the airport, the two of them were merrily breaking into email accounts all over the country, reading more and more messages as they put together the same information Swan had. And, quite probably, in the same way she had. Unlike her, of course, the Doctor and Bob were prompted by the purest of motives.

Bob stirred some coffee into his chocolate milk and sucked the muddy result through a straw while he watched the Doctor at work. Every so often the Doctor would ask him a question, checking some technical point. Bob would gush an answer with far more information than the Doctor needed.

They were deep inside a university on the west coast when the messages started to come. As well as sending email anywhere in the network, you can send a short 'msg' to someone else on the same system, a sort of internal mail. The Doctor had tiptoed in: he took a snapshot of the computer's current list of users, then altered its 'who' command to show that list instead of actually checking who was online. He was, in short, invisible. So he was suitably surprised to be challenged:

```
Hellooo! Who have we here?
```

'Don't answer it,' said Bob, putting down his mocha milk.

'There's little point in putting our heads into the ground,' said the Doctor. 'They can obviously see us.'

'Then let's get out,' said Bob nervously.

```
Cat got your tongue?
```

The Doctor had already typed the who command. There were only four users logged on that Christmas morning: the Doctor, a couple of sysadmins, and zydeco.

The Doctor opened the file he had edited to disguise his entrance to the system. Sure enough, there was no record of zydeco's login. 'It's another hacker,' he said. 'And what a coincidence they should happen to be on the same system as we are this merry Michelmas morning.'

Bob gulped. 'Swan.'

Amused, the Doctor typed:

```
Good morning. Are you working your way
```

backwards through the dictionary?

You can run, replied Swan, but you can't hide.

'Oh please,' said the Doctor aloud.

No matter where you go, typed Swan, whenever you pick up a phone or dial into the net, I'll find you. You may be able to hide from the authorities, but you can't hide from me.

Speaking of the authorities, replied the Doctor, they could be very interested in your connection to the death of one Charles Cobb.

'Who he?' said Bob.
'Just one link in the chain of people who brought Swan her little collector's item.'

Nothing to do with me, said Swan. I'm not threatening you. We should work *together*. You won the first round. I respect your skills. Let's combine our talents and our information. We'll both benefit.

The Doctor hammered out, You don't have the slightest idea of what you're dealing with, do you? What did you think that device was? Did you run any tests? Take any precautions?

Tell me what it is.

You're like a little child who finds a detonator, said the Doctor. Take my advice: just this once, leash your curiosity before anyone else gets hurt.

Now you're threatening me.

The devices are the threat. Go back to your hacking and phreaking and leave well enough alone.

No more messages came from Swan.

Two

'There's only one thing for it,' declared the Doctor. 'We'll wiretap the wiretapper.'

'You want us to bug Swan's phone?' said Bob. 'Waitaminute. You want *me* to bug Swan's phone?'

'I have every confidence in your ability,' said the Doctor smoothly.

We were standing around at a rest stop on the I-95, stretching our legs, halfway home from Baltimore. Peri got a grape soda from a vending machine. 'I love this stuff,' she confessed. 'And the places we visit, you usually can't get it.'

'My ability to get screwed by Swan when she finds out,' grumbled Bob. 'I'm no phone phreak. I could use the test set to listen in through her bridging box, but that's kind of conspicuous. And she probably visits that box about as often as she visits the bathroom.'

'Do we even know her phone number?' said Peri. 'We'd need that, wouldn't we?'

'C'mon,' said Bob. 'She's not gonna be listed, is she?' He suddenly made a gesture as though turning his own head backwards. 'On the other hand, maybe she's that cocky... hang on.' He got up and went to a payphone nearby.

Bob came back. 'She's ex-directory,' he said. 'So I did a CN/A on her. Couldn't believe it. First time lucky.' He showed us Swan's phone number, scribbled in ballpoint on his arm.

'You did what?' said Peri.

'I called up a Customer Name and Address operator and told her I was a linesman,' said Bob. He shook his head. 'Never done it before. But she was only too happy to give out Swan's address and phone number.'

Peri shuddered. 'Is there any way somebody can keep their private information private?'

Bob grimaced. 'Not when people are really determined. Question is, what do we do now? I know there are ways of bugging someone from inside the telco, but I don't know how it's done.'

'Peri,' said the Doctor, 'why don't you and Bob go and get some lunch? I want to have a word with Mr Peters.' The kids wandered off to the kiosk to see if it was open.

'Peri doesn't seem too happy about tapping Swan's phone,' I ventured.

'Extreme situations call for extreme measures,' grumbled the Doctor. 'I don't think it's possible to appeal to Swan's better nature. The question is, can we appeal to her common sense? Her desire for self-preservation? Or will we have to simply bludgeon her into giving up?' He scowled. 'I never like to be reminded that simple rational argument, simple facts, are not enough to convince people.'

'If you learned something you could use to blackmail Swan, would you?'

'If it became necessary, yes I would. After all, we all have secrets we'd rather keep to ourselves.'

The little hairs stood up on the back of my neck. I usually only felt that just before I got into a fistfight with someone. 'Are you threatening me?' I said.

The Doctor stopped, surprised. 'Nothing was further from my mind.'

'Oh, boy.' I shrugged, trying to get my shoulder to un-knot.

'Well, Swan could make some serious trouble for me. She thinks I'm investigating you, helping her out. If she realises I'm just a neutral party –'

'Are you a neutral party, Mr Peters?' said the Doctor. 'Is it possible always to be a neutral party?' This was what he'd wanted to talk to me about.

'Call me Chick. Staying neutral is the journalist's job. We don't make the news, we just report it.'

'And yet, isn't there sometimes the temptation to interfere?'

I sat on the bonnet of the Pontiac. I thought of a story I'd been doing in Los Angeles about traffic safety. 'Well, you know. I wouldn't just stand there and let a kid get run over by a car, or something like that.' Even if it would make one hell of a story.

The Doctor nodded. 'But what if the stakes were higher than that?'

'Higher than a child's life?'

'Much higher. The lives of every child, woman, and man on the planet.'

My secret for dealing with people who are either mean or crazy is to imagine them in their underwear. I tried to imagine the Doc in his underdaks, and failed. 'Right,' I said, uncertainly. 'Because of the extraterrestrials.'

'If you prefer, imagine the device we found to be the product of a secret weapons laboratory, years ahead of other research.'

'So it is a weapon,' I said. The damn thing was in the trunk of the car. I slid off the bonnet.

'It could be used as one,' said the Doctor. 'By someone who penetrated its secrets.'

'But if it's so far advanced, wouldn't it be like a caveman trying to figure out how, I dunno, an electric toothbrush works?'

'A persistent enough caveman will eventually find the on-switch,' said the Doctor.

'OK,' I said. 'I can go along with that. So what's your angle?'

He raised his eyebrows. 'You're working for the "Eridani", right?'

'Not in the sense you mean. They asked for my help, and I was more than happy to help clean up the mess they'd got themselves into.'

'And the mess they've got our vulnerable little world into.'

'Indeed.'

'So, altruism.'

'If you like. Or think of it as involvement. My people – most people simply sit back and watch the universe go by. I prefer to roll up my sleeves and plunge my hands in. Get them wet, or dirty. Whatever's required.'

I was grinning. 'I bet in school you were the kid who always ate the Playdough.'

'Something like that,' he said.

'I've got my hands plenty dirty,' I said, seriously. 'I've done all the hard living I plan to. I've earned some time to sit back.'

'How old are you, Chick?' asked the Doctor.

'Thirty-three,' I said. 'Sometimes I feel about a thousand.'

'Hmmm.' He began the elaborate process of extracting a peanut butter cup from its wrapping. 'You and I have both seen more of life than either Bob or Peri. Their enthusiasm and idealism hasn't been worn down against the grindstone of time.' I wasn't so sure about Peri's enthusiasm, but I held my tongue. 'When you're young, it's hard to grasp the fact that other people can and will hurt you. It seems so unfair. We're both old enough to know that someone like Swan doesn't care about abstract ideas like fairness or privacy. When she wants to attack someone, nothing will stop her. If she gets hold of one of those devices, Mr Peters, I promise you that no-one's personal affairs will ever be private again.'

'Ah shoot – now what?'

'I want you to give someone a little advice,' I told Mondy. I heard him sigh at the other end of the phone. 'He doesn't know who you are, and he doesn't need to know. And I'm not going to ask you to do anything. I just want you to let him pick your brains for half an hour.'

'What if Swan's listening in?'

'I know you can find a safe place to talk somewhere in the bowels of Ma Bell. Come on, Mondy. You owe me one.'

'If Swan finds out I'm even talking to you,' said Mondy, 'I'm a dead man.'

'Well, I'd better hand you over then,' I said. I passed the phone to Bob.

Three

Our glorious return to the nation's capital: two rooms in a hotel slightly less crappy than the last one. Oh well, appreciate the advantages over home: room service, no housework, and a soda machine down the hall. If I'd had a spare shirt I've have sent it down to be laundered.

This time Peri butted in while Bob was talking to the receptionist, and insisted on having her own room. I think it just hadn't occurred to him or the Doctor that she might like a little privacy. After this morning's bathroom gymnastics I was tempted to get a room of my own as well, but I wanted to be able to eavesdrop.

Bob rented another car and buzzed off to see about tapping Swan's phones. I was torn between wanting to accompany him to see how it was done, and wanting to hang around the Doctor to see what he'd do next. In the end I decided to stick with him, if only to minimise the chances of being spotted by Swan.

Peri also insisted on having something to do. 'I might not be a computer expert, but I've got a brain,' she reminded the Doctor. 'There must be some way I can help. Anything's better than watching you guys play with that chunk of plastic.'

'Yes indeed there is, young Peri,' said the Doctor, brightening. We were sitting around in his room while he fiddled with the Apple II. 'I'm going to do a little investigating of my own into Miss Swan's affairs. That's going to mean sifting through quite a bit of information, but the results could be invaluable.' The

Doctor gave the Apple a reassuring pat. 'But first, I have an errand for you to run.'

Peri jumped up and saluted. 'What is it?'

He handed her a wodge of cash. 'Go and buy a printer for this thing,' he said. Peri stuck out her tongue, but she went.

And so began the hackers' version of legwork. I drove Peri to a computer shop and dropped in at my apartment for a change of clothes. By the time we got back, the Doctor had broken into Swan's credit card records. (He was more worried that Swan might notice than that the credit company would.)

The Doctor printed out page after page of Swan's credit card transactions – almost a year's worth. The printer chewed steadily through the paper we'd bought, until the last sheet fluttered out onto the floor.

'Oh well,' said the Doctor, 'that should be enough.' He gathered up the bundle of dead tree and handed it to Peri. 'Your job is to look for anything interesting, anything unusual. Anything which might tell us something useful about Swan and her activities.'

Peri flipped through the first few pages of the massive printout. 'Looks like she spends most of her money at computer stores.' She sat down, already absorbed in the thickly printed lines, twirling a highlighter pen around in her fingers.

And there we sat for the next few hours, while Peri muttered to herself and made the occasional mark on the page, and the Doctor stared into the Apple's screen and made little 'aha!' noises. I would have liked to borrow the machine, dial up my news service, and type up a report, but they'd have killed me.

The Doctor fooled around online for a little longer, then went back to fooling around with the Eridani's plastic ball. I took a nap. Only two things interrupted the boredom of the next few hours. One was a delivery of a dozen red roses, which the

Doctor sent back as it wasn't for us. The other was Bob's triumphant return from the land of phone crime.

'How did you get on?' said the Doctor.

Bob gave him a thumbs-up. 'Mission accomplished. We can listen in to Swan's phone calls any time we like.'

Peri looked up from her pile of printouts. 'I hope we're doing the right thing.'

Bob knew it was a bad idea, but he reckoned that with his sandy hair stuffed under a toque and in the rented car, he was pretty difficult to identify. So on his way back, he had driven past his house, just to take a look.

Everything looked just like it did any day. There were no police cars or crime scene tapes, no-one in the street. His house looked fine. Bob cruised past again, trying to see if anything inside had been touched.

He couldn't stand it. He had to know if they'd confiscated his computers. He especially couldn't stand the thought of losing that brand-new, five-grand IBM PC. The driveway was full of snow: he parked in the street and crept in through his back door.

The study was untouched. His notes and books and hardware had not been shoved into cardboard boxes and carried off by the Feds. Bob relaxed. Nobody had been in here since their panicked run to Baltimore. At the time, bolting had seemed like one hell of a good idea, especially after finding that tap. Bob gave his phone an evil look as he passed it on the way to the kitchen.

Bob actually leapt backwards through the kitchen door in fright. Taped to the fridge was a huge occult symbol drawn in thick red and black marker.

He was gripped by several conflicting urges: tear the thing

off the fridge door, run out of the house, run back into the study to check again everything was OK, run through the house to check there wasn't a dead snake in his bathtub or a live snake in his bed, grab the phone and call the Doctor (argh! no!), or just stand there slack-jawed and try to analyse the symbol.

He pulled the paper off the fridge with shaking hands. The seal was drawn freehand, but extremely neatly. It was all contained in a circle; inside that, a ring of Greek writing; inside that, another circle, divided into four by arrows; inside each quarter, a square crammed with more symbols, alchemical and astrological. It was damned complex. But talismans never were very elegant.

Bob stumbled into the study and grabbed some of his books. No, he was right – it wasn't from the Goetia, or the Key of Solomon, or the Heptameron. But nor was it just a scribble by someone trying to be spooky – it was too well-constructed, the work of someone who knew what they were doing.

Bob laid the symbol down on the kitchen table, carefully. He didn't want it near the phone or the computer. He didn't want to bring it with him, either. He made a quick sketch of it on the back of some printer paper, folded it up, and stuffed it into his jeans pocket. Maybe the Doctor could work it out.

Before he left the house, he dug his Sixth Pentacle of Mars out of a bedroom drawer and slung the talisman around his neck on a leather thong. No sense in taking any chances.

Unfortunately, he'd already taken one. And blown it.

Swan had lived in her station wagon, parked down the street, waiting for Bob to return. She had popped caffeine pills to stay awake, making sure she didn't miss a moment of the nothing that was happening in the street. She'd read the *Washington Post* from cover to cover by the time her prey showed up.

Swan waited while Bob went inside. She ate a cold, limp taco without taking her eyes off the house. Finally he emerged, looking nervous, and climbed back into his rent-a-wreck.

Swan followed, keeping well back. Bob never noticed her. She hoped her little message had rattled his mind.

She spent a few minutes driving around, looking for a parking spot near the hotel. No need to hurry. She strode in through the front doors carrying her suitcase and went to the little florist's shop.

'I'd like to send some flowers to one of your guests,' she said. 'Robert Salmon.' The florist gave her a card to sign, and she scribbled, 'Best wishes for your bar mitzvah. Florence.'

Swan had guessed Bob would sign in under his own name. If he were the sort to have a fake ID or two, she would have known about it. As it turned out, she didn't have long to sit in the lobby before a bellhop went past carrying the massive bouquet.

Swan quietly got up and followed the bellhop into the elevator. She watched from the vending machine niche down the hallway as someone answered the door. 'I'm afraid these aren't for us,' said a voice in an English accent.

Swan made her way down into the basement, where she found the bridging box for the whole hotel. A couple of cleaners gave her an odd look, but she just went on as though they weren't there, and they left her to whatever she was doing.

Which was attaching a DNR to the Doctor and company's phone line. The Dial Number Recorder would print out every number they called.

Early that evening, the Doctor plucked a fob watch from the inside pocket of his jacket. 'It's time,' he said, getting up from the Apple II and stretching. 'I've got to call the Eridani and arrange our delivery.' Bob, who'd had nothing to do all afternoon except watch the idiot box, eagerly leapt onto the abandoned machine.

Swan watched the Doctor leave, by himself, with a cardboard box tucked under his arm. He never noticed her, sitting at a glass table in the café area, downing an extra caffeine pill with her second coffee.

Swan could have followed him. Maybe she could even have got the device off him – I can easily see her as a mugger, vibrating with stimulants and cold anger, wielding one of the Japanese knives I'd seen in her kitchen. But instead, she decided to borrow the power of the law.

Swan went back to the basement and looked at the little roll of tape in the DNR. It had registered a single number. Swan clipped her linesman's test set to an outgoing line and called up a C/NA operator. Then she called the police.

The three of us almost walked into Swan as we exited the elevator. We were on our way to dinner. She was just stepping out of the other elevator, on her way back from the basement.

We stared at her: Bob and Peri and me, looking guilty as hell with our mouths hanging open. Swan looking guilty in her own way, her face forming a protective blank mask.

I expected a sarcastic remark, the sort of thing passed in the hallways in high school, a little flourish of superiority. She had found us again. She had proved her electronic omniscience and caught us with our computational trousers down. At the least she could have given us a knowing smile before floating out of the building.

Nothing. Just that blank stare. The personality she had shown in cyberspace stopped there.

'Come on,' I muttered to my partners in crime. We backed into the elevator, its doors still yawning open as though in surprise. They slid shut, cutting off Swan's empty glance.

'The Doctor,' said Peri, as the lift slid silently upwards. 'Do you think Swan knows where he's going?'

'She's not following him, that's for sure,' said Bob.

'She found us again. Maybe she found out where he's headed, too. That could mean the Eridani are in big trouble.'

'We'll call them,' said Bob.

'But what if Swan is listening in!'

'What difference is it gonna make?' Bob leaned his forehead against the elevator's mirrored wall, looking squashed. 'Man, she knows everything. It doesn't matter what we do. She knows it all.'

One

'*¿Hola?*'

'Luis? It's Sarah.'

'Sarah! I have some wonderful news for you.'

'Don't tell me just now. I need an eyeball, *en seguida*.'

'No problem. Let's go to the park, like spies. I'll be carrying a red rose.'

'How about the Mall? Lots of people around.'

'OK, opposite the Smithsonian Castle. I'll bet my news is bigger than yours.'

'I'll see you there in an hour, if the traffic is merciful.'

Luis Perez was ten years older than Swan, a greying Mexican who had met her on the conference calls when he first emigrated to California. They had hung out together on the phone system for years, never meeting in the flesh until Luis moved to DC to be closer to his relatives.

Luis worked in a library in Adams Morgan. For him, computers and phones were still just a hobby, while they'd become a career for Swan. He still used his phreaking skills to place free long-distance calls to his garrulous *abuela* in Puebla. But these days his main interest was collecting. His flat rivalled Swan's own home museum of things electronic.

Luis was waiting for her on the well-trodden grass of the Mall, wrapped tight in a grey wool coat, a single baby rose clutched in a gloved hand. The National Mall is a two-and-a-half-mile line of sight between the Lincoln Memorial and the Capitol, with the Washington Monument sticking out of the middle like a stray nuke. Half a million people line the Mall each year for the Fourth of July fireworks.

DC is low, with long lines of sight, boxy classical architecture mixed with weird sixties curves. Driving around in it you go from pompous to funky, wealth to poverty, business to tourism. The whole thing is very slowly sinking into the swamp plain it was built on.

Luis gave Swan a mock bow and handed her the flower. She looked at it. 'I gotta talk to you about that thing I got in western Maryland that time,' she said.

Luis looked at her in surprise. 'I also want to talk to you about "western Maryland".'

'Well, I hope you're having more luck than I am. I've got a bunch of smartasses on my tail who ripped me off. I've just set the police on them.'

Luis was getting more surprised by the moment. 'The police?' he said, looking around.

'I told them it was a sculpture. Worth a fortune. If they can't get it back I might just strangle the little bastards with my bare hands. They're good, Luis, really good for a change. We've been playing cat and mouse for days and I'm not sure whether I'm the cat or the mouse.'

'What can I do?'

Swan looked at him. 'I didn't call you to ask for help. I wanted to warn you. They might come looking for you.'

Luis nodded. The great Sarah Swan never asked for help; she only made bargains, collected favours. He put a gloved hand on her arm. 'Yes, I have been having more luck than you,' he said. 'Come with me. Come and see.'

* * *

Two months previously, Swan and Luis had driven together in his little red van to a farm in Allegany County. The family was auctioning their equipment, their land already sold. Luis and Swan walked past a small crowd examining the tractors and trucks that would be up on the block later that afternoon. The genuine auction was a cover for a rather less ordinary sale taking place in one of the farm's big sheds.

There were a dozen people there, sitting on folding chairs they had brought with them. Luis spread his big jacket on a bale of hay and he and Swan sat down side by side.

She recognised some of the faces. Swan had only a rough idea of who the other buyers were, a mix of collectors, incognito scientists, conspiracy theorists, and spies. These little auctions were held on an irregular schedule, always masked by some other big sale: last time it had been an office building selling off its desks and filing cabinets. Swan and Luis had sold one or two items over the years, but usually, they were here to buy.

The lots were presented by a soft-voiced young man in a dark suit who mostly looked at the ground; he always made her think of attendants at a funeral, their insistent solemnity. The resemblance would have been better if it hadn't been for his punk hair, a wave of metallic red that sparkled with golden highlights. Despite her not inconsiderable efforts, Swan had never managed to find out exactly who he was.

Today's selection was fairly typical. Plenty of circuit boards with suspicious pedigrees. A box of floppy disks that bore the label of a major researcher – bidding was fierce for that lot. More disks and some printouts of stuff downloaded from milnet. Part of what looked like the controls of a helicopter, labelled in Cyrillic script. Some of it had been brought by the bidders, but mostly it had filtered down through a grapevine of thieves and collectors. The auctioneer set a starting price for each. He had a reputation for scrupulous fairness when it came to estimating the values of his wares.

The young man always saved the most eccentric items until last, like a sort of dessert course. They often included odd little inventions, specially modified computers, and things the auctioneer admitted he could not identify. People ventured the last of their mad money on cheap gewgaws which might turn out to be anything from an amusing toy to a genuine innovation.

Swan rarely bought anything at the auctions; she and Luis joked that she was waiting for the pearl of great price. He was mostly interested in antique technology; the little gems of early computing that sometimes surfaced at these sales made it well worth his while to attend. That day he bought a RAMAC 305, gloating over the primordial hard drive while the spies battled for the military stuff.

'Our last item, ladies and gentlemen,' announced the auctioneer. He wore contact lenses that made his eyes appear an unnaturally bright blue. 'Two objects of extraterrestrial origin.'

A little polite laughter as he displayed the two gadgets. They looked nothing like the serious machinery he had been selling all afternoon. They looked like gift shop baubles, or kid's toys.

'I would like to start the bidding at five thousand dollars,' said the soft-voiced man.

That stopped the chuckling. The bidders glanced shyly at one another. What did the auctioneer know about those gizmos that they didn't?

Swan put up her hand for the first time that day. 'Five thou,' she said loudly. The other bidders looked everywhere but at her.

'Five five,' said someone, half-heartedly.

'Six thou,' said Swan. Luis was grinning and nodding at her. There was nothing he loved better than a surprise, some mystery machine he could pull apart at home and decipher.

'Um, six one?' said the other buyer, but Swan knew she had it.

'Six five,' she said firmly.

Silence. 'Going, going, gone,' murmured the auctioneer.

'Dutch?' said Luis.

'Of course,' said Swan.

They were each wearing a money belt tucked under their jackets. Luis had a thirty-eight special in his pocket as well, 'Just to balance the weight of the money,' he always said. They counted hundred dollar bills into a manila envelope and handed it over to the auctioneer, who passed back a box containing their purchases without ever looking them in the eye.

That night, they flipped for who got what in the parking lot of a Denny's.

Luis's apartment always smelled of cinnamon, coffee, ozone, and dustbunnies. The spare bedroom where he kept his collection was tidy and clean to the point of sterility, but the rest of the flat was always in need of vacuuming and polishing. Swan found the smell comforting, the smell of a place that's lived in. Her own house smelled of paint and empty rooms.

They hung up their coats and Luis went to the kitchen to boil up some strong Mexican coffee to warm them. The cardboard box they had brought home from the auction all those months ago was sitting on the living room table.

Swan opened the box, gingerly. The device Luis had chosen was still inside, nestled in layers of blue crepe paper. Its dark green-blue surface was covered in lighter tracings that looked like a cross between printed circuits and Tolkien's Elvish writing. It was bigger than her fist, maybe six inches long, a round shape pointed a little at one end.

And it was broken. When Swan had last seen it, it was a heavy handful. She had assumed it was nothing more than a decoration, like one of those polished crystals you could get, with some artist's idea of circuits etched into the surface: an artsy gift for the computer lover. She had been more than happy to leave it in Luis's hands and take the much more intriguing multicoloured device for herself.

Now the object had cracked into three large pieces. Instead of a single weighty lump, all that was left were those three chunks, maybe a quarter of an inch thick; the centre was hollow. Swan picked up one of the pieces. It was tough, smooth on the outside except for the lines of etching, crinkled and wrinkled inside. The inner texture made her think of the whorls and soft complexities of a brain.

Luis grinned at her from the kitchen doorway as she looked up at him. 'Your Easter egg hatched,' she said.

He raised his eyebrows, enjoying her surprise. 'More about that later,' he said, putting down a cup of rich coffee in front of her. 'Tell me about these smartasses who are making your life difficult.'

'They read my email. They read my frigging *email*, man,' she said. Swan took a long drag on the coffee, seemingly not bothered that it was seething hot. 'They broke into my work machine and they kicked me out while they were doing it.'

Luis was the only person in the world she would ever admit something like that to. He listened quietly as she outlined the Doctor's antics, how he had taken away the device from under her nose, how she had followed Bob. 'They know stuff about western Maryland that we don't,' she said. 'I have worked and worked on the device, and I've got no idea of how it works or what it's supposed to do. I've pestered collectors all over the country. All I've found out is that there are supposed to be three more of those devices. Five components making up a single machine.' She pushed the heels of her palms against her eyes. 'I think the Doctor is working for the original owners. They want their crap back.' Luis shrugged with his face. 'Don't gimme that!' said Swan. 'We paid good money for those items. It's us against them. And we're gonna be the ones who win.' She slammed both palms down on the table. In the dim light her pupils looked like a pair of black marbles.

'¡Cálmate!' said Luis. 'Think it over. They have given themselves away to you. You'll be able to learn from them where the other parts of this strange machine are. And in the meantime, we still have one of its components. A good one.'

'Luis,' she said, looking down into the box, 'what the hell was inside this thing?'

With a conspiratorial wink, he got up and crooked a finger to her. Swan put the box down on the table and followed him.

Luis put his finger to his lips. Very carefully, he turned the knob of the bathroom door. Swan craned her neck, trying to see around him. Luis trod softly into the cramped bathroom and, very slowly and gently, began to pull back the shower curtain.

The first thing Swan saw were the gadgets lined up on the rim of the tub. There was one of those plastic trays across the tub, piled with half-disassembled radios, Walkmen, circuit boards, Tandy hobby kits. There was more stuff in the dry tub.

It took her a long moment to see, really see, what was sitting in the bath along with all that junk. Her first thought was that Luis had fished a mermaid out of the half-frozen Potomac.

The thing in the tub was shaped roughly like the letter 'Y'. It had long, raised scales, or perhaps short, stiff feathers. What

Swan had taken for its tail seemed to actually be its head: a long cylinder rearing up above the other two limbs. Each of those held several pieces of an autopsied television set, as well as a couple of screwdrivers and some lengths of wire. Swan couldn't see how it was hanging onto so many things at once – she couldn't see hands, or fingers. Perhaps the scale-feathers did the gripping?

It didn't have a face. There was a truncated beak the colour of mahogany that looked as if it had been pushed into the flesh behind the dirty yellow feather-scales. She couldn't see eyes, ears, a nose, anything but the dull beak.

'Jesus, Luis,' she said. 'What do you feed that thing?'

Luis put the toilet lid down and sat on it. 'The only thing it seems to like is Kosher Pareve fruit loops.'

'You can't give it human food.'

'It wouldn't eat anything else. Anyway, think of how little the egg was. It's thriving.'

Swan stared at the animal. It didn't stare back, turning a piece of circuitry over and over at the end of a cylindrical limb. 'Do you think it knows we're talking about it?'

'I don't think it cares. All that interests it is mechanical things, electronic things. I gave it an alarm clock and a child's toy telephone and it plucked them apart.'

Swan leaned against the wall, the towelrack pressing into her back. 'OK,' she admitted. 'You got me. I'm impressed.'

'We should leave it alone,' said Luis, but he didn't get up. 'That coffee must be done.'

'I don't want to go out,' said Swan. 'I want to watch it.' She gave a little shudder, as though waking up out of a daydream. 'I guess I want to convince myself it's real.'

'It's a fascinating little thing, isn't it?' said Luis. 'Sometimes I find myself watching it for hours. I watch it take some appliance apart and put it back together again, over and over.'

'Just like its daddy,' said Swan. Neither of them moved, and in the kitchen, boiling coffee sludge escaped its saucepan and spread across the stovetop.

Bob called the number for the Eridani's bolthole again and again, but each time all he heard was ringing, a click, and a sort of screeching that got louder and softer.

'Do we have to move again?' said a weary Peri, stuffing her few possessions into a shoulderbag.

'We've gotta get off the grid,' said Bob. 'Isolate ourselves. Swan's all over the phone system like a rash.'

We went through the whole routine one more time: checkout, sneak out the back way leaving the rent-a-car in the parking lot, taxi to yet another car place. Bob paid cash for the remains of a '71 Travco ('designed and appointed to assure the finest in plush living for two people') and loaded it up with what remained of his nuclear survival kit. The RV looked like the unnatural offspring of a caravan trailer and a school bus. 'We got one heavily armoured recreational vehicle here, man!' enthused Bob.

'How are we going to find the Doctor?' said Peri.

Bob said, 'We're gonna mail him a letter.'

Meanwhile, the man in question was sitting in his rented Mercedes, looking up at a cop.

He had got out of the Eridani's apartment building with seconds to spare: just as he was about to knock on their door, he heard the elevator doors ping across the hallway and saw the blue of uniforms inside. He hoofed it down the concrete stairs of the emergency exit two at a time and slid back into his car in the basement garage.

He was sure there was no way the police could have spotted him. But he was pulled over not five minutes after leaving the building. The police car and his car were sitting on the shoulder of the Beltway, the rest of the traffic shooting past in Dopplered spurts.

'Can I see your licence? Please? Sir?' said the cop. He and his partner, sitting back in the patrol car, were a pair of grim blond body-builders who looked like they'd been stamped out of the same mould, like Smurfs.

'Of course, officer.' The Doctor fished around in his jacket pockets, pulling out all sorts of identity cards, spare change, and junk, until he found a wallet containing four American dollars, ten Scottish pounds, an autographed picture of Grace Murray Hopper and a current Maryland driver's licence. The policeman wordlessly wandered back to his car and handed the piece of plastic to his clone.

In that moment when their eyes were off him, the Doctor reached over and opened the glovebox. He knew it was a dangerous thing to do; if they noticed the movement, they would assume he was reaching for a weapon, getting it ready to use.

He was.

The cop was back. 'You don't mind if we search the vehicle, sir?' he said.

'Of course not, officer. Always more than happy to co-operate with the authorities in pursuit of their duty.' The Doctor got out of the car and stood near the bonnet while the pair of patrolmen sniffed around the trunk and then the glovebox.

The cop straightened up and showed his partner the Eridani device over the roof of the car. 'What do we have here?' he said.

'Seems like we found what we were looking for,' said the other cop. 'I'm going to ask you to come for a ride with us, sir.'

* * *

The kids were so raddled that I offered to drive. Bob dozed in the passenger seat, occasionally emitting directions, until we arrived at a post office. 'Pull over, pull over.' His slurred speech sounded like backmasking.

Bob jumped out of the campervan while I kept the motor running, dashed up to the post office boxes, fumbled with the keys, and pushed a postcard into one of the boxes. He looked up and down the street once, startled, as if suddenly remembering we were supposed to be on the run. Then he collapsed back into the passenger seat and erupted into mighty snores.

Somewhere around here, I realised I'd forgotten all about Trina's birthday. I slapped my hand against the car door and cussed. I'd promised to take her out for surf 'n' turf. There was nothing I could do about it now – I couldn't even phone her.

We headed out along 270, past the tatty yellow ribbons still tied to telephone poles, until the strip malls tapered out into houses and then into nothing, just the highway.

TWO

By midnight we felt safe enough to stop and sleep.

Peri and Bob had got so used to my quiet presence that they talked as if I wasn't there. I sat in the passenger seat of the Travco, trying to make myself comfortable, while they lay in the sleeping bags in the back, muttering about whether the Doctor was OK and if he could find us. Centre of their world.

Boy, it was brown back there in the Travco. Brown brown brown. The national colour of the Seventies. Bob had chivalrously taken the sofa under the mangled venetians, while Peri got the 'bedroom'. They had the heater on full, running off the generator. I suppose I could have stretched out on the floor, but I didn't fancy being trodden on.

We were pulled over in a scenic lookout. Other than their murmuring, it was deadly quiet. I had a view of pine trees standing like dark giants, rearing up from the hillside and staring down at the gravel arc of the lookout. There was no moon. If I ducked my head a little, I could see a skyful of burning stars.

Oh yeah. I stretched out my legs on the driver's side, my jacket pillowed under my head. The dark is good. It's always good. I remember burning out of Los Angeles in a little Citroën I later crashed in a ditch and left for dead. The California emptiness looked like a video game, looked like Night Driver, just lights in the sky and lights marking the edges of the road, a big black screen. I was invisible then. And the three of us were invisible now. Even Swan couldn't see through the thick black muffler we were wrapped in. I nodded off in my diagonal position, warm and toasty in the blast from the van's heater.

I woke up as the sound of another car carried through the night air. A moment later we heard the crunch of tires on gravel. I ducked down, peeking through the passenger window. The other car was parking in the lookout, a little distance from us.

'It's OK,' I said. 'It's the Doctor.'

Peri and Bob wriggled loose from their sleeping bags and opened the side door of the campervan. The Doctor got inside and closed the door. They scrunched up to make room for him, banging on the back of my seat.

'Thank you for the postcard, Bob,' he said.

'Are you OK?' said Peri, sleepily.

'Manifestly,' said the Doctor.

'Well, how did everything go?'

'Almost without a hitch. I did have a little run-in with some officers of the law.' Peri and Bob's eyes grew huge. 'Fortunately, with the device at hand, it wasn't difficult to persuade them to sit quietly in their patrol car until I had made good my escape.'

'You did what?' I said.

He said grimly, 'I was not exaggerating when I said that, in the wrong hands, the device could be used for mischievous ends. In any case, it's out of the picture now. The device has been safely returned to its owners, and they have retreated to a safer location. I suggest you all get a good night's rest, and tomorrow we'll begin our search for its twin.'

Some time later I opened my eyes and saw that the Doctor was standing in the lookout, uh, looking out. His hands were clasped behind his back. Standing so still, in his black suit, he looked like one of the mountains out there in the night, solid and ramrod still. I slipped out of the car, pulling on my jacket, and went to stand beside him.

The air was crisp and clean as though it had just been washed. American forests *smell* different, they have a rich, dirty, wet smell you could cut with a knife. Australian forests have their own delicate, dry smell. It's like comparing coffee to tea. And the sky... instead of the sparkling cross, there's the huge, empty shape of the plough, cranking its way around the northern pole of the sky like a giant handle.

I lit up. In the freezing air, the cigarette felt like it was burning my fingers. The Doctor glanced back towards the car. 'How do you think they're managing?' he asked quietly.

I took a deep, deep drag of that tasty smoke. 'They're knackered,' I said bluntly. 'I think the excitement is wearing off, even for Bob. Peri's just coasting. It's like she's used to things sucking, she expects it.'

The corner of the Doctor's mouth scrunched into an angry look. 'That young lady has seen me through some very troubled times. And that young man has a great deal of courage and determination. They both deserve better than running from place to place in a constant lather.'

I shrugged. 'If either of them really can't take it, they'll just step out for a packet of peanuts and never come back.' He looked down at me. 'They'll survive,' I said. 'They both believe this is incredibly important.'

'It's more important than I can tell you, Mr Peters.'

'Chick. Please.'

'Chick,' he said. He looked out across the valley again, breathed in that cold clean air. 'May I?' the Doctor reached for my ciggie. I handed it over. He flicked his hand in the air, and suddenly it was gone. He went on as though nothing had happened. 'It's so hard to believe this little world is balancing on the edge of a knife. Every day, any day, at a moment's notice, the sky could fill with deadly lights.'

'I know. Now this thing with Poland. You know, my neighbour's kid plays Missile Command. That home video game. He's still too young to get the joke.'

But the Doctor was shaking his head. 'It's not your petty wars I'm worried about,' he said. That startled the hell out of me: one of the facts of life, living in Washington DC, was knowing you were standing in one of the world's biggest nuclear targets.

'Oh, I get it,' I said. 'The aliens. The UFOs are going to come and get us if we don't return their toys.'

'A distinct possibility,' he said. 'Though I'm far more worried about what human beings might do with Eridani technology.' He raised a hand to stop me before I could ask again what the devices were supposed to do. 'A cageful of mischievous and belligerent monkeys. And someone throws in a hand grenade for them to play with. There's one more component out there. One more. I'm convinced Miss Swan knows where it is. She will be more determined than ever to keep it out of our hands, to discover its secrets.'

'How much harm can Swan do?' Where the hell had he put the lit cigarette? 'Even if she finds the last pieces, won't it be useless on its own?'

'It may actually be *more* dangerous without the other components to control it.'

'Doctor,' I said, 'did you invent it? Is that what this is all about?'

He give me one of his piercing blue looks, and suddenly that safe lambswool feeling of the darkness just flew away, and I had the same feeling I had had with Swan: this was a person who could look right through you and see all your secrets. He lived on another plane, rich with information, with a million data points you had no way of accessing. Like a four-dimensional monster that can see you when you can't see it.

'Still trying to come up with an explanation you can put into print,' he said.

'Well, I've already decided you can't be a Ruskie, or you'd have found some way of getting rid of me.' I had a sudden flash of being chucked down the side of the mountain in the dark. 'Before now,' I added.

'I see,' said the Doctor. 'And what are your other theories about my identity?'

I ticked them off on my fingers. 'Corporate agent. Industrial spy. UFOlogist. Undercover military investigator. Pseudologue. A major unknown hacker – that goes without saying. Art thief.'

'Art thief?'

'Well, the "devices" really could be stolen artworks for all I know. So, am I getting warm?'

He just smiled, and went back to stargazing.

'Which of those is Epsilon Eridani?'

The Doctor's finger swept up to point instantly at the star. 'That one,' he said. 'The "Eridani's" jumping off point for your volume of space.'

I suddenly seemed to see the lines between the stars, the paths taken by all those imaginary starships, hopping from one to the next to the next to the next. 'So how come they haven't taken over the world?'

'Without faster-than-light travel? Very uneconomical. Besides, the ecology is all wrong. Mars would be more their cup of tea, if it wasn't already taken.' He spoke not with the feverish excitement of a true believer, but casually, like a lecturer sketching in the basic details for a student.

'So I suppose they're the source of all the UFO sightings.'

'Certainly not. The Eridani have been slingshotting craft

through your solar system for centuries, studiously avoiding drawing attention to themselves. It's only now that the human race has developed radio that this mighty bungle has occurred.'

I was getting interested despite myself. His story was so straightforward – no ancient civilisations, no higher planes of consciousness. 'So why did they screw up?'

'They simply didn't notice that anyone was here. It only takes eleven years for radio signals to reach Eridani from Earth, but by the time they get there, distance has watered them down to a billionth of their original strength. Put simply, they didn't care and they weren't looking. To them, the Earth is just the equivalent of an interplanetary traffic cone.' I had to laugh at that, but he looked deadly serious. 'And just about as disposable. There must be a world for Peri to come home to,' he breathed.

The back door of the campervan creaked. I saw Bob climbing out, stretching his gangly limbs in the freezing morning air.

The Doctor reached behind my ear and extracted the cigarette, still lit, with a flourish.

'Doctor,' said Bob. 'There's something I need you to take a look at.'

He took a roughly folded sheet of paper out of his pocket and uncrumpled it. The Doctor snapped on a flashlight as Bob laid the sheet flat on the bonnet of the campervan. 'And what have we here?' he asked.

'I found this on my fridge. Not actually this. I found this diagram taped to my fridge. This is just a copy.'

'When was this?'

'Yesterday afternoon,' admitted Bob.

The Doctor ran a finger over the diagram, tracing its geometry, its symbols. 'Quite a professional job,' he murmured. Bob was shivering. It was weird to watch the Doctor shift frames like this – science fiction one moment, fantasy the next.

'Someone meant to give you a good scare.'

Bob relaxed a little. 'So you don't think it's for real,' he said. 'It's just meant to spook us out.'

'When it comes to the occult,' said the Doctor, 'there's real, and then there's real. Your intruder, and I think we can safely assume it was Miss Swan, may have had one of three intentions. One, she noticed your interest in things arcane and thought she would use superstition against you. Two, she is a believer herself and hoped to harm you in some paranormal way. In either case, you have nothing to worry about.'

'What's three?' said Bob.

'She actually has a command of paranormal powers, and this symbol has some genuine and measurable purpose,' pronounced the Doctor. 'You know, it's amusing – in the theatre, the term *machinery* is sometimes used to mean the supernatural elements in the play. Gods and goblins produced from the stage machinery.'

'I don't get it,' Bob said. 'Do you believe in this stuff, or don't you?'

The Doctor leaned against the desk, holding Bob's scribbled impression of the seal in his hands. 'The world is full of real and strange powers. It is also full of cheap and shallow imitations of those powers. Half-remembered keys to the energy of the universe. Half-invented rituals. Mental practices that have become detached from the cultures that made sense of them.' He looked up at Bob. 'Your *Key of Solomon* and *Goetia* are the equivalent of watching a television with the plug pulled out. The form is there, but not the content.'

Bob had a death-grip on his personal talisman. 'What about the device? What if it gave her some kind of power?'

'I think we'd know about it already,' said the Doctor simply.

Cold rain started to fall, carrying the fresh promise of snow to follow. The Doctor went back to his rental and turned on the radio, catching a little distant opera between the crackling of static. I don't think he slept – he was just waiting for the rest of us to wake up. I crawled back into the passenger seat of the RV.

Bob stayed looking up at the sky for a while, pulling on a beanie against the fat, chilly drops of rain. We were miles from the nearest electrical power, the nearest phone. But Bob was surrounded by energies he couldn't see or touch. Like the rain, falling everywhere, those energies connected everyone. He wasn't safe in the dark, but vibrating in a network of power like a bug fished out of the air by a spider's web. He would never be invisible.

The Doctor had brought about a million chocolate bars for breakfast. He kept finding more and more of them in the pockets of his suit, along with a bottle of chocolate milk for Bob. We sat in the campervan, shivering our socks off. 'I'll never be mean about a hotel room again,' said Peri.

'What's on the agenda for today?' said Bob.

'Our goal now is to follow Swan's movements without her being able to follow ours. That means we keep moving and we stay anonymous.'

Peri said, 'So how do we know what she's doing if we can't use the phone or computers?'

The Doctor raised a finger. 'Actually, we can do both. We just have to be very careful about it.'

There was a line of telephone poles sticking up from the forest floor, their wire-laden heads looming over the road. Bob and the Doctor picked their way down the steep slope, grabbing onto trunks and shrubs to avoid a long bum's rush into the wet undergrowth below. Peri and I spread a map on the bonnet of the campervan so we'd have an excuse if anyone pulled over. The occasional car cruised by, but no-one disturbed us.

The Doctor came into view a few minutes later, halfway up one of the poles. He was climbing awkwardly, wearing a pair of gardening gloves, keeping a death-grip on the metal steps. We could see a long coil of wire looped over one of his shoulders, and a leather satchel, like a kid's schoolbag, over the other.

At the top, he stuck a set of instructions onto the wood of the pole with a bit of blu-tac, and went to work with tools from the leather bag. Peri and I leaned over the safety rail to see what Bob was doing. He appeared to be setting up his computer down there, spread out on a picnic blanket.

We looked at one another. 'How the hell's he gonna run it?' I said.

But the Doctor had thought of everything. After clambering down from the pole, making Peri bite her lip and mutter curses, he hauled himself up the slope carrying some spare cable. Shortly afterwards, Bob's computer was running off Travco power.

I followed the Doctor back down the wet bank, slipping and sliding in melting snow. Bob was hunched awkwardly in front of the Doctor's Apple II. 'We're in,' he said. I crouched down, shading my eyes so I could read the screen. He'd logged into his university account. The modem was connected to the phone lines by a cable that ran right up the telephone pole. It was the most awkward, overproduced, jerry-rigged lashup I'd ever seen. But it was a thoroughly anonymous way into Swan's private electronic world – provided they could get through the door.

He and Bob spent the next hour trying to break back in to the TLA mainframe. Last time, it had been like a hot knife into the butter. Now, nothing from the Doctor's bag of tricks could crack Swan's security. She had gone back in and nailed shut every doorway, every window, every trapdoor in her system.

I got bored watching them try and went back to the cabin of the campervan, where Peri was dozing in the driver's seat. We had a lovely view of the misty valley. I checked my look in the rear view mirror and we talked for a bit, swapping favourite films. Mine's *Key Largo*. Peri's is something called *Ghostbusters* that I've never heard of. She told me a funny story from her first year of college: one day she was out walking beside a road when she saw a little white dog come out of a church parking lot. It was tiny, a toy dog – Peri knew it wasn't a poodle, although she didn't really know what it was. It trotted along, surprisingly fast, its little pink tongue flicking in and out as it bounced along the pavement.

A moment later the little dog had wandered out into the road. It was a suburban street, but busy. Peri expected the dog's owner to come running out of the parking lot. But no-one appeared. The little dog trotted across the road and was up onto the opposite pavement before any more traffic came along.

But now the dog was running around in the gas station! Peri reached the big intersection, waiting at the lights, watching as two people started calling the dog. A woman in a pleated skirt knelt down, whistling. But the dog took no notice, this time heading for the four lanes of the main road.

Peri's heart sank as she saw it scoot out into the traffic. It was so small, surely none of the dozens of drivers queued up could see it, let alone the drivers rushing past on the other side of the road.

No – there it was! It had somehow emerged on the other side, without having been crushed into street pizza or causing a ten-car pile up. Peri felt her shoulders sag in relief.

Oh, for God's sake, it was back out in the road again! The

light had just changed, and the first car was moving slowly enough that they could brake to avoid killing it. The two cars behind it braked and honked. Randomly, obliviously, the tiny dog darted sideways through the traffic, constantly moving, jaywalking until it was back on Peri's corner.

It trotted down the pavement, tongue still dangling, as though nothing had happened.

Peri watched it go. If the dog had stopped for a moment, frightened by the traffic, it would have been run over. But it just kept moving, and the cars just kept missing it. It was almost, she thought, as though the dog hadn't been killed because it had never occurred to it that it was in danger.

'Sometimes that dog reminds me of the Doctor,' she laughed. 'And sometimes it reminds me of me.'

'So,' I said, 'do you think you'll keep on travelling with him?'

The smile slid off Peri's face. 'Well,' she said hesitantly, 'I don't think there's really much *point*.'

'You know,' I said, 'all this would be more fun if we were actually going somewhere. Road trips usually go in a straight line, not round and round in circles. And then we end up sitting here while the geeks have all the fun.'

'It's not that,' said Peri. 'You know that old saying about flying – that it's hours of boredom plus minutes of stark terror? Being with the Doctor is like that. Sometimes it's horrible, but sometimes it's so exciting... but when it comes to the crunch, the only thing I can do is sit here. I don't know anything about computers. Or aliens either. The Doctor is always having to pull me out of some scrape. I'm pretty much useless, really.'

We sat there for a few moments. I said, 'You know, I think in a way he's doing all this stuff for you.'

She turned to look at me. 'What do you mean, "for me"?'

'Whatever's going on with these devices, he takes it very

seriously. He even thinks it could be the end of the world. The end of your world.'

'My world? You mean he wants to save the States?'

'Because it's your home,' I said.

'He doesn't even *like* America.'

'He likes you.'

'We can't seem to get along.'

'You like him, don't you?'

The smile inched its way back onto her face. 'Yeah. I do. He can be a pain in the ass, but he's a lot of fun to be around.' She told me about her first time on board the Doctor's boat. 'I have a little white room all to myself,' she said. 'That first morning I woke up and I swear I didn't know who I was. Never mind where, I couldn't even think of my name for about half a minute. I just lay there in a kind of daze, staring at a white wall and wondering what was going on. I mean, I'd woken up in hotel rooms all my life, but this was different. Like I had turned into somebody new. I was starting a whole new life.'

At that moment, we heard another car. I looked in the side-view mirror. 'Oh, shit burgers,' I said. 'It's the police.' They pulled in between us and the Doctor's car.

Peri gripped the steering wheel. 'What're we gonna *do*?' she squeaked. She pushed her hair out of her face, screwed her courage to the sticking-place, and told me to put my arm around her.

'What?'

'You heard.'

I slipped my arm around Peri's shoulders as an officer of the law armed with a pistol and a vast moustache strode over to the parked campervan. Both of us must have been silently uttering the same prayer. Please don't let him see the cable. Please don't let him see the cable.

He tap-tapped on the driver's side window, and Peri wound it down, giving him her big, perfect smile. 'Good morning,' she said.

'Good morning to y'all,' said the officer. 'Just wanted to make sure you're all right out here.'

'Oh, we're fine,' said Peri. 'Just admiring the scenery.'

Officer Moustache didn't answer. He was giving me The Look. My heart dropped into my stomach and slid from there down to my boots. I had seen The Look many a time before, and it always meant trouble.

'Step out of the car, please,' said Officer Moustache. He took a step back so Peri could open the door.

'Is there a problem, officer?' said Peri, all nineteen-year-old timid friendliness, sending out the vibes of a good kid from a good family who would just, you know, like, *die* if she ever got into trouble.

'Come on and step out of the car. Both of you.'

We got out. Officer Moustache herded Peri around to the passenger side and stood us next to one another. He took a good, long look at both of us, as though he was comparing us.

He undid the catch on his holster, so his pistol was handy. 'Don't you make any sudden moves, now,' he said.

Very suddenly, his meaty hands were undoing the button on my jacket. 'What the hell!' I yelped, slapping them away. 'What is this, a strip search?'

'You shut the hell up and keep still,' he said. He grabbed hold of the jacket and ripped it open, sending buttons popping off into the snow.

This was the point at which Peri, her back braced against the car, lifted her right foot and extended her leg like a harpoon tipped with a high-heeled shoe right into Officer Moustache's beefy groin.

He bent over and uttered a stream of imprecations that I'm not gonna repeat in case there are ladies reading. As he came back up his hand was reaching into his holster.

I applied my trusty right hook, aiming for just below the moustache. He went down into the gravel and slush without another dirty word.

Peri crouched and snatched the gun out of his holster. She held it like it would explode at any moment. 'You take it,' she gasped.

I went to the police car, pulled the keys out of the ignition, wiped them and the gun clean with the inside of my pocket, and locked the gun in the trunk. Then I chucked the keys out into the valley as far as they would go.

'Whoah.' Peri was bent over a little, her hands on her knees, like she couldn't get her breath. She was looking down at the policeman we'd knocked out. 'Whoah, *shit*. What the hell was that all about?'

'I don't want to know what the hell that was all about.'

'You know, he never even noticed the cable.'

We looked at one another, and both of us ran to the railing, waving our arms and shouting, 'Doctor! Get *up* here! You get up here *now*!'

65

One

I switched off the radio when *Long Distance Runaround* came on. Peri, who had been dozing, woke up with a start in the abrupt silence. 'Can't stand that album,' I muttered.

We had been driving since early morning. Peri offered to take a shift behind the wheel, but I could see how much she needed a nap, so I chivalrously insisted she try to get some Zs in the Travco's small bunk. She had switched on the radio, keeping it down low, saying that the familiar music would help her to sleep.

The Doctor sat on the bunk bed. He was building something back there, and had been for hours. He had interrupted our journey three times to run into stores he spotted out of the window. The bunk was strewn with bits of metal and tools, probably arranged in a careful order that the Doctor understood but which, to anybody else (me, for example) looked like a jumbled mess.

We had dropped Bob off in a motel in Frederick. The Doctor insisted that someone should stay near a phone line while we made out great expedition down the Delamarva Peninsula. Bob would stay connected to his email account via an Anderson Jacobson A211 acoustic coupler – a chunky beige modem with padded rests for the phone receiver. He set up the tap on Swan's phone to forward to his home answering machine; if she made a call, it would be recorded, and he could play back the messages by calling the machine. (Before we paid for the room,

Bob checked that its phone was touch-tone and not rotary-dial.) Every two hours, we would call to see if our efficient spy had any new information.

It was the tap that had sent us on the long drive eastward. She had phoned Luis Perez to let him know she'd be away for a day or so. She said she was going to 'visit' Charles Cobb, the deceased collector, in Ocean City. (The Doctor was at first disbelieving and then amused when Bob assured him there *is* a place called Ocean City.) Neither Swan nor Luis mentioned what was living in Luis's bathroom: for that sort of exchange, they'd use payphones or a face-to-face meeting. We didn't have a phone book for Ocean City, so I bullied Mondy into coughing up Cobb's address. 'His number's been disconnected,' the phreak reported. 'But I looked at the last couple of bills.'

Bob had been happy to stay wired to the network in the motel, but the Doctor had also wanted to leave Peri behind. 'This expedition is going to involve not just a tedious trip from one side of the state to the other, but some real-life breaking and entering,' he told her. 'There's not only the risk of another confrontation with the police, but with Swan. I'd rather you kept Bob company while I confront them.'

'No way,' said Peri. 'I'm not sitting in some motel while you have all the fun. I've never been to Ocean City.'

'Peri!' He could pack her name with a world of irritation. 'It's the middle of winter!'

'You're not leaving me out!'

'I'll never understand you! First you complain about being put into danger, then you're upset because I want to keep you out of it!'

Peri won that one by getting into the passenger seat and refusing to be budged. The Doctor threw up his hands and got into the back. I took the wheel, remembering the time my dad made me drive my two bickering cousins to Orange. I had solved the problem of their constant noise by dumping them by the side of the road and driving off, returning half an hour later to pick up a couple of very quiet kids. Thankfully we sat in a disgusted silence until Peri balled up her jacket between her head and the window and dropped off.

The Doctor spoke softly, so as not to disturb his slumbering fellow traveller, but I could make out every word. 'Your world is reaching a turning point here, Mr Peters.'

'How do you mean?' I murmured.

'At the moment, any electronics hobbyist worth their salt can hold everything there is to know about a computer in their head. They can know a program intimately, down to the individual lines of machine code – even know the system firmware which supports it just as intimately, and the hardware down to the individual circuit paths. One human being can still design an operating system, write a video game, follow all the actions of a microprocessor. They can take the same pride as a Victorian engineer does in oiling every piston and gear of his steam engine. Or a motor enthusiast, who can trace a problem from its largest-scale effects down to the finest detail of a sticking valve.'

I was pleased; not many people have seen past the geek surface. 'I know the guys you mean. The ones with furnaces for brains.'

'It won't last. In just a few years, even the circuit diagrams for an oven or a car will be vast and inscrutable. Huge chunks of logic will be locked inside little black boxes. Chip diagrams will become too huge to trace or grasp. The world becomes as formalised at the microcomputer end as in systems hundreds of times the size of Bob's Apple. Programmers will become teams, teams will become bureaucracies, the ribs of a lean harmonious system will be lost under a layer of flabby toolkits and libraries and protocols. All proper and correct and fully functional, of course – but leaving no room for the elegant shortcut, the blinding efficiency of the intuitive leap straight from the large to the small. They can do so much... but nothing with the bare-metal directness of the one who understands. It's a dying art, Mr Peters, a dying art.'

I said, 'That doesn't look like a computer you're designing back there.'

He gave me one of his small, knowing smiles. 'It isn't.'

I switched the radio back on, in time to catch the swirling beginning of *Tom Sawyer*.

We stopped somewhere near Annapolis for our first call to Bob. We had just started to lose the DC radio stations in a haze of static. I twiddled the dial, trying to find something worth listening to, while the Doctor and Peri crammed into the phone booth. She fed it coins while the Doctor shouted down the crackling line at Bob.

'I've found Cobb's account on a BBS[5],' Bob told the Doctor, his voice a mix of excitement and professional cool. 'There was a message from him in those emails of Swan's you downloaded. The number was in his .sig file.'

'Ah,' said the Doctor. 'When you say "found"...'

'Cobb was no hacker,' said Bob. 'His password was "secret"! I've saved about half of his email onto diskettes. His account

---

[5] A Bulletin Board System is a meeting place for computer users. It's not a network, but a single machine: the users can connect via modem, leave public messages and send and read private email and swap files. Bob showed me the BBS in question, a private bulletin board for a clique of technology collectors, with an unlisted number. Since Cobb had inadvertently made it so easy for Bob to break in, I don't think they ever realised he had visited. There must be hundreds of accounts on BBSes and the ARPAnet where the owners never see the footprints of intruders.

hasn't been used for a while – Swan must not have reached Ocean City yet. In fact, she may end up not going there at all. She called her friend again to say she was going to meet someone at the Delaware State Fair.'

'The what?' said the Doctor.

'It's in Harrington. Lots closer than Ocean City. Get Chick to look it up on the map. Swan said she wanted lots of people around, for safety. Look up the State Fairgrounds, that's where she'll be. You guys must be an hour ahead of her – it was at least an hour between the two calls I taped, so she was still in DC. I'll bet she's still at the fair when you arrive.'

We stood around the van for a few minutes, stretching our legs and puzzling over his new development. 'Who's she meeting?' Peri wanted to know. 'I thought you said that guy was dead.'

'That's right,' said the Doctor. 'Cobb tried to arrange a meeting between one of the Eridani and one of his fellow technology enthusiasts, with appalling consequences. The Eridani still aren't clear on exactly what happened. Certainly someone tried to betray someone else... perhaps Swan is planning to meet the third party.'

'But they couldn't have another one of the components. Could they?'

'No. The Eridani retrieved it after the disastrous meeting, along with...' The Doctor saw me listening. 'Swan is on a wild goose chase.'

'Well why are *we* driving all this way then? Why not just let her waste her time?'

'For information,' said the Doctor.

'But can't Bob just get that off Cobb's computer?'

'Not if it isn't *on* Cobb's computer. Not everything is out there in the great green and black void, you know. Swan had to invade Bob's filing cabinet to get his details. It will be some years before she could rustle up the same information over a phone line.' The Doctor stretched his arms above his head and yawned. 'Besides, I want to meet Swan eye to eye.'

'Let me guess,' said Peri. 'You figure that if you can talk to her in person, she'll come around to your point of view.'

'It has been known,' said the Doctor, with dignity. 'If nothing else, once we make contact with her, she'll find us very difficult to dislodge. And that will make it harder for her to do anything with us knowing about it – or stopping it, if it comes to that.'

I'd never driven over the Chesapeake Bay Bridge before. It's the strangest thing – two four-mile ribbons of road floating a couple of hundred feet above the water. It's actually two bridges side by side, so there's a lot of empty air between you and the cars going the other way. The feeling that there's nothing between you and the water is eerie.

'You know,' I told the Doctor, 'when I was a kid, we always spent our holidays driving around the outback, staying in caravan parks. We'd spend all day driving to get somewhere. But it wasn't much like this.'

Despite that, sitting behind the wheel on a trip across the US countryside was, surprisingly, not much different to sitting in the back on a trip across the Australian countryside (or more often, lying down with my bare feet pressed against the window, watching the gum trees rush by). You still ended up in those long, thoughtful silences – not quite highway hypnosis, but some relative of it.

I found myself imagining what if would be like if Mr Ghislain's extraterrestrials were real, trying to pursue the consequences of that. (I guess I was looking for a contradiction to catch the Doctor out with.)

Imagine if they were out there right now, circling the fifth brightest star in the constellation of Eridanus. Think of the time scale on which they'd have to operate: their civilisation would function over distances which make Columbus' voyage look like a trip to the soda machine. A better analogy: imagine if Columbus had no boats that could harness the speed of the wind – imagine if he had to swim to America.

So does that mean they're incredibly long lived – even immortal? Do they shoot one of their 'slow packets' out into space the way we would post a letter – confident that it will be delivered and replied to quickly enough to make it worth the effort of licking the stamp? Or is it a monumental event, a moonshot?

Ghislain claimed they had to hire a faster boat from another bunch of aliens, ones who did know the secret of faster-than-light travel. Are the Eridani jealous of their neighbours? Can't they scrape up enough cash to buy their own starships? Or do they scoff at those hotrods, the way we might smirk as a teenager roars down our street in his first hoon-mobile? I can't imagine human beings carrying out a mission that spanned centuries – politicians can barely see past the next election.

I found myself trying to imagine the great, cold minds who could operate at that speed, and had to snap myself out of the reverie. 'What is that thing you're building?'

'You've heard of elegance in software design,' said the Doctor. 'Programs which rely on cleverness to solve problems in the quickest, cleanest way possible.' He hefted the machine he had built. 'This represents the opposite of that approach.'

'Brute force,' I said.

'Just in case we need it.'

When we got to Harrington, we drove around for half an hour

trying to find the State Fairgrounds. There were grounds, all right, but no Fair. We all looked at one another. 'I guess we better ask someone,' said Peri.

A gas station attendant looked at us as though we'd asked for directions to the Martian Embassy. 'The State Fair is only on in July,' he explained. 'You're kind of late. Or maybe kind of early.'

Peri said, 'Maybe she meant she was going to meet someone at the fairgrounds, not the Fair.'

'We drove all over,' said Bob. 'There was nobody there. Have we ever been had. What a bunch of hosers.'

'Swan has discovered the tap on her phone,' said the Doctor. 'We'll have to let Bob know – there's not much point in monitoring her calls if she's going to use them for disinformation. Blast. That's quite a useful resource, gone!'

Peri and I exchanged glances. I wonder if she was feeling a little relief that we wouldn't be using the tap again, the same as I was. Computer crime is too new to give you the creeps the same way that eavesdropping on someone's phone does.

'So, after that little diversion, it's on to Ocean City,' said the Doctor.

'We're on our way,' I said.

'She knows we're going there,' said Peri. 'If she found the tap on her phone, then she must know we heard her earlier calls.'

The Doctor didn't have a reply to that. 'Do you want to take that turn behind the wheel?' I asked Peri. We pulled over and they both got into the front. I stretched out in the back seat. I wished I could take my shoes off and press my feet against the window.

Ocean City is basically one long street, several miles running down the finger of a peninsula, with cross-streets travelling just two or three blocks from the oceanfront to the bay. In December it's almost but not quite a ghost town – there are still cars, but far too few to justify eight lanes of road... closed miniature golf courses, boarded-up diners. The average age of the people in this town goes up twenty years in the off-season, and every one of those years seems to be added to the age of the town itself. The sky is grey, the houses are grey, the sea is a slab of slate.

Cobb's house was a faded clapboard relic of the '50s, off on the bay-side down near the Route 50 bridge – standalone, but not much elbow room between it and the neighbours: land is scarce and pricey on a glorified sandbar. More and more of the sand is being eaten away on the ocean side: eventually the big hotels are going to end up on stilts. Back in the '30s a hurricane actually carved a channel through the peninsula, the sea charging in to reach the bay, turning the lost bit into an island that's gradually fleeing south over the years.

Swan knew she was risking a wasted trip. It was likely that Cobb's house would have been picked clean by now, emptied and swept out ready for resale. She parked in the driveway and used her home remote to roll up the garage door. There were no cars parked inside, and she could see through the windows of the house that at least some of the furniture had been taken.

Swan put on her gloves, took a crowbar from the garage, went in the back of the house and jemmied open the kitchen door. Inside, she flicked the light switch just once, to make sure the power was still on. She put the crowbar down on the counter, then slipped a tight sportsband onto her left wrist and slid a small flashlight under it. She kept the light pointed at the floor as she moved around the dead man's house.

She picked up the phone in the living room. No dial tone; Cobb's relatives had done that much, at least, unless the phone company had cut him off for non-payment. The shelves in the living room and study were still packed with Cobb's possessions. Swan wondered idly what percentage of the books – mostly chunky hardbacks – he had actually read. She hadn't even bothered to unpack most of the books she'd moved with in her house in McLean.

She had made a mental list of the most likely places to look for the device. If he wasn't worried about keeping it a secret, then it would probably be in his study – there was no workshop in the garage or basement. The filing cabinet was locked; she retrieved the crowbar and opened each of the drawers. Nothing but personal papers, the accumulated paperwork of life. If he was worried about keeping it a secret, then try under the bed, under a floorboard beneath a rug – no chance there, everything was carpeted except the kitchen and bathroom. Less likely were the boxes in the closets. A problem was that she didn't know precisely what she was looking for, even how large it would be, although she was guessing it would be around the same size as she and Luis's original purchases. Smaller than a breadbox, she thought. Around the size of her fist.

Swan worked patiently down her list. She didn't put the boxes back in the closet, but she didn't throw them around, either. Only people frustrated Swan. Even a clunky computer system or a badly written program couldn't faze her: she dropped into what she thought of as her work mode, and systematically tackled whatever tangled mess she had been presented with. Chip Cobb's house was merely another problem that required a systematic approach.

All right. Either the device wasn't here, or Cobb had hidden it too well for her to find it in a casual search; they were both possibilities. Cobb was no longer around to ask, but that didn't mean he hadn't left the information where she could find it.

The study was a veranda – what the Yanks call a porch. A brand new IBM PC adorned Cobb's tidy study desk, its Pastel

Denim Binders standing to attention on a miniature bookshelf. Swan glanced at the modem: there was a dial tone. The family hadn't thought to disconnect Cobb's second line.

She pushed the DOS disk into the A drive, and flipped the big red switch. She went to the kitchen to make herself some coffee while it booted up.

Cobb had written the password to his BBS account on the inside of the DOS manual. Swan systematically read through his email, including his sent-mail, which included messages to her. There were several messages which mentioned an item which had to be the third component. Swan sat forward, putting down the coffee cup.

There was mention of meetings and money. Cobb had been helping someone calling themselves The River find the missing item for a hefty fee. Had he delivered the item before he had died? Had he put it in safekeeping somewhere? There was no mention of an agreed drop, but the device might be in a safety deposit box.

Swan paged through a box of five and a quarter inch diskettes on Cobb's desk. Each was labelled with a range of dates. She slid one into the PC, and confirmed her guess: this was a record of Cobb's correspondence, downloaded from the Internet where it would be safe from hacking eyes. He had never been able to download the last week or so's worth of mail.

Swan smiled wryly to herself. Only recently had she learned what it was like to have someone else rummaging through your private email and files: a lot of people had tried, but only the Doctor and his friends had succeeded. It seemed as though there was no safe place for communications, not the network, certainly not the phone system. With no laws to stop hackers, you had to assume everything was an open book. From now on, she would keep all her messages and files encrypted. One day those laws might come into existence, and she no more wanted the Feds reading her disks than the Doctor. But in any case, reading Cobb's email couldn't do him any harm now.

Still... the little hairs on the back of Swan's neck were bristling. She had the deep and instinctive feeling of being watched. She found a blank diskette, slapped it into the drive, and waited impatiently while the last of Cobb's mail came down the modem.

When she had it all, she made a backup, swapping diskettes back and forth in the single drive. Then she deleted all of the remaining email, including all of the copies of messages Cobb had sent. She could have gone on to disconnect the machine from the ARPANet, to make absolutely sure no-one else could get at the goodies; but that would have been enormously conspicuous, at least to the local users of the machine and its sysop. No, she had what she wanted, and now she could read it at her leisure.

When we next called Bob, he had the exciting and unexpected news that Swan had discovered the tap on her phone (she had called herself and left a filthy message on his answering machine). 'Where have you been?' he demanded. 'I've been dying for you guys to call! God, we should have got a phone for that car!'

'We couldn't find a public telephone before now,' said the Doctor. 'We've been driving all over the Delaware countryside trying to find one.'

'Well why didn't you just knock on some farmer's door?'

'We were just about ready to try that,' admitted the Doctor. 'Then we came across this life-saving petrol station. But when we did call, your number was engaged!'

'Well, I'd given up and logged back in, hadn't I! It's not like I have more than one phone line to choose from.'

Peri had arrived bearing melts. I knew what a mess the sandwiches made and didn't want to start mine until we were back on the road, but she was already tucking into hers, getting onions and grease all over her face and hands. The Doctor put his into the pocket of his jacket and smacked the receiver against his forehead. 'How frustrating it is to have the laws of physics dictate how you can move and communicate!' he sighed.

Two

Piece by piece, diskette by diskette, Swan put together the story of the supercomputer and its components.

The computer's owners had lost their grip on it somewhere in West Virginia, close to the border with Maryland. (Cobb had no information on where it might have been before that.) Somewhere in the countryside, apparently; although the emails were vague on this point, Swan guessed that a vehicle carrying the device had run off the road, and a local – possibly a farmer – had got hold of the pieces of the machine. There were five parts. Swan guessed input, storage, CPU, memory, output – although if this really was a new kind of computer, the old architecture might have been irrelevant. Which parts had she and Luis bought?

The hypothetical farmer had looked to make a quick buck from his find. It hadn't been quick after all. Swan had long been familiar with the underground of collectors, spies, and suspicious types who traded in esoteric and forbidden technology, but of course the farmer had never heard of them. His initial efforts to sell the components had got him nowhere. It was almost two years before news of their existence trickled out to the grapevine.

Over the following months, a gaggle of collectors and suspicious types turned up, looking to beg, borrow, or steal the components. The farmer quickly realised that what he had given up on as junk had a real value. He played coy, pretending he had already sold some of the items, making sure that each customer only got one piece of the puzzle.

Swan was surprised when she put these events onto a timeline. The computer had fallen off the back of the truck, or what have you, in 1970! All this time, its bits had been out there, becoming more and more separated. Why had its owners waited so long to retrieve their property? The only explanation was that they simply hadn't known it was there. When it fell off that truck, to them, it became invisible. That was a bit of luck for her imagined farmer. One of Cobb's pals hinted darkly that the owners had visited the original finder and they hadn't exactly brought him candy and flowers.

1970. Swan spun the chair back and forth, thinking. One hell of a lot had happened in computer technology since then. Could the components really still be valuable after all this time? The auctioneer had certainly thought so, and she had learned to trust his judgement. An awful lot of freaks and hobbyists thought so too – they had pursued the components from one end of the country to the other.

That clinched it. If the technology was outdated and worthless, they'd never have bothered to come after it eleven years later. Perhaps losing it had stalled a research project, something truly revolutionary which could now continue. More likely, the research had continued, and now there was a risk that the secrets of a new computer might be revealed if the early prototype was reassembled.

Swan closed her eyes for a few moments, massaging her eyelids. The picture of the thing in Luis's bathtub kept drifting into her mind.

Who were the original owners? It was a toss-up between a big corporation and a spy agency. Swan guessed the latter – more likely to have the resources and the drive to find and recover the components, more likely to need to keep its technology dark.

They had already got three. One from California, where it had been undergoing testing in a Silicon Valley lab. As far as Swan could tell, the owners – represented by 'River' – had broken in and taken it. One had got as far as Arctic Canada; it had been bought back at an exorbitant price.

And then there was the component Chip Cobb had been hired to retrieve. Swan had met him once, and they had swapped a few emails; he was a hub in the collectors' grapevine, best known for his ability to get hold of information about prototype computers (and very occasionally, the prototypes themselves). The components would have been right up his alley. River had been talking to him in email, promising cash and circuit boards if he could locate the device. (Cobb had spent a lot of time trying to trace River's email connection. Only once had he been able to track his employer back to a pirated account at a defence contractor – only to have River shut down that account and turn up again from a different direction. 'He seems to be everywhere and nowhere,' a frustrated Cobb had told a friend.)

River was certain that the remaining three components had stayed on the east coast – in fact, had probably not gone far from what he once called the 'crash site' (confirming Swan's theory that a secret transport had been involved). Although collectors were keen to get their hands on the devices, they eventually realised that they simply couldn't do anything with them. Swan recalled her own frustration with the loopy plastic ball. So they had moved slowly through the grapevine, sold at auction or in private transactions. But one of the three, discovered Cobb, had been sold only once – from the original finder to an obsessive collector in Salisbury. The guy was famous for never playing with the toys he bought – just shrinkwrapping them in plastic and locking them away in a vast array of filing cabinets in his basement. Even if Cobb hadn't been able to trace the sale of the component to Salisbury, he might have guessed it had ended up in the black hole of the guy's collection.

Cobb's job was to wrest that component away from the guy in Salisbury. River provided a slush fund in four figures to help persuade the collector to give up the goods. Cobb had dealt with the man before; he knew the chances of prying the item away from his bosom were pretty low, especially once the collector realised it was valuable.

Over a period of six months – always begging more funds from River – he tried everything he could to win the component. He offered the collector all sorts of bribes and trades. He paid him a 'consultation fee' (large enough to make Swan whistle) just to whet his appetite. When his patience started to run out, he switched his tactics. Small hints became minor harassment became outright threats. The collector found his phone disconnected and phone books for exotic countries delivered to his door, COD. His home number mutated daily, making it impossible to call him. Finally, Cobb hired a thug to break into the collector's basement. The thug didn't even get close; the place was wired and armoured like the vault of a bank.

Cobb was astonished when River decided the best idea was to talk to the collector in person. His employer had somehow got it into his head that where greed and fear hadn't worked, simple honesty would. River would sit down with the man, explain everything, and the collector would be only too happy to hand over River's property.

Cobb had never seen River in the flesh. He turned out to be

a bland-faced man in his thirties, wearing a dark suit and hat. He had a pet parrot which went with him everywhere. It was the only strange thing about him; everything else was entirely forgettable. In an email to a friend, just before it all went wrong, Cobb admitted he had trouble remembering what the man looked like.

River arrived early in the morning and knocked on the door until Cobb tumbled out of bed. The man was happy to sit in the living room, in the dark, while Cobb got a final couple of hours of sleep. When the sun had come up, they set out for Salisbury.

That was where Cobb's emails ended. The rest of the story Swan was able to piece together by breaking into the accounts of the people he had shared his secrets with, and reading their emails. One quoted an entire news article, which told her everything worth knowing about what happened next. The collector was dead. Cobb was dead. Even the parrot was dead. Of the component and River, there was no sign.

On the long drive, the Doctor and I swapped travel stories, while he tinkered with whatever it was he was making.

When I was small, my family would stay in a caravan park in the country town of Parkes. Or was it Forbes? Or perhaps it was the small city of Dubbo, and my childhood memories are even vaguer than I thought. I must try to find an atlas with enough detail of the New South Welsh countryside to work it out.

Anyway, the point was that we would drive from Parkes to Forbes (or was it the other way around?). My father said that the two towns were exactly eleven miles apart; he would get the three of us to watch the odometer, counting down the miles.

But the biggest thrill was always the visit to the thirty-one flavours ice cream shop in the town of Orange. One flavour for each day of the month, a sign said. 'I remember we arrived in

Orange late one night after a long day's drive. I bawled my eyes out because the shop was closed. I've been to Baskin Robbins, sure. But it's not the same thing.'

Peri said sleepily from the back seat, 'Did you ever see a horseshoe crab?'

'Ah, we don't have 'em Down Under.' As if on cue, that bloody song came on the radio. I flipped the dial impatiently. 'I did see a lot of jellyfish at Bateman's Bay, though. I could never understand the point of going on a beach holiday where it's too dangerous to swim. I saw a dogfish and a manta ray there, too. And a spider with orange legs that lowered itself in the back of the car and made my little brother scream.'

'We used to turn them over,' said Peri.

'What? Spiders?' I said.

'Horseshoe crabs. It was a game. You got fifteen points every time you found one on its back and turned it the right way up again. Maybe they're from space.'

'Nonsense, Peri,' said the Doctor.

'They look like they're from space.'

'The Cambrian Epoch may have been another world, but it wasn't another world. They're no more extraterrestrial than you are.'

'The ocean is just like outer space.' She was murmuring now, half-asleep. I was suddenly reminded that she was only around half my age. Just a kid. 'One day all the weird creatures in there will come and invade us.'

'There are some people who believe this has already happened,' said the Doctor.

There was something about this silly conversation that was making the small hairs on the back of my neck stand up. Maybe it was the image of the Earth as a little beach on the edge of an impossibly huge sea full of monsters. And these two travellers, the sorcerer and his apprentice, floating about on that cold sea in their little ship.

'You're like a horseshoe crab, aren't you?' said Peri.

The Doctor glanced at me. 'Peri –'

'I meant, a living fossil,' she said cheekily.

'Go to sleep, Peri,' he told her. A few minutes later he said, 'Hmmph. A living fossil indeed. In ten years' time – in *five* years' time the computers that are far beyond Peri's comprehension will be fossils themselves. People these days chuckle at the tiny brain of ENIAC. Soon they'll have a new joke every few years. And a new computer to buy. Perhaps future archaeologists will discover a layer of discarded personal computers – all that's left of your young civilisation.'

'America's not doing too badly,' I said. Sometimes you have to stick up for the Yanks. 'Not if they're producing technology at a rate like that.'

'Electronic digital computing is only one way of organising a civilisation,' said the Doctor. 'There are many other ways to manage information at high speeds – much better ways. And besides, the human race has managed without any of them for most of its existence. Most human beings are still doing just that.'

I shrugged. 'I read somewhere that most people on Earth haven't even made a phone call.'

'That will remain true for a long time,' said the Doctor. 'But computers have a habit of getting in everywhere. Like the vermin that follow human beings as they stride around the Earth.'

'Computers are rats?'

'Perhaps a little more useful.'

'I can't work out whether you *like* them or not.'

'As long as they're useful, I like them perfectly well. When they start pretending to be people, that's another thing.' He paused to consider. 'On the other hand, I've known some quite charming computers.'

I had to grin. 'I'll bet you have.'

'Oh, good heavens.'

'What is it?'

'That sandwich Peri gave me. I'd forgotten all about it.' The Doctor extracted the cold and sodden melt from his pocket, sniffed at it, and then stuffed it into the glovebox. I watched out of the corner of my eye as he struggled with the contents of his pocket – it seemed to be crammed with toys and coins and bits of junk, all of which needed wiping after their encounter with the sandwich. It was the equivalent of Mondy's bat-belt, an engineer's collection of tools and spare parts.

I was nodding to myself. The Doctor was obviously involved in the design of new computers which would make the current crop of high-tech gizmos look like junk – not just faster machines, but machines with a completely different basis.

The Doctor seemed to guess my thoughts. 'Oh, I think the electronic digital computer has some life left in it yet,' he said. 'Electricity is quite a fast way to move information around. Of course, there are faster ways.'

'Like what?'

'Light, for example. You can't get faster than that.' I suppose he meant fibre-optic cables. 'Or if you must use physical things, then you keep making the components smaller and smaller – to speed up the movement of information, you see – until at last they are so small that quantum mechanics becomes a consideration.' He touched the back of my hand with a finger. 'Something like that already operates in your DNA.'

I shifted uncomfortably. 'That's enough about me. So where are you from?'

The Doctor raised an eyebrow at me. 'It's best not to know everything about a person. A little mystery is a good thing.' I couldn't interpret his smile.

We arrived in Ocean City not long afterwards. Peri sat up and peeked out through the venetians.

'Grim,' commented the Doctor.

'I don't know,' she said. 'I kind of like it.' Which made me wonder what kind of places she usually visited. 'It reminds me of being a kid. Do you think maybe when this is all over we could come back here?'

The Doctor hesitated. 'Perhaps in summer.' It was hard to imagine him on the miniature golf course, that was for sure.

'Maybe,' said Peri, in a small voice. I think they had both just remembered that they might not be together once this was all over. 'It'd be nice to just look around and not have to rush off because the planet's going to blow up.'

We parked several blocks from Cobb's house. The Doctor packed a dufflebag with equipment from the back of the RV: I could see the weight of it as he hefted it onto his shoulder. The machine he had built on our trip was inside, obviously. But what else had he stuffed in there? We followed him, Peri breaking into short bursts of running to keep up with his long stride.

The phone rang.

Swan froze at the sound. Literally froze, every inch of her skin turning blue-cold. The dead phone in the living room had come to life.

Years ago, Swan had seen an episode of some black-and-white anthology show, in which a phone junction box came to life and started calling people. Her younger self had been equal parts fascinated and frightened – too scared to touch a phone for weeks, but secretly jealous of the monster and its power to mock the human voice. She had played its role many times since: the unseen, threatening caller, the voice which could be coming from the next room or from thousands of miles away. Now, for a second, she was that kid again, jumping every time she heard the phone ring.

Swan got up from the desk and stomped into the living room, furious with herself, ready to tear the ears off whoever was on the other end of that line. If it was some blundering telco technician, she was going to wish 'em into the cornfield.

Swan snatched up the receiver and said nothing. After a moment, the Doctor said, 'Ah, there you are. I'm afraid you beat us there after all.'

'You freakin' idiot,' said Swan. 'If you hadn't told me about Cobb, I'd never have come out here. What'd you think you were doing?'

The Doctor was silent for a long second. 'I assumed you knew one another.'

'Of course we knew one another. But he never mentioned anything about this.'

'Oh, good grief,' said the Doctor.

While they were arguing, Peri and I were marching up the street to Cobb's house. I was carrying the duffle bag, which wasn't light.

We both saw the veranda, and the office equipment inside, at the same moment.

'Stay back,' said Peri. She was tugging the Doctor's ramshackle device out of the bag. 'I'm gonna torch the porch.'

'You're going to do what?'

Peri hefted the long machine. 'Like this,' she said.

Fire erupted from the end of the thing with a heavy kerosene smell.

'Shit!' I scuttled sideways like a startled crab.

The window burst inwards. Peri let go of the trigger for a second, startled. Then she got a crazy smile going and stepped up to it, pushed the blunt nozzle through, and pulled the trigger again.

'Jesus, girl, what are you doing?'

Peri started to turn towards me, making me jump back even further as the line of flame followed her motion. She realised and turned back to the window. 'Well, what does it look like I'm doing?' A pile of papers on Cobb's desk erupted with a crackling roar.

This time she held the trigger in, holding the Doctor's improvised flamethrower with both hands, moving it back and forth in quick little jabs. The desk erupted like a warzone in puffs of orange and black. The box of diskettes issued a hideous chemical smell as it began to melt and char.

The screen of Cobb's PC burst inwards with a terrific crunch. Peri yelped, jumping back and letting go of the flamethrower's trigger.

Swan dropped the phone the instant she heard the window go, knowing instantly that she'd been had. She ran back towards the study.

She reacted just as quickly when she saw the flames: she ran like hell in the other direction, bursting out the front door of the house. We never even saw her, running like hell from the back of the house.

She ended up watching from a couple of streets away as the fire engines rolled in. The trip hadn't been wasted; she knew far more than she did before. The ruse with the phone tap had been worth it, although it meant she could never again use that method for disinformation. If the Doctor and co had arrived only a little earlier, she would never have had the chance to learn so much. But Cobb had never had the component at all, whatever he may have hinted to his fellow collectors.

California, Canada, Salisbury. The components she and Luis had bought were the only two left. Correction: the component Luis had hatched in his bathtub was the only component left. The Doctor was obviously playing the same role as Cobb had, acting as the original owner's agent. And she had let him take away something that was worth scouring the continent for, something that was worth killing for.

There was only one thing to do now.

The Doctor had watched until he was satisfied with the level of destruction; then he pulled a pair of miniature fire extinguishers out of the duffle bag and set about dousing the conflagration before it could spread further.

'As a matter of fact,' he assured me between cold bursts of white vapour, 'I called the fire brigade to warn them of my intentions just before we set to work. They're taking longer to arrive than I had expected. Perhaps they thought it was a prank call.'

We had made a hasty exit, climbing over a fence and running through the concrete at the back of a garage to avoid the neighbours' eyes. (The Doctor has a surprisingly light stride.) We ran through the blackness to the Travco, still parked safely where we had left it.

None of us spoke until we had been on the road for several minutes. Peri sat on the bed right at the back, watching for police lights through the venetian blinds. Nothing. We had got away with it.

'So,' said Peri. 'The real point of all that was to get rid of anything Cobb had left behind about the Eridani.'

'The other motives were real too,' said the Doctor. 'That was quite well done.'

'Gee thanks,' said Peri. How long had they been planning that little stunt? What else was going on that they weren't telling me?

'Doctor,' I said, suddenly alarmed. 'You didn't trash Cobb's house to prevent *me* from getting a look at the info – did you?'

'Far from it,' he said. 'The most sensitive information would have been dangerous only to those who believed in it.'

'You know everything Cobb did – don't you?'

'There's quite a lot I can still tell you. On the trip home. Let us absquatulate. In fact, why don't I take a turn behind the wheel?'

'You comfortable with driving on the wrong side of the road?'

'You seem to have got used to it.'

'Yeah, but I've had years of practice.'

'Trust me,' he said.

'Uh,' I said. 'It's OK. I'll drive for a while.'

Route 50 begins two blocks from the Atlantic, and runs the whole way across the country. As we left town on the Route 50 bridge, passing under the "Sacramento CA 3073 miles" sign, I glanced in the rear vision mirror and got a glimpse of the ocean. It felt like the waves were gaining on us. And the rain started to fall, the first fat, dusty drops.

70

One

Swan contemplated her plan long and hard. It had to be flawless. There was no margin for error; if Luis realised her intentions towards his new toy, there would be no getting it away from him.

She considered setting up an automatic program that would email him at intervals, convincing him she was somewhere she was not. Maybe even an ELIZA program that could chat with him in real time over the wires, feigning a human conversation just well enough to hold his attention. She could build in a subroutine that imitated typographical errors to make it more convincing.

In the end she rang him up and asked him to meet with her right away. When he went out, she went in and stole the monster.

Luis had given her a duplicate key to his apartment when she had first arrived in DC; she had stayed with him for a few weeks while house-hunting. (As far as I've been able to find out, romance did not bloom as a result.) She had a heart-in-mouth moment when she pushed the key into the lock – had he changed it? But the innocent door opened up for her.

Swan stalked into the apartment and into the bathroom. The creature was sitting happily in the tub, playing with Lego and munching on breakfast cereal. She stuffed handfuls of Lego and half a box of cereal into her backpack, plucked Luis's dressing gown from the back of the door, and wrapped the monster in it. It didn't react in any way when she touched it, stuffed it into the threadbare fabric, and hoisted it into her arms. It was too busy pushing two blocks together and pulling them apart again, over and over.

Swan locked the door behind her, walked down the back stairs to her station wagon, and drove off with the monster hidden under old clothes in the back. It was as simple as that.

Luis waited for her in a nearby coffee shop for fifteen minutes until he realised what was going on. He sprinted back to his apartment, faster than he had ever run anywhere, arriving on the stoop with lungs wheezing and legs trembling. He still loped up the stairs two at a time.

When he saw the empty tub, he actually screamed. The sound was forced out of him involuntarily, the way it had been just once before when, as a child, he had been riding his bicycle and turned to discover an immense dog trying to bite his leg.

He searched the apartment, knowing full well that Swan had come and taken the creature, hoping like a lost child that he would find it if he only kept looking for long enough. It was not under the bed or behind the sofa and it certainly wasn't in the fridge.

Luis sat down for a moment. He felt sick. Not just queasy at this betrayal by an old friend, nor shaken by his hyper-ventilating race home. His hands trembled, he couldn't focus on anything, and the floor felt as though it was falling out from under him.

After several long moments in this limbo, he realised why Swan had done it. The craving he felt for the monster had overcome her. She had not been acting out of her own will, any more than he was when the urge to find the child propelled him up from the sofa and made him pace the flat, forcing himself not to just run outside and search and search at random until he found it. Swan didn't mean to deprive him of the child, she couldn't help herself. In fact, she needed help. And he was the only one who could help her.

Luis's fists clenched and unclenched. He went out, slamming the door behind him, unlocked. There was nothing left worth stealing.

He sat in his car for five minutes before he realised that he had no idea where Swan lived these days.

Two

And so we were on the road again, leaving a trail of mayhem
behind us. Around four hours later, we picked up Bob from his
motel room. We could have used some rest, but the Doctor
insisted we keep on the move. Peri drove while the Doctor
navigated. They argued pretty much constantly about where
we were and which road to take. Bob and I exchanged a smile;
it was like being the kids of an old married couple, listening to
them bicker from the front of the car.

I held the radio from the police car in my lap. The Doctor ran
a cable from the cigarette lighter to power it. So far I hadn't
heard anything to suggest our little encounter at the lookout
had sparked a state-wide search: it was always possible that an
embarrassed Officer Moustache had decided to keep the details
to himself. I was still nervous as hell tooling around in such a
conspicuous vehicle.

Exasperated, Peri said, 'It would help if I knew what you were
trying to find!'

The Doctor said, 'Somewhere safe and private to hide away
for a few hours. I have arranged a meeting with Sarah Swan.'

Peri slammed on the brakes. The campervan rolled onto the
side of the road and stopped there, engine grumbling. We all
looked at the Doctor.

'Not out here,' he said. 'Inside the world of the computer.'

'Well what would have been wrong with Bob's motel room?'
she said.

'Peri. If it's at all possible, I'd like to be somewhere that no-one knows we are.'

She took a moment. 'You're not thinking of breaking into a house or something, are you?'

'Certainly not!'

'I know electrical power isn't a problem, but we are going to need a phone line. And I think somebody might notice if you shimmy up a pole in the middle of town.'

'Hmmm, yes. I'm afraid that publicly accessible computers are some years away yet.'

'God forbid,' Bob sniffed.

'Ah! Stop!' Peri startled and braked rather suddenly, jumbling us about. 'Shangri-La!' he declared. 'Utopia! Solla Sollew!'

We stared out the campervan's windows at the damp grey wreckage of a gas station. It looked like it had been abandoned for months, maybe years – long enough for weeds to carpet the concrete and a ragged forest of shrubs and shaggy trees to have sprung up in the wasteland around it. Patches of snow lay around, mostly melted by the cold rain.

Peri piloted the campervan around a pile of rusting rubbish and parked it in back of the building. With the engine off, the silence was deafening.

'Some Shangri-La,' said Peri.

'There should be a phone line somewhere inside.'

'Come on, Doctor. There's not going to be a working phone.'

'We only need the line,' said the Doctor. 'Bob, your task will be to use a public telephone in the town to bring our borrowed line back to life.'

We hopped out of the campervan, stretching our legs. The back door of the gas station was shut with a padlock and chain. The Doctor fiddled with it for a few minutes, using an unbent paperclip and then a knitting needle. Then he sighed, stood back, and stiff-armed the door. It popped neatly off its hinges. He caught it by the handle before it could fall backwards into the station, and laid it neatly beside the doorway. 'A somewhat unorthodox entry. Remind me to repair that before we leave.'

Peri looked around the inside of the station. 'Honestly, Doctor, I don't think anyone's going to care.' It was mostly empty, but trash was piled against the walls, yellowed newspaper plastered over the windows. An entire car engine had been left sitting where the cash register once must have been. The place had a rich smell of mouldy rags and oil.

We carried the computer equipment into the place in cardboard boxes while the Doctor ran a cable from the campervan's generator. 'You know what would be cool to have,' said Bob, hefting a box onto the counter. 'One of those computers you can fold up into a suitcase.'

The Doctor began to unpack the computer equipment, giving the deceased engine a look of annoyance. 'Phone jack's right here,' said Bob, crouched on the floor behind him.

'Very well. Young Bob, make me a miracle.'

Bob gave him one of his serious, frowning nods, and scooted out of the station. We were maybe ten or fifteen minutes' walk out of town. Privacy, just as the Doctor had ordered.

The Doctor fussed over the computer. Peri got bored and wandered out, and I followed her, in hopes of an uninterrupted smoke.

Behind the station, Peri sat scrunched in the open door of the Travco. She held the camp stove in her lap. 'All right?' I said.

'I'm fine,' she said, with an attempt at a smile.

'I bet you kick a police officer in the garbanzo beans and torch some house every day of the week.' I pulled out my ciggies. 'Got a light?'

Peri had to laugh at that. 'I was kind of thinking of making

166

some coffee,' she said, turning the camp stove around. 'Or maybe a cup of soup.'

'Do we have any coffee?' I said.

'No, and we don't have any cup of soups, either.' She turned and dropped the stove back inside the campervan. 'What are we doing out here?'

'Staying invisible, I guess,' I said.

'It doesn't matter where we drive to, does it? Swan is always just a phone call away.'

She was right. The net was always there, in the same place. We could have dialled in from California and Swan could have called from Germany and the net would still have been in the centre. There's a Chinese proverb which says 'Heaven's net may look loose, but nothing can escape getting caught in it'. For a moment I knew how Bob had felt, looking up at those stars: we were surrounded.

'It's not gonna do any good, just talking to Swan,' Peri was saying. 'The Doctor always thinks he can talk people out of things. If they'd only listen to reason... but they never do.'

'Never?'

'Pretty much never,' said Peri. She held out her fingers, absently, and I passed the cigarette to her. She took a drag and started coughing and wiping her eyes. I took the butt back. 'I haven't done that for a few years,' she wheezed apologetically. She glanced at the station, like the Doctor might catch her smoking in back of school.

'What is it with you two?' I said.

Peri broke up, half-laughing and half-coughing. 'We are *not* a couple!' I back-pedalled like crazy, but she didn't seem offended. 'I did have kind of a crush on him once. He was a lot younger then... but it was like the crush you get on your high school teacher.'

I already knew they weren't together; all those little touches and glances and familiar words that two people build up, none of those were present. It wasn't even like an intimate friendship – that also has that secret, shared vocabulary. But I said, 'No offence. It's just that you sound kind of like my parents used to.'

Peri gave a little laugh. 'I guess we do sound like an old married couple sometimes. But we're just good friends.' She saw my quizzical look. 'The Doctor is the smartest person I know. I have a lot of respect for him. The problem is, he's also the smartest person *he* knows.' She dropped into a gruff-voiced impression of the Doctor. 'I cannot agree with those who rank modesty among the virtues.' In her own voice she said, 'He just can't stand it when other people can't keep up. Mostly me,' she sighed. I nodded at her to go on. 'You know, mom used to say that I wanted to be a botanist because I wanted to be alone. Just me and the plants. It's a lonely profession, she said. I think she was really talking about archaeology, though. Just her and the artefacts. Listening to dead people.' She took another puff from the fag and managed to keep it down this time. 'She actually called it that once. Listening to dead people.'

'I get the same impression when I talk to hackers,' I said. 'They spend most of their time talking to computers. Sometimes they're not so good at talking to other people.'

'Bob's like that, isn't he? He always gives me the feeling I'm wasting his time.'

'They can be a little wrapped up in themselves. A little impatient with everybody else,' I said. 'I think they get disappointed when the rest of us aren't as smart as they are.'

Peri took the fag out of her mouth, which was curling into her slow, wry smile. 'I think I know somebody like that. You're writing an article about us or something, aren't you?'

'I don't think the *Post* is going to be too interested in aliens

168

from Epsilon Eridani.' She handed the smoke back to me and I took a puff. 'Mostly I'm just curious, though. I can't pin the Doctor down at all. I can't pin down your relationship. You seem distant and close at the same time.'

'We are close. But more like... I know. Once mom and I got stuck in the subway in New York. The power went out, there were no announcements or anything, and we were there for about two hours with a couple dozen people who didn't know each other. We all ended up talking like old friends, though – we even sang "happy birthday" to an old lady who just turned seventy-eight. We were all best friends because we were going through a bad thing together.'

'They call that "crisis syndrome".'

'Yeah. That's it. The Doctor and I are always going through one crisis after another.'

Bob rounded the corner and glanced at us. Peri looked awkward all of a sudden, but he didn't seem to register anything. We followed him inside.

The Doctor was saying, 'We have a dialtone. Bless you, Bob,' and feeding a phone number to the modem. 'The sun reflecting upon the mud of strands and shores is unpolluted in his beam,' he declaimed. 'Now it's time to test that theory and wallow a little in the MUD with Swan.'

'Doctor,' said Peri, 'what are you talking about?'

I knew that one. 'Multiple User Dungeon,' I told her. 'It's a space inside a computer, like a map in a game of D&D. You can walk from room to room, look at what's there, and meet other people and talk to them. The mud program runs everything, like a Dungeon Master.'

'Neutral ground,' said the Doctor. We watched over his shoulder as the Apple II's modem shook hands with another modem somewhere else in the States.

The first step was to create a 'character' that would represent him in the miniature imaginary world. The Doctor didn't bother with details like appearance or even gender, just a code name, Merryman. The MUD was set up so that guests could appear as anonymous wraiths in the public areas of the game. Normally participants would go to great lengths to create their appearance. For Swan and the Doctor's meeting, play-acting wasn't necessary.

The Doctor's featureless character appeared out of nowhere in the imaginary world:

```
Welcome to the Dungeon of Doom. You are
standing in a forest clearing facing
north. In front of you is a cliff wall.
In the wall is a large opening, the
doorway to the Caves of Catastrophe.
```

'Well, you obviously don't want to go in there,' said Peri. We all looked at her. 'It was just a joke.'

'I doubt there's anywhere else to go,' said the Doctor. He typed:

```
go north
```

A few moments later, the computer answered:

```
You are standing in the entrance cave.
Passages lead off to the east and west.
You can see daylight through a doorway
in the south.
```

'Well, this could take all day,' said Peri.

'Ah, but I know a way to speed things up.' The Doctor typed:

```
Ziz-zy, zuz-zy, zik!
```

The computer responded:

```
The genie appears in a puff of smoke.
'Welcome, guest,' he says. 'Where would
you like me to take you?'
```

The Doctor typed:

```
genie living_room
```

And the program responded:

```
You enter a pleasant living room. There
are comfortable chairs scattered about,
rugs and lamps, and a roaring fireplace.
Fionnuala is here.
```

```
The genie departs in a puff of smoke.
```

'Fionnuala,' said the Doctor. 'A woman changed into a swan in Irish legend. She's just where I asked her to be.'

From time to time, the net, even just the phone gives me a case of the profound heebie-jeebies. It's a feeling of being watched. Have you ever had a prank phone call, and been really creeped out by the fact that someone could just call you up like that, enter your home in a sense, and you had no idea of where they were or who they were? Worse still, have you ever had a call where someone said 'I can see you through the window, I'm outside your house?' I haven't, but Sally did once. We agreed it was probably bullshit, but she insisted on sleeping at my place for a week.

I had that feeling as the Doctor joined Sarah Swan for their little chat in the living room of the imaginary house. There was something unnerving about Swan waiting for him there, another pseudonymous, abstract creature. It could, in theory, have been anyone. We could have been anyone. It was only our agreement, our mutual acceptance that this was a place and we were going to meet there and talk, that gave any of it any substance, any meaning at all.

Imagine them sitting in that sketch of a room – the black, silent, empty space inside the network. Imagine the edges of walls and objects drawn in lines the same livid green as the writing on a monitor. Their chairs are luminous stick-figures. They are only outlines of words, a conversation punctuated by electrical lacunae, their shapes traced by the flicker of the cursor as it darts across the screen.

'What is it you want, Sarah Swan?' asks the Doctor.

Between each line of their dialogue there is a pause, as if they are gathering their thoughts. It's actually the slow motion of the machines and the miles of wire that connect them.

Swan says, 'I want to own something that no-one else in the world has.'

'What are you willing to pay for that privilege?'

Swan responds, 'Ha ha ha. I ALREADY HAVE IT. It's too late to demand payment.'

'That's not my meaning,' retorts the Doctor.

'???'

The Doctor says, 'What will be the cost to yourself? Since no-one else in the world possesses what you possess, no-one can give you advice about it. No warnings, no rescue.'

A very long pause. Then, 'You warn me.'

'I can only warn you to give it up. You know you don't know what you're dealing with.'

'Every human advance is dogged by nay-sayers and doom-sayers.'

'This is not a HUMAN ADVANCE!' thunders the Doctor. 'This is an intrusion from well outside the human sphere.'

'Ha ha ha ha ha.'

'If that's too extraordinary to squeeze into your mind, then consider this: you did not invent this thing. You have no way to understand its workings. Rather than an advance, this is a leap into a realm riddled with unknowns.'

'The problem is not me,' argues Swan. 'It's you. You have the knowledge and you won't give it to me. It's your fault if something goes wrong.'

'Then let's meet in real life.' (In real life, the Doctor was ranting about Swan's cheap manipulation of ethics.) I can help you understand the component, assess the danger.'

'Ha ha ha ha ha.'

Swan stands up from her imaginary chair and walks out of the room. The Doctor doesn't hesitate, but follows her through the exit:

```
The   door   opens   into   a   large   unlit
cavern.   You   can   hear   the   sound   of
running  water.  An  unlit  torch  is  here.
Fionnuala is here.
```

The Doctor has nothing to light the torch with. He stands in mathematical darkness, aware of Swan's presence but unable to see her. It doesn't stop him from trying to get the message across.

'Your petty greed will not only endanger yourself and those you come into contact with – think of the consequences if those with ambitions beyond your own take your toy away from you. Just for once, think of something larger than yourself.'

Swan doesn't reply. He talks about danger, but doesn't give her a shred of evidence. She's simply waiting for him to agree, confident he'll have to give in.

```
Luis enters the cave.
```

'SWAN!' shouts the newcomer. 'I KNOW THAT'S YOU. FOR GOD'S SAKE TALK TO ME.'

'Get lost, Luis!'

The Doctor picks up the unlit torch, ducks back into the living room, and thrusts it into the fireplace. He hastens back to the cave, where Luis and Swan are arguing.

```
The door opens into a large cavern. A
river runs through the east part of the
cave. Fionnuala is here. Luis is here.
```

The Doctor types 'Look Luis'. The computer responds:

```
Luis is just a grey figure, an outline
without any details.
```

'it's gone,' says Luis. 'did you take it?? tell me!'

'You should have been more careful,' says Swan. 'Anyone could have got into your apartment and discovered it.'

'u have to give it back!'

'Luis, get out of here.'

'give it back!!!!!!'

'I'll talk to you later.'
'GVIE IT BAK OR I'LL KILL U!!!!!!!!!!!!!!"

Everything stops, for an interminable moment, on that agonised, muddled threat. The Doctor thumps the keys. Nothing. It's as though the intensity of Luis's need and fury has brought the computer world to a halt.

Then Swan speaks again.

Sorry about that. I kicked him out.

The Doctor types furiously.

What's happened to your friend, Swan? Is he always like that?

A long pause. Then:

Maybe it gives you an idea how determined I am to hang onto what I've got. Goodbye.

The Doctor grunts in anger, bangs the counter, and pounds out:

Wait!

But she doesn't.

The Doctor and Bob tried to squeeze information out of the computer. Swan was gone, and just as both sides had planned, there was no way to trace one another. Luis, on the other hand,

didn't give a damn about covering his tracks. The Doctor and
Bob were tracking him through the network, using the genie to
poke around in the guts of the mud's software. When suddenly:

```
You are standing in a large cavern. A
river runs through the east part of the
cave. Luis is here. Luis is just a grey
figure, an outline without any details.
```

'Oh, good grief,' said the Doctor. A brief struggle ensued over
who was going to use the keyboard, which the Doctor won.

```
Luis, we need to talk. I need your
help.
```

The silhouette stood motionless on the other side of the
cave. 'Where's Swan?'
'I don't know,' the Doctor said. 'I have to find her.'
'She needs help. That thing is affecting her mind. You're a
doctor. You have to get it away from her.'
'I intend to. But I need to know more.' There was a pause, as
though Luis was trying to decide how much to tell us. 'Where
did you get it?' prompted the Doctor.

```
Ritchie ... w MD ... National Pike
```

Bob scribbled it down on his arm. The Doctor asked, 'How
did you find it?'

```
Swan and I @ collector s meeting.
```

'Can you put me in touch with whoever sold you the item?'

An address crept across the screen.
'Luis: try to stay away from Swan.'

I have to find her. She needs help.

The Doctor scratched at his forehead with his thumbnail. 'I wish I could tell him that the craving he's feeling will pass. But it's possible his brain has already been permanently restructured.'

'You're not talking about brainwashing, are you,' said Peri. 'You mean more like brain surgery.'

'I'm afraid I do.'

There was something so fundamentally vile and butcher's-shop about that. For a moment, I could actually believe that aliens were behind the whole thing, monsters who were happy to play with the most private of human offal.

'This guy should be in the hospital,' said Bob.

'I doubt very much that they would be able to help him.' The Doctor typed, 'Stay put. I give you my word we will track down Swan and take the stolen goods away from her.'

You have to give it back to me.

Before the Doctor could answer,

i need help.

Ritchie was a spot on the map somewhere near Frostburg, just outside the fog belt, surrounded by low and stony mountains carpeted with snowy trees. US 40 narrowed to two lanes as we drove past clapboard houses and brick boxes. We passed a red Amish barn. 'Hex sign,' noted the Doctor, making Bob sink a little deeper into his seat.

We arrived that night, parked the Travco on a bit of disused gravel between the railway line and the old canal. B&O coal-hoppers clanked past, leaving dark lines where the rails cut through the Christmas snow. The next morning I stood outside the van, pulling hot smoke into my lungs, taking in the view. You could see from one side of the town clear to the other, the way I could see right across Canberra as a kid. It was just the place for an alien invasion.

You want to know how small Ritchie is? The local Mickey D's has only one arch out the front. I'm serious – it's tucked into an awkward bit of land between two intersecting narrow roads. The building is shaped like a slice of pie and there's only enough room for one of the golden humps.

We headed inside for camelburgers and hot coffee. The Doctor refused to sully his palate with the stuff, but he quizzed the server about anything interesting that had happened around town.

I summoned my courage and called Trina to apologise for missing her birthday. I tried to explain that I really had been incommunicado all this time, that I was following up the story she had given me, but it only made her madder. 'You could have called me if you had just remembered to,' she said. There was no arguing back to that. She gave me quite an earful. I tried imagining her in her underwear, but that didn't really help.

The Doctor joined us at the cramped plastic table. 'There's something the matter with that young woman,' he said.

I craned my neck. She was a redhead with a shape even the Scottish Restaurant's uniform couldn't ruin. 'She looks just fine to me.'

For once, the Doctor said nothing. I strolled over to the counter, where the lady in question was waiting for her next customer. She didn't seem to see me coming, her eyes focussed on the blank plastic in front of her.

'G'day,' I said. She blinked a little and looked up into my face. 'I could use some more hot coffee. You know, in Australia, it's the middle of summer right now.'

Usually this led to some cute questions about koala bears. Instead, she spoke slowly, as if trying to remember each word: 'Do you ever get that feeling, when you go into a room and you can't remember why you went in there? Maybe you're in the kitchen, and you sort of wake up, and find yourself staring into the fridge. Does that ever happen to you?'

'Oh yeah, all the time,' I said.

'Or do you ever get that feeling when you know you had an idea just a minute ago, and you feel something kind of speed up and crack inside your head, and you know you're going to forget what you just thought of, and then you do?'

'I guess I know what you mean,' I lied.

'Or do you ever feel like there's something missing from your life? Something really important, something that would make everything complete, but you just can't put your finger on what it is?'

'Jesus, lady, are you all right?'

She blinked again, slowly, and turned to pick up the coffee pot from the burner. It made me nervous as hell to watch her handling the scalding liquid, but her autopilot saw her through. She even asked me if I wanted fries with that. I didn't.

The Doctor gave me a querying look as I squeezed back into my seat. 'That's more than just too many hours flipping burgers,' I said. 'It's not like she's a vegetable... but something's missing.'

'Something is constantly claiming her attention,' said the Doctor quietly. 'Something which is no longer here, and never will be again.'

We drove out to the farm at the address Luis had supplied. To no-one's surprise, the place was abandoned, 'for sale' signs dotted around. The barn had, after all, only been a staging post for the auction that had sold him a hunk o' furry brain damage. The Doctor spent upwards of an hour sniffing around for clues, but came up empty-handed and grumbling.

We meandered around the town a bit, taking in the sights, such as they were. The Doctor oohed and aahed a bit over a restored railway station. He had a surprising ability to strike up a conversation with anyone he bumped into – whether they liked it or not.

There were people with the faraway look everywhere we went. The owner of a Chevy dealership, his flock of used cars huddled under a white awning. His wife came out to talk to us, patting her distracted husband on the shoulder. He hadn't been himself for more than a month, she said. She mentioned the doctor he had been seeing.

We found a doctor's surgery, a brick building with a colourful flag of birds and flowers hung outside. The receptionist wouldn't let us talk to him unless it was an emergency. I asked to use the bathroom and caught a glimpse of him in his office, fiddling with the bits of paper on his desk, staring out the window as if trying to spot something in the distance.

There was no real pattern to it, no transmission from person to person, nothing they all had in common except that they lived here in Ritchie. If some poison, some bit of radioactive waste had fallen from one of the trains that clattered through the town, you might have seen something like it – people spattered by the invisible fallout all around.

We sat on the steps of the public library – closed – and breathed plumes of steam into the air. Bob shifted uncomfortably on the cold, dry stone, and said, 'Can we get a medical team in here or something?'

The Doctor just shook his head. The cold didn't seem to bother him at all. In fact, I don't think his breath was even misting. That English constitution. 'To the Eridani's technology, the human brain is only another form of hardware. Something that can be tinkered with and modified as required. Human medicine cannot yet say the same.'

'Well what about us?' said Peri. 'We've been carrying it around all this time...'

'It hasn't been switched on,' he said – a little nervously, I thought. 'Well, only briefly. None of us have suffered any ill effects.'

'That we're aware of,' said Peri. The Doctor made an impatient gesture as though he was chasing away her needless worries. He was probably worrying about the pair of cops who'd pulled him over. 'We know those components have been all over. You think somebody would have noticed by now... all those people...'

'I suspect that the components only became dangerous around the time of the auction,' said the Doctor. 'The auctioneers probably tampered with them before selling them. I doubt they realised what they had on their hands.'

We crammed back into the Travco (Bob had started to refer to it as the 'white elephant'). I volunteered to drive again, knowing they'd speak more freely amongst themselves if they thought I had my mind on the traffic. But they weren't in a chatty mood. Peri announced she wanted something to take her mind off of things, so she sat cross-legged on the narrow bed, going through another pile of printouts with her highlighter pen.

'Doctor,' she said, 'Have a look at this.'

She passed it forward to the Doctor in the passenger seat. He hunched over it, running a finger down the columns of figures to the data she had marked.

'How very interesting,' he said. 'Our Miss Swan seems to have developed a sudden interest in security equipment.'

'Looks like she bought half a dozen security cameras and an alarm system,' said Peri.

'Now, what does that tell us?'

For a moment they looked like teacher and pupil. Peri answered, 'Swan is keeping the final component at her own house.'

The Doctor nodded. 'I should have realised at once. She could have hidden it anywhere. But she's beginning to withdraw into herself, losing her trust in everyone else – not only trust that they are on her side, but trust that they can do anything as well as she can. She has become the only person she can rely on.'

'Is that good or bad?' said Bob. 'I mean, from our point of view. If she's paranoid, does that make her more isolated and vulnerable, or more careful and dangerous?'

'Perhaps a little of each,' said the Doctor.

Three

We pulled into the parking lot behind my apartment building in Arlington at around six o'clock that night. I went up first, then flashed the lights a couple of times to let them know it was OK to come on up.

Peri looked around dubiously. My flat is a bunch of horizontal surfaces covered in stacks of books and newspapers and in-trays made out of cereal boxes. 'You sure nobody's been searching in here?'

'Relax. I have my own filing system. If they'd moved one piece of paper I would have spotted it right away.'

'Where can we set up, Chick?' said Bob, who was clutching his much-travelled Apple in its protective cardboard box.

I unplugged my IBM Selectric typewriter and hauled it off my writing desk with an 'oof'. Everything else had to come off as well, to make enough room for the computer and its peripherals: the stacks of paper, my Walkley award, the statue of a raven on a branch. I relocated it all to the kitchen counter, where Stray Cat was stealing leftovers from a dirty dish. She gave me a cynical look and one of her monotone meows.

I phoned for takeout while Peri took a shower and borrowed some of my clothes. (I had to stall her long enough to hide the porno mags in the bedroom.) She emerged from the bedroom in high boots, a cowboy shirt, and jeans that were slightly too tight. She stopped towelling her hair, and gave Bob a meaningful look.

He sniffed at his tuxedo tee. 'God, I better change this thing,' he said. He pulled it up to reveal another T-shirt underneath that said FLEX YOUR HEAD and went back to the keyboard.

I put *Ghost in the Machine* on the turntable. It seemed appropriate.

'Hey, Doctor,' said Bob, a few minutes later. 'Come and have a look at this.'

The Doctor grabbed a kitchen chair and sat down next to him at my desk. He gazed over Bob's shoulder at the screen.

It was literally gibberish – a great block of random characters. I could see from the headers that the computer in Swan's kitchen had sent all this garbage to her email account at the office. Bob tapped the keys. There were more of the gibberish messages. Dozens of them.

'They're all exactly eight K,' said Bob.

'Maybe it's camouflage,' suggested Peri. 'She's deliberately sending nonsense messages to confuse us.'

'Maybe it's the aliens talking to one another,' I said. I expected a sarcastic response, but Bob and the Doctor were too intent on their new discovery to notice either of us.

'It must be some form of encryption,' mused the Doctor.

'Oh! Slaps forehead! I know what this is!' Bob started hammering the keys. 'It's uuencoded binary data. No problem. Just let me uucp a copy of uudecode over to my account.'

We waited while he copied the key program that would turn the garbage back into some kind of information. The Doctor had assured me there was no way their calls could be traced to my number. Tired of running back and forth, he and Bob had come up with a way of confusing their trail through the phone system. Anyone trying to trace them would find a succession of connections between trunk lines, bouncing back and forth like reflections in a hall of mirrors.

'I think it's some kind of graphics file,' said Bob. 'Wait, I'll see if I can display it in Applesoft.' The Apple's screen manifested something that looked like a spray of coloured dots.

'I know what it is,' said Peri. We all turned to look at her. 'It's pictures from Swan's security cameras. Look, that's the edge of a table, that's the window over the sink. Move back to where I'm standing and I bet you can see it better.'

She was right. It was like looking at a newspaper photo up close, all those dots and blobs. But with a little distance, and you could make out what the picture really was.

'Good heavens,' muttered the Doctor. 'Swan has invented the Webcam.'

Now we all looked at him. The Doctor fluttered his hands in a 'never mind' gesture. 'It appears Swan has fed the output of her cameras into her personal mainframe. It then encodes the images so they're compatible with email, which can only carry text, and sends them to her work account.'

Bob was decoding one image after another and displaying them on the screen. 'These are screen dumps from another Apple II. It handles the graphics and the mainframe does the rest.'

Peri said, 'So she set up the cameras to send her a picture every so often, so she can keep an eye on things while she's out of the house?'

'Looks like it,' said Bob. 'Look at the time stamps on the messages.'

'They don't all match, though,' said the Doctor. 'She may be using motion sensors to trigger the emails. If someone broke into the house, she'd see a sudden rush of messages. It would act as a very simple alarm system.'

'So if Swan isn't home, what was moving in those extra images?' said Bob. Again his fingers went chocka-chocka-chocka and brought up one of the rough pictures. There were only six colours in them, making me think of those fluoro hippie posters.

'Kind of looks like the bathroom,' said Peri. We all stared into the image, trying to work out what was important about it.

'It's a still frame, of course. Wait until I bring up a couple more,' said Bob.

There was something disturbing about seeing the inside of someone's house like this. I've looked through enough windows and listened in on enough extensions that my stomach no longer tightens when I drop myself invisibly into someone else's private life. What was creepy was the idea of pointing cameras at your own house. At the front yard, sure. But the kitchen? The bathroom, for God's sake? Swan had become her own Big Brother.

'She could watch herself walking around in there,' I muttered. 'See what she did the day before. You know, where did I put my keys? Just rewind the tape and see.'

'There,' said Peri. 'There's something in the tub.' She used the same tone of voice you might use to say *There's something in my sock and it's moving*.

A quick succession of possibilities – a corpse – but it's moving – flies? – a visitor?

'Look at the timestamps,' said Bob. 'Whoever's sitting in the bathtub, they've been there all day. I think the curtain is drawn, over to about here. We get a snapshot whenever they move back far enough that the curtain isn't in the way and the camera sees them move.'

He tapped a key, and the bathroom images cycled. There was something wrong about the shape in the tub. Peri had seen it at once, but I was having trouble making it out.

'It looks like a crippled kid,' I said. 'Maybe an injured dog. No arms. Or no legs, maybe. It's probably trying to get out of the tub.'

'It's what Swan took from Luis, isn't it?' said Peri.

'Take another look at the times,' said Bob. 'A group of images every fifteen minutes. Then, for about the last four hours, nothing.'

The Doctor sat back, steepling his fingers. Sometimes his face would go blank for a few long moments, as though his eyes were seeing some internal chalkboard where he was mentally writing out equations, trying to solve some problem. Peri had obviously learned to wait for him to snap out of it. Bob and I exchanged annoyed glances.

'Bob,' said the Doctor abruptly, 'see if you can hack into Swan's account. Check if she's removed our email forwarding program.'

'Right. What are you going to do?'

'I'm going to give the Eridani a call,' he said.

The Eridani, apparently, had retired to their space craft, which was lurking in one of the Earth's LaGrange points.[6] They were able to transmit and receive by hijacking communications satellites, hiding their own messages amidst the flood of traffic passing through. Supposedly, then, the Doctor's conversation with his alien pals was travelling along a channel that started with a satellite at one end, meandered through the international phone system like breath through a tuba, and emerged from a speakerphone on my desk. Not exactly a Close Encounter.

The Doctor seemed to have a lot of trouble getting the connection to work. There was that annoying delay you always get with satellite phone calls (supposedly made a lot worse by the Eridani being around five light seconds away) but there were also a bunch of whooping and shrieking noises. The

---

[6] A stable orbit point between the Earth and the sun, ideal for placing satellites.

Doctor listened patiently to these, like a blind phreak listening to the phone system's language of clicks and clunks.

Finally the conversation got going. The Doctor brought the Eridani up to date. They seemed relieved that we knew where the missing component was, even if it was in Swan's hands. And they confirmed what we thought we'd seen in Swan's crude camera pictures: it was alive. The ideal way for their colony to make more of the machines, they said, was for at least part of it to be able to reproduce itself.

'The component forms a close bond with its user,' said Ghirlain's voice through a background hiss of space static. 'Swan won't harm it. She will have an instinctive sense of how best to take care of it.'

The Doctor was scribbling comments on a bit of paper for our benefit. 'INSTINCTIVE?' he wrote, and underlined it a couple of times. He was impatiently doodling up and down the margin of the sheet while Stray Cat lolled in his lap like the slut she was. 'Can I assume you will collect your property at the first available opportunity?' he asked.

A few moments of static. Then: 'Breaking the bond may damage both the component and the organism to which it has bonded. It would be safer to wait for the component to mature.'

The Doctor sat forward. 'And precisely what happens when it reaches maturity? Do we have any alarming physical transformations to look forward to?'

Ghislain seemed to be groping for the right terms. 'It is a nymph, not a larva. There is no metamorphosis. Only, the development of its nervous system will be complete. It will be ready to interface with the other components of the system.'

Bob cut in. 'Will it be sentient? Come to think of it, is it sentient now?'

Crackle. Hiss. 'Not in the sense that you understand the word.'

The Doctor pounced. 'And just what do you mean by that?'

'Its nervous system is extremely specialised,' said the Eridani. 'It is expert in certain tasks, but incapable of others.'

'If we're going to contain this situation until it's safe to wean the creature away from its foster "mother", I need to know precisely what it's capable of,' said the Doctor.

'Without the other components, its abilities are limited,' said Ghislain. 'Its task is to analyse systems and adapt itself to them, or them to itself.'

The Doctor didn't like the sound of that at all. 'What do –'

The voice cut him off. 'There is a further cause for concern. The component will have initiated its own gestatory process while still *in ovo*.'

'It's parthenogenetic?' said the Doctor.

'As will be its offspring.'

Peri saw me looking lost. 'It's born pregnant. And its kids will be born pregnant. I guess they wanted to get their factory conveyor belt rolling,' she added bitterly.

The Doctor was saying, 'Not only have you unleashed a mind-altering living computer on this bumbling little planet, but you've placed a miniature horde of them into the hands of a sociopath!' He stabbed at finger at the speakerphone. 'You said the creature can adapt systems to itself. There's more to this than a clutch of baby components running about. That "specialised" creature can modify machines. Computers. Heaven only knows what Swan might be able to do with it.'

Bob said, 'What does that mean, it can modify computers?'

'Think of it as the ultimate programmer. It can acquire computer languages the way an infant acquires a human language. A native speaker of hexadecimal. Hacking a system – in either sense – would be as natural to it as playing with blocks. As natural to it as giving birth.'

Bob slowly said, 'Do you mean it could make a copy of itself into a computer? A machine language version of itself?'

'That's precisely what I mean.'

'It is true,' admitted the Eridani's crackling voice.

'The human race is just entering a phase of its history in which it relies heavily on computers,' the Doctor told the speakerphone. 'And you have introduced this spanner into those delicate works.'

'The device will not operate without commands.'

'Swan is right there to give it those commands. Intuitively, remember? Your ham-fisted contraption –'

'All right, CUT IT OUT!'

The Doctor swung around. Stray Cat leapt out of his lap and ran for the safety of the kitchen. Peri was standing with her fists planted firmly on her hips. 'I can't believe I'm hearing this!' she said. 'You're both as bad as each other.'

'Peri, I'm in the middle of a very delicate negotiation,' said the Doctor.

She emitted an exasperated hiss. 'Listen to you, talking about that poor little thing in the tub as though it was a machine.'

'It is a machine,' said the Doctor. 'Of sorts.'

'You wouldn't talk about some poor kid like that. You know, one of those autistic kids who's a mathematical genius. Whatever that little alien guy can do, it's still a living, breathing creature. It's got rights. I mean, for heaven's sake, it's just a baby.' The Doctor's shoulders were progressively slumping in the blast. 'It's not a stolen computer, it's a kidnapped kid. And you and those other guys have to get it back before it gets hurt or sick or Swan makes it do something awful. And that goes for its babies, too.'

'Peri,' said the Doctor, 'we're not talking about a lost puppy. The component has the potential to wreck your civilisation in a very short space of time. What's worse, it's affecting Swan's already unpleasant mind.' He steepled his fingers. 'It probably interferes with the brain's opiate receptors. Like a particularly powerful addictive drug. You saw how desperate her friend Luis was to retrieve it.'

'It makes them want to own it?'

'That's right. For our lost *idiot savant*, it's become a survival mechanism. It needs to be sheltered and fed and supplied with technological toys.'

Peri said firmly, 'I want to talk to those guys.'

The Doctor sat back from the speakerphone. Peri hesitated, but Ghislain's voice said, 'We are listening.'

'What will you do with it when you get it back?' she asked.

'We will return home with it. It will be put to normal use.'

'What about your colony world?'

'A new slow packet has already been launched. Its guidance systems now include Earth and its radiosphere on their charts.'

'What is normal use, anyway?'

'Be assured the component will be healthy and busy, as will its offspring. Such devices are an integral part of our society.'

Peri looked as though she'd tasted something sour, but the Doctor said, 'Is it worse than training a dog for police work?'

She admitted, 'It's gotta be better than whatever Swan's planning to use it for. All right, Doctor. Let's send that kid back home where it belongs.'

'If it's sitting in Swan's bathtub,' I said, 'why don't we just go and nick it?'

'Because I wouldn't advise it,' said the Doctor, and wouldn't say more.

Four

Swan was well aware that something was happening in her head. Her guess was that the creature was releasing pheromones, those chemicals bugs use to attract mates.

It took to the terminal in her kitchen like a fish to water. It seemed to understand the keyboard moments after the rippling tentacles in its fur had moved across the letters. It began to type commands, imitating what it saw on the screen, generating one error message after another, faster and faster, until its commands began to make sense and the machine began to respond.

Swan watched, leaning back against the kitchen sink, both hands gripping the cold metal rim. It was just an animal. How could it possibly understand letters and numbers? How could it possibly turn them into commands? What kind of secret superproject had she got her hands on?

The monster was *programming*. It had created a file and was pounding in lines of code as fast as the machine could take them, building up a huge set of instructions. Swan could only catch snatches of the code as it flashed past. The monster seemed to be debugging as it went, running little bits of the program over and over until it was satisfied with them, then adding them to its massive project. It was learning only slightly faster than it was producing output.

The system crashed a few times as the big hairy bug tested its lengthy program. Each time it restarted the machine, massaged it a little to fix whatever it had broken, and then started its tests again.

Swan was cold and her arms were stiff by the time her furry baby was done. It just stopped, with the same abruptness with which it had started, and sat back a little from the machine. The rippling in its fur quieted for the first time she could remember.

She wasn't sure how it would react when she picked it up out of the seat, but it seemed quite happy to be carried back to its bathtub. She poured in the milk crate of Legos. At once it started picking them up, the tentacles moving them along its surface until it was half-covered in coloured plastic shapes.

She sat down at the computer in the kitchen. The seat was still a little warm.

Swan tried to analyse the code, but she couldn't seem to stay on task. She played with pens, she rearranged the mess of cords behind the table, she even washed up some coffee cups. Twice she found herself halfway up the stairs.

If she was going to get any work done, it would have to be at the office.

Three times she had to stop herself from turning the car around and racing home. But after a few hours in the office, she was sure her head felt a little clearer, she had more perspective.

Somewhere deep in her head, she knew that no-one was going to take the creature away from her. It was hers now, and it knew it.

It took Swan about fifteen minutes to hack a program for her Unix box that would display the pictures from her home cameras. After that, every quarter of an hour, she checked on baby. Improve the picture quality, add some sound, and you'd have a dandy software package to sell to nervous parents.

She picked through the creature's code. The printout ran to hundreds of pages; she had stuffed them into a couple of binders. She had forgotten the last time she slept. Teaspoons full of instant coffee held under her tongue helped keep her focussed on the problem.

The simplest thing would be to just run it and see what it did. Swan wasn't quite ready to take that step yet. Not on her computers. And not on the network, where any weird effect was liable to spread from one machine to another, all of them pointing back to her. She didn't want to let this puppy loose until she was sure she knew how to control it.

Swan sat back from the screen, scratching her scalp with a ballpoint. The start of the program didn't make sense. It poked around in the computer's memory, as though trying to make a map of it, finding out things which it must already know. But it was tightly written, deliberate. The hairy bug had refined and refined the code until it was pared to an elegant minimum.

Was this program the whole point of the monster's existence? By planting it in front of her home terminal, had she detonated its payload?

It didn't make the slightest bit of sense. If the Reds or anyone else wanted to sneak a program into American computers – or vice versa, for that matter – a hormone-secreting, Lego-obsessed *Sesame Street* monster was not the way they would try to accomplish it. I mean, who would think to put it in front of a computer in the first place? Or would it have waited for her to take a nap, and then clumped down the stairs to reach her machine? Or had its cloud of chemicals somehow instructed her in what to do?

Was she being used?

The temptation to fire up the program and let it run struck her, and she couldn't be sure if it was some sort of mind control, or curiosity, or just plain exhaustion. No. She'd keep decoding the program until she knew what she was playing with.

It was instinct that told her the mainframe was running a little slowly, a subconscious awareness that commands were taking a fraction of a second too long to be executed, a change in the rhythm of the machine.

She brought up the logs on her screen. They didn't show anything unusual – no-one else on the system, no record of anyone trying to dial in from outside.

Swan stepped out of her office and headed for a printer in the corner of the cubicles. She had inserted a command into the system that printed out a hard copy of the logs every five minutes. She lifted a handful of the blue-lined tractor-feed paper and ran her eyes over the last half-hour's records.

There. A fourth person was logged into the system. He had immediately edited the logs when he arrived, leaving only the paper copy to give away his presence.

Look at his connect speed! He wasn't coming in over a modem. He was talking to the mainframe through one of its terminals. Swan's scalp prickled. He had to be *right here*. But where? There were around forty terminals in the building.

It took her a few more minutes, a little more digging in the system, to work out which terminal he was using. She couldn't use the normal commands any sysadmin could use to find out who was where doing what: he would have noticed her in a moment, and fled. She finally grabbed the information from an error log, a single line written by the system when he'd made a typo.

The noise of the compute centre, the breathing of all those machines, was enough to mask the sound of the door swishing open. She could see the backs of three heads, three people working in the company's mainframe. She knew the number and location of every terminal in the room.

She walked right up to Bob. He was so intent on what he was doing that he simply didn't notice her. She watched over his shoulder as he patiently tried one trick after another, trying to grab root. Each time, he bumped up against one of her security fixes, and crossed off his tactic from a hand-written list.

Swan caught her bottom lip between her teeth. There was one she'd missed – he was in her account! Without a pause, he listed her files, spotted the new and huge program created by the monster, and set up an ftp session to transfer a copy of it somewhere else. She had to restrain herself from grabbing his shoulders and flinging him away from the terminal, spinning in his chair. She had to see where that file was being sent to.

He only looked up when the security guard she'd called clumped into the room, his billy club banging against the doors as they slid open. Bob froze when he saw her, his mouth locked open in shock, his hands curled over the keyboard like claws.

80

Robert Salmon Snr was not impressed.

He drove from the centre of Washington to meet us in a parking lot in Crystal City, close to TLA. The Doctor, looking serious in his dark suit, shook hands with Salmon Senior. 'It's good to meet you face to face at last. I only wish the circumstances were better.'

Bob's father was a scowl above a moustache, keeping his temper under control while he dealt with the crisis in good military fashion. When the Doctor introduced Peri and I, he dismissed us with a glance. 'Maybe you can explain why my boy is in trouble with the police. He was mighty vague about it.'

'Mr Salmon,' said the Doctor, 'Bob has been helping me to investigate a serious threat to your nation's security.' He was choosing his words carefully. 'He rose to a similar challenge as a very young man.'

'Yes, he did. But everything we did five years ago was authorised. There was never any reason for the police to be phoning me about my son.'

'I can't say too much,' said the Doctor, 'but the stakes are much higher this time.' Mr Salmon's eyebrows lifted; last time the stakes had been nuclear blackmail.

'You can say a whole lot more, Doctor. You can explain why it's necessary to involve a vulnerable young man in your mission. You can explain just what threat makes that a responsible thing to do.'

197

The Doctor said, 'For one thing, Mr Salmon, your son is an adult capable of making his own choices. And for another –'

Peri said, 'Shouldn't we go and get Bob out of jail?'

The Doctor and Mr Salmon both glanced at her. Peri's voice dropped, but she stood her ground. 'He is waiting for us.'

'You're right, of course,' said the Doctor. 'Mr Salmon, I'm quite prepared to pay for Bob's release from custody.'

Robert Senior wanted to say 'Don't be ridiculous,' but instead he said, 'That won't be necessary.'

And so young Bob was extracted from the clutches of the law, having spent an educational night in the tank, and driven back to his parents' house in the 'burbs. Father and son didn't say a word to one another in the car, but Bob asked, 'Is Mom here?' as Salmon Snr rattled the keys in the lock.

'No. I didn't call her.' Bob sagged with relief into a kitchen chair, but his father said, 'It's up to you to tell her yourself.'

'Oh.'

Mr Salmon pulled out a chair, then stood for a few long moments, his hand on the back of it, stroking the wood. Finally he sat down.

'As soon as you moved out of this house,' he began, 'your life was your own. If you want to skip work and run around the countryside chasing UFOs, it's none of our business.' Bob knew better than to interrupt. 'But as soon as your mother and I become involved, it's our business too.'

Pause. 'Dad,' said Bob, 'I have never bullshitted you in my life. Have I?' Mr Salmon's mouth flattened beneath his moustache in a look of irritation. Bob rushed on, 'You know I would never do anything like that without a meaningful reason. I wish you could have been with us when we visited Ritchie.'

'Who's this Richie?'

'It's a place,' said Bob. 'A little town. A piece of technology got loose there and it's done a lot of damage. We're trying to stop it doing any more damage.'

'When you broke into that building,' said his father, 'did you understand what you were putting on the line?'

'I didn't break in. I just walked in. All she's got on me is trespassing.'

'That could be a lot if you're trying to convince a computer company to hire you,' said his father.

'I know. Swan has got me by the prairie oysters. She can make a lot out of that little charge. I knew when I went in there that she could wreck my career or my chances of college. A couple of days ago I wouldn't have dared to get anywhere near her. But she's got something that's at least as dangerous as what Professor Xerxes tried to put in your program when I was fifteen.'

'Convince me,' said Robert Senior.

'Xerxes was only aiming to corrupt one program. Imagine if he had been able to install a trapdoor in *every* machine. The military, the colleges – and it doesn't matter which box they have or what system they're running on it. Swan has something that can break into all of them. And once that thing gets loose on ARPAnet, it'll be like the tapeworm in *Shockwave Rider*. There'll be no way to stop it or stamp it out except to kill the net itself.'

'What about vaccinating the computers before that can happen?'

'To do that, we need to analyse what Swan's got. That's why I went in there.'

'All right,' said his father. 'But Xerxes' trapdoor would only have affected computers running the new software. Sounds like Swan's program, or whatever it is, will only affect computers on the ARPAnet. That's only a couple hundred machines.'

'But it's growing all the time,' said Bob. 'In the future, there could be hundreds more, even thousands of them connected through the network. Imagine if someone was prepared to wait twenty or forty years to take over all the military and science computers. They'd have a backdoor into every computer on the net – all that tactical and research information. Or they could simply cripple the net. Kill all those projects, and the military's alternative communications capability.'

Bob's father nodded slowly, digesting that. 'If we can prove what Swan is doing, the charge against you will look like a well-meaning mistake instead of a crime. I may be able to pull some strings to get a search warrant. But I'd need some solid evidence. Have you got that?'

Bob shook his head. 'Nothing that would convince the police. I mean, that's what I was there to get.'

'Then what can I do to help?'

Bob said, 'Let me keep helping the Doctor. He needs a programmer he knows he can rely on.'

Mr Salmon took a good, long look at his son. 'I don't want to have to bail you out again,' he said.

Bob gave him a shy grin. 'I don't want to have to be bailed out again.'

'Do we have an agreement?'

They shook hands. Bob's dad went to the freezer to fish out some frozen Chinese food for the pair of them.

'I'm glad I don't have to deal with that on a regular basis,' said the Doctor.

Peri agreed. 'My parents would've strangled you ages ago.'

The Doctor had been unusually quiet on the journey back to my apartment. Letting Bob take risks was one thing, but having to deal with an angry dad was quite another. I wondered if the

Doctor just didn't think of the danger, or if he trusted his sidekicks with their missions enough to let them face it. More likely, I thought, the magnitude of the problem wiped any thought of personal consequences from his field of view.

There was an email for the Doctor waiting in Bob's university account. It was Swan, making her gambit:

Trespassing can easily lead to industrial espionage. I'll forgive your trespasses if you'll hand over the instruction manual (or point me to it).

The Doctor barked with laughter. 'She doesn't know what to do with it! She's asking us!'

Peri was chewing on the lid of her highlighter pen. 'Hey,' she said. 'Why does she think you would have the manual? Doesn't she know it's from another planet?'

'She must assume it's a product of military research,' mused the Doctor. 'In which case, she's probably searching the ARPAnet for information about it.'

I said, 'She must know they wouldn't leave classified info lying around on ARPAnet where anyone could get at it.'

'Hence her demand that we tell her where to look,' said the Doctor. 'But she would also know that if she searches long and hard enough on the unclassified systems, she might put together enough clues to tell her where to look off the net. I doubt even a classified military computer would be a great challenge for Swan.'

'Then why ask us at all?' said Peri.

'It would be far more efficient if we just coughed up the info,' I said.

'The crucial thing is that she doesn't know what she has or

what she can do with it. Not yet. The Savant hasn't told her. Which is interesting in itself... ah.'

A new email had arrived in Bob's account. The Doctor opened it up: it was from Swan, but this time, it was just a list of Internet addresses. Each of the curt acronyms represented one machine, one node on the net.

'What's she trying to tell us now?' said Peri.

The Doctor looked like the cream-swiping cat. 'Bob's mission was a success after all,' he purred. 'This is a copy of a file which Swan saved in coded form a few minutes ago. Before she caught him, Bob installed a program on her system which quietly sends us a readable copy of any file she encrypts.'

'So we get to read anything she doesn't want us to read?' said Peri.

'Exactly.'

'We're gonna need more diskettes,' said Peri.

The Doctor was saying, 'In this case, I assume we're looking at a list of the Internet sites she's already searched.' He ran his finger down the screen. 'Which would mean...' he began to hammer at the keyboard in earnest.

We watched as he spent a few moments breaking into a poorly guarded college computer. 'Not here,' he said. 'Then...' He used the telnet command to leap from that machine to another. This one had no protection at all; he simply logged into a maintenance account with root privileges. He stabbed a finger at the screen. 'There,' he said. One of the users listed on the system was our friend f i o n n u a l a. She hadn't even bothered to disguise her presence.

The Doctor sent her a text message: 'You won't find a manual because there is no manual.'

I could imagine Swan's response – surprise, followed by hindbrain rage. Whatever she was feeling, she let none of it show on the screen. 'Hand it over or you know who will suffer the consequences.'

The Doctor responded by sending a message to the sysop, warning him of intruders on his system. The sysadmin took the message seriously: a few minutes later, while Swan was in the middle of searching through the system's files, both she and the Doctor were kicked off.

The Doctor glanced at Swan's list of computers again, and compared it to Bob's map of the net. 'Logically,' he said, 'her next destination should be... here.'

He jumped to the next computer, took a moment to break in, and started searching for signs of Swan's presence. 'She's set up an orderly search pattern,' he muttered to himself. 'I doubt she has the imagination to break out of it now. There.'

This time Swan had hidden herself from the list of users currently logged on, but the Doctor found her through the tell-tale signs of her activity. 'No-one knows how to use that thing safely,' he told her, again in a text message. 'Least of all myself.'

Swan shot back 'GO AWAY!!!' It was the first time we'd seen her be anything but reptile cold. The Doctor was starting to get under her skin.

She jumped again. The Doctor followed her again. It took him two tries – ten minutes – to find the system she was on. She was in the list of users again, working carelessly and fast, rummaging through the files for anything that might give her a clue as to what she could do with the Savant.

It went on that way for an hour. The Doctor would lecture Swan, Swan would leap away to another computer somewhere on the net, the Doctor would find her again. Her text responses became more abusive, then stopped all together. She simply could not believe that he could find her again and again, following her through the maze like Theseus guided by his string.

I couldn't help thinking of the time I'd watched Stray Cat playing with a mouse she caught out on the balcony. Instead of just killing it, she kept patting it, or pretending to ignore it – all to see if it had any energy left. Even a mouse can give a cat a potentially fatal bite if it isn't exhausted before the cat goes in for the kill – I saw it go for her face more than once. Stray Cat kept her head well back, and used her paw to tap it and tap it again, wearing it down until it couldn't fight back any more.

Swan broke her search pattern and started jumping around randomly; that only meant it took him a little longer to track her down. Outside the fortress of her own mainframe, she was less like a god of the net and more like a rabbit on the run. In the end she sent him an obscene email and logged out in disgust.

'Are you really sure that was such a good idea?' said Peri. 'Won't she get mad and land Bob in hot water?'

'I can't let her hold that over us. I mustn't.'

'But –'

'I have no intention of letting her harm Bob,' said the Doctor. 'I must make her see that's she's helpless. As soon as she accepts that she needs my help, this miniature catastrophe will be over.'

'What about the Savant's grip on her mind?' I asked. 'Can she get past that?'

'Swan's an intelligent woman,' said the Doctor. 'Single-minded and malicious with a dash of megalomania, but intelligent. She must be aware of what's happening to her. In a way, her demand for an instruction book is a cry for help.' He looked up at his companion. 'We're almost there, Peri. We're *this* close.'

My phone rang. I hit 'answer' and told the speakerphone, 'Shoot, it's your dime.' Then I flinched, expecting Mr Salmon.

Christ help me, it was she. 'Mr Peters,' she said, sounding a little hoarse. 'This is Sarah Swan. I'd like your help with something.'

'Uhhhhhhh.' I said. It was the plummeting moment of stage fright when your lines are just *gone*.

'I don't trust the phone right now.' It should have sounded like knowing cynicism, but instead, it sounded like weary fright. 'Let's meet.'

The Doctor opened his mouth, and Peri just about shoved her fist into it. He subsided onto the couch. Swan had no idea they were there. I said, 'Uh, at your house?'

'No!' She named a shop at Tyson's Corner. 'Right now,' she said. 'I'll be waiting for you.'

'I'll be there.'

I hung up the phone. The Doctor exhaled loudly. 'I'll go,' he said.

'You know, I think it might be better if I go,' I said. The Doctor put his hands on his hips. 'She still thinks I'm neutral in all this.'

'And are you neutral, Mr Peters?' said the Doctor, looming over me. 'After everything you've seen?'

'I guess I am.' I lit up, obliging him to get out of my face. 'I'm still an observer.' The Doctor always looks grouchy, but Peri's disappointed glance cut to the quick. 'Someone has to be,' I insisted. 'Or there wouldn't *be* any meeting with Swan. I'll see what I can get out of her.'

Mr Salmon dropped Bob off at my apartment, and Peri let him in. She said, 'How was your dad?'

Bob blew out a combination sigh and whistle and rolled his eyes. 'I think he'll let us live.' The Doctor showed Bob the email he'd received from an unknowing Swan. 'The more cautious she becomes, the more information she'll give away.'

He insisted on waiting until they heard from me, but the lack of action was driving the Doctor buggy. He straightened out the papers on my desk (wrecking my filing system), played a couple of games of chess with Bob (substituting pennies for the pawns missing from my set), inspected my fridge (a bottle of ketchup, half a lemon, a packet of cornflakes), scratched Stray Cat's rump while she dragged herself about on the carpet with her claws, and finally went back to the Apple, to try to trace Luis based on the information he'd given away during the MUD session.

Peri tried to comfort a depressed Bob. 'You could come with us, you know.'

Bob's eyes got very big. 'Really?'

'I don't think the Doctor would take much persuading. We've got plenty of room.'

'You know, he asked me,' said Bob. 'Back in '77. He asked if I wanted to travel with him. It was a crazy question. My mom would have had kittens.' Peri had to grin. Bob said, 'So he told me he'd return for me in a few years and ask again. When you turned up at my office, I thought it was because he'd come back for me.'

Peri's grin softened into a smile. 'So how about it?'

'I don't want to miss the next ten years of computing!' Peri thought about that. Ten years of living in the same place, watching it change around you a day at a time. She had never had ten years in a row like that. 'History is happening right now, and I've got my hands on it.' He mimed typing at a keyboard. 'It's too exciting to go right now. Maybe in ten years?'

'Maybe,' said Peri. She gave him a pat on the arm.

Bob hovered at the Doctor's elbow until he came out of his computer trance. 'Er,' said Bob. 'I drew this up for you. For protection. Just in case.'

He handed the Doctor a slip of paper on which he had constructed an elaborate occult symbol. The Doctor unfolded the paper, raised an eyebrow, examined the complex diagram drawn with ruler and compass and ringed with angelic names and alchemical marks, carefully folded it up again, and inserted it into his coat pocket.

'Thank you, Bob,' he said. 'That was very thoughtful of you.'

'Uh, Doctor?' said Bob. He was pointing at the screen of the Apple. Letters and numbers were flowing across its screen in a flood of symbols. 'I have never seen anything like this. What'd you do to it?'

'It's not me,' said the Doctor. 'It's something on Swan's Eclipse. I was trying to make her system crash to root, and suddenly something reached out and grabbed the modem.'

'Well, disconnect it!'

The Doctor caught Bob's hand before he could yank the modem's plug. 'Just a moment. Look at it. What's it doing?'

Bob said, 'It looks like it's running the same instructions over and over again. You know, it looks like a diagnostic test... a program checking out the Apple's system, poking into all the nooks and crannies. I do not like this.'

The scribble on the screen meant nothing to Peri. Everything she had seen up to that point had been in kind of stunted English, the high-level command languages which let human beings talk to the machine: a translator takes words like PRINT or RUN and turns them into the microcode that the computer can understand. Now the Apple was receiving instructions in its own tongue, and gleefully running them through its little circuits just as fast as it could.

They watched as the program refined itself. 'It's using a sort of evolution,' said the Doctor. 'Inputting its best guesses, then running them through 'natural' selection to refine them. Each generation of the program is a little better than the last.'

'There's no way the Apple has enough oomph to do that,'

said Bob. 'The actual program that's doing this must be running on Swan's mini.'

'Using the Apple as its testing ground.'

'Well, what's it trying to accomplish?' said Peri.

'A good question,' said the Doctor. He reached over and plucked the cord out of the modem. Instantly, the characters on the screen of the Apple froze.

Bob picked up a diskette and fed it into the slot. 'Let's do a core dump,' he said. 'Find out what Swan was trying to do to my machine.'

The big fear about the people who break into computers is that they could bring civilisation tumbling down. They're forces of chaos, pulling the rug out from under the order we've created with our machines. Trust me, the hackers aren't going to trigger World War III. They just don't think that big, even when their philosophy tells them to screw the system before it screws them. No, what they cause are little miseries. Dumb pranks, mostly against one another. A few thousand dollars bilked from Ma Bell or the credit card companies isn't enough to blow the walls down. Oh, in theory they might be able to kill a few people by blowing away 911 or messing up a hospital's records, but even that's not enough to end life as we know it.

I couldn't believe that Swan was as dangerous as the Doctor was making out. I could see her growing fat and ugly on petty thefts, petty revenge. But she'd always be a parasite, living around the edges instead of pulling strings from the centre. Let her keep the little monster; if the Ruskies really wanted it back, or the CIA really wanted to get their paws on it, Swan would just turn up missing one day, simple as that.

That's what I was thinking on my way to the mall.

I met Swan at a coffee and pastries shop. She had a junk look about her, a pale twitch. The thing that was scraping at her mind would soon be flaking away the health of her body.

'Tell me where the Doctor is,' she said.

'Hold on!' I said. 'What makes you think I know where he is?'

'I practically walked into you when you were with his pals.'

'But I was only interviewing them,' I bullshitted.

'Mr Peters,' she said, 'if you're not with me, you're against me. Is that clear?'

'Miss Swan,' I said, 'what's clear to me is that you're sick. I do want to help you. Let me take you to your doctor.'

Then Swan called me a name which made up my mind about her. 'You dumb faggot,' she said. 'Do you know how much trouble I'm going to get you in?'

I sat back in my little plastic chair and stared at her.

'This is the biggest opportunity I've ever had,' she told me. I wasn't sure if she thought I knew everything, or if she just didn't care to explain it to me. 'I'm sorry, but I'll break anybody to make the most of that windfall. Does your editor know the LAPD still want you for bashing your editor there?'

'Lady,' I said, 'I didn't bash anybody. Someone throws a punch at me, I throw it right back at them. Seem fair to you?'

'You won't be throwing any punches at me.'

'I won't be throwing any crumbs your way, either.'

'Can't you guys understand?' Swan's voice was creaking. 'I'm going to wreck you. I'm going to crush you. Anybody you like, anybody you love, I'm going to take them down too.'

'You'll try. And we'll push back three times as hard as you push us. You don't know when you're outclassed.' I stood up. ''Scuse me. I've got some shopping to do.'

* * *

It only took three tries with the air gun to shoot out the

209

camera above Swan's doorway. I managed it easily from the sidewalk. From our little expedition into Swan's security set-up, I knew I was invisible where I stood. Through the curtains of the house next door, I could see a family eating miniature chocolate bars from a bowl and playing with a new chess machine. They took no notice of me. It gave me the creeps to be standing by their front yard with a toy gun, and them all unawares.

Swan was back at the office; I'd phoned before I'd driven out to McLean, hanging up when I heard her voice. The broken camera would warn her anyway: I didn't have long to take the obvious step of busting a window and making off with her prize.

Swan had absolutely isolated herself. She never spoke to her neighbours, she was friends with no-one at her office. She had bullied every hacker and phreak in the greater DC area, but now she couldn't trust any of them, even her old pal Luis. She couldn't even use social engineering to rustle up some support from unsuspecting technicians; Swan's style was strictly anti-social. She was on her own. That made her very safe in one way, and incredibly vulnerable in another way: she couldn't even have someone guard her house. I wrapped my hand in my pocket, and busted the window on the porch.

I had a rough map of Swan's house in my head built out of glimpses. I only wish I'd had a genie, like the Doctor's guide in the mud, to carry me straight to my goal. There wasn't a lot of light inside, but I knew the areas she was watching had to have their bulbs lit. I crept up the stairs – not an easy thing to do, when you're in a blazing hurry – and located the bathroom where Swan was keeping her prisoner.

The air gun claimed another camera as its victim. The shape in the tub didn't even flinch when I shot the lens out. It wasn't easy to see in the dim yellowish light and behind the grubby shower curtain, but then, I wasn't looking at it too closely.

There was no putting it off. I held my breath and ripped back the slimy plastic barrier between me and the monster.

It didn't look at me, too busy with the guts of a pushbutton phone and a hand-held football video game to care. I could see its fur rippling with tiny appendages, like the legs of a caterpillar or a wormy slice of meat, keeping a firm and elegant grip on the components it was toying with.

It never looked up, but I still had an intense feeling of being watched, of being looked back at. The longer I stood there, the more intense that feeling got, as though I was the most important thing in its little echoing bath-tubby world. It was the kind of warm and important feeling you get as a kid when you're the centre of everybody's attention. All that, and it never so much as glanced at me.

The thing was about the size of a six-year-old, and as light as though it really was just a stuffed animal. When I bent and scooped it up out of the tub, it just kept right on playing with its new toys. I had expected it to be warm, but its fur was as cool as the tub it was sitting in.

I caught sight of myself in the bathroom mirror, holding the thing, and almost dropped it. It looked so bloody *wrong*. There isn't anything on Earth that's shaped like a Y with banana-yellow fur for fingers. If it had been a trained monkey or a mutant crocodile or even a disfigured human child it wouldn't have been so disgusting. If you've ever got a big spider, like a huntsman, on the end of a broom, only to have it run right down the handle into your hands, you know the feeling I had at that moment. I wanted to throw the thing away from me while my whole body shrugged back in the opposite direction. But that nauseating flinch was overridden by a new and different feeling: I wanted to hold onto the thing, grip it tightly, keep it as close to me as possible.

I snuck out of the bathroom and headed for the dark stairs. Was this how Luis had felt about the monster? And now Swan? Was the monster clouding up the air around me with irresistible pheromones? Or was it doing something directly to my grey matter? The urge to toss it away rose up in me again, like the first thump in your stomach when you know you're going to chunder and nothing can stop it. But something did stop it. The ugly fear that I was being reprogrammed faded into the background, beaten by my need to get the monster somewhere safe and start feeding it breakfast cereal.

Swan met me at the bottom of the steps. I was so wrapped up in my furry armful that she just stepped out of nowhere and hit me across the back of the shoulders with a baseball bat. All my muscles stopped working for long enough that she could take hold of her alien baby and shove me back onto the uncarpeted stairs.

The thump of wooden angles into my spine seemed to break the monster's spell. Swan gripped the thing tight against her winter coat, and I had no jealousy, no urge to take it back from her. I could have got the baseball bat out of her awkward grip in a moment, but instead I just lay there, propped up on my elbows, waiting to see what she'd do next.

Swan cussed me out in no uncertain terms and added, 'I'm going to ruin you, freak. Just ruin you.'

'Screw you, lady.'

'You must've realised the call at the office would warn me.'

'I can't believe you just left it there. Not with everybody that wants it.'

'You'd never have got it out of the house,' snorted Swan.

'Is that right,' I said, hauling myself to my feet. I was in her face, but she didn't so much as take a step back.

> I am lying on that second-floor bed in Los Angeles, naked
> as a snake, sunshine slanting in hot white beams across the
> room. I am yelping in time with *Heart of the Sunrise*. The
> record player is under the bed, speakers tipped onto their
> backs, so the sound is coming to me from another planet,
> through a wall of springs and mattress and bedclothes and
> my own skinny, helpless flesh. Each time the guitar starts
> its merciless climb and fall, like a race car driver
> accelerating, I am shouting out CHRIST JESUS and bursting
> frozen sweat through every pore. I'm riding a bull, naked,
> bareback, I'm flying and leaping over as it tosses me away
> again and again, circling round to land on its back, like a
> piece of stretched elastic snapping home. The bull will not
> stop, its buck and plunge matching the rise and fall of the
> guitar. The acid I have taken has turned out to be angel
> dust and everyone I know in the whole city is peeking in
> through the crack of the bedroom door.

I landed back in the present again, sitting on my ass at the
bottom of the stairs. Swan and her baby were gone. Every inch
of me was soaked, as though I had been covered in snow and
thawed out. For a paranoid moment I was sniffing my own
sleeves, nervous that Swan had doused me with petrol. After a
moment I realised I was covered in sweat, my hair heavy with
it and glued to my face.

I had never, never been able to remember that shit before.
People had told me a little about it, looking at the floor while
they hinted at what had happened that afternoon. Now I had all
the details in hi-fi stereo Technicolor.

I could hear Swan upstairs, cooing to her little mutant baby in the bathtub. I disappeared out the front door, not giving a damn about cameras, and shot through.

90

The Doctor bit my head off when I confessed. 'The Savant could
have done irreparable damage to your brain!' So could the angel
dust, I thought, but I kept that to myself. 'It's obviously bonded
deeply with Swan. It was just beginning that process with Luis
when she stole it away from him. Threatened with being
snatched from her side, it responded with a mental attack. A
very low-level one, happily, for your peace of mind.' That was
low-level? I was there, absolutely there, as though every
molecule of the event had been recorded somewhere in my
body and played back like a tape. 'Why do you imagine we
simply didn't knock the door down and purloin the
component? Why do you think the Eridani haven't done it
themselves? No, now that the Savant has fallen into the
proverbial wrong hands, we've got to handle this with the
proverbial kid gloves.'

He seemed to have run out of steam. I had been sitting on the
arm of my sofa through the whole speech. Now I slid down
onto the cushions. My head was freezing cold after walking
through the winter air with my hair full of sweat. In a few
minutes I'd take a hot bath and try to forget about the whole
thing.

I said, 'I still don't get your angle, Doc.'

'What?' he huffed.

'What's in it for you? Besides whatever the Eridani are
paying.' He sniffed at that, like it was an insult. 'I could really

believe you'd do this even if they didn't have a red cent. For a good cause. Or just to put Swan in her place.'

'That certainly needs doing,' he said archly. I thought of Swan's speech about the food chain. The Doctor was making a mess of the whole concept of stronger beats weaker, winner takes all. I wondered what kind of card player he was. 'Peri was right,' sighed the Doctor. 'In the end, this is about taking a lost child home. An enormously dangerous child.'

'I gotta tell you – the thing looked perfectly happy with Swan to me.'

'She simply cannot care for it,' said the Doctor. 'No matter how slavishly devoted she may become to its needs, only the Eridani have that expertise. There may be nutrients it requires that aren't even available on Earth – it could be starving slowly to death for want of them. Its neurological development will already have been stunted by lack of contact with the rest of the components, particularly the control unit.' By now he was talking more to himself than to me. 'No. We must restore it to the Eridani, whatever their purpose for it.'

'Couldn't we get them to hand over the manual or something?'

The Doctor raised an eyebrow. 'And do you fancy raising the Savant to maturity?'

I hauled myself up off the sofa. 'The only thing I want in my bathtub right now is me.'

Swan was as good as her word. She phoned my editor at home, where he was relaxing with his wife and three kids, and told him all about my adventures in LA. She convinced him to check the news archives over his modem. He spent half an hour digging up the little news item about how I'd slugged the editor of a well-known west-coast newspaper.

Swan called him back the moment he logged out. 'Well?'

'You're right about the assault charges,' he said. 'But there is no way that man is a fag.'

'You saw what the paper said.'

'I don't *care* what the paper said. I've met three of Chick's girlfriends.'

'Camouflage,' she spat.

'Bullshit. Maybe one lady, sure, but three? Now if someone in San Fran called the man a pussy, I can understand why he might take a swing at them.'

'Better make sure he doesn't take a swing at your ass.'

'You've got a dirty mouth, ma'am. What'd Chick ever do to you?'

'I'd be more worried about what he might do to you,' said Swan, and slammed down her phone.

Swan ground her fists into her temples. Nothing was working. Nothing was helping. The Doctor seemed unmoved by her threat to destroy his young protégé's life. Her threat to wreck mine had hit a dead end. There wasn't the slightest hint of a shred of information on the network about her precious windfall, and even it was out there somewhere, the Doctor would pester and plague her every step.

She ought to be on top of the world, and instead she was boxed in on every side.

Bob could be crushed simply by pressing charges. There must be more to my story than she had been able to find, something she could use to turn my editor's stomach the way it had done in Los Angeles. And the Doctor, what could she find out about this Doctor, what was there about him that he would never want the authorities to know? She would dig and scrape and claw until she ruined us.

* * *

217

It didn't take the Doctor long to find Luis Perez. He traced the MUD connection back to a forged university account, had a word with the sysadmin and got help tracing the connection back to a second forged account on another machine, and left a message in that account with a request for Luis to email him at Bob's account.

Luis asked for a meeting in a cafeteria in one of the Smithsonian buildings. It had a sort of conveyor belt on which the food went round and round, and you snatched what you wanted. Kids stood next to it, watching all those desserts cruising past, just out of their reach.

The Doctor had insisted we all stay behind; he didn't want to intimidate the man and he wasn't sure if he was dangerous. Bob and Peri protested a little, but it was obvious they were going to do as they were told. Not so me. I wasn't going to miss a thing.

'You got to remember,' said Luis, raking at a bit of hair over his ear. 'You got to remember what Swan has is a *reputation*. She's supposed to be able to do anything. If word gets out that some other guy can beat her, that she can't even do her thing without you peeking over her shoulder, then she's got nothing.'

'Good,' said the Doctor. 'Then she must realise that the only way to get rid of me is to hand over the Savant.'

'She can't do that, man.' Luis's fingers tightened around that lock of hair. 'She can never let anybody beat her. If it happens once, it could happen again. If anybody even gets close to winning a bout with her, she crushes them down so hard they can't get up again.' He looked up at the Doctor. 'That's what she's gonna do to you.'

The Doctor said dryly, 'She is welcome to try.'

'If she can't hit you, she'll hit the people around you. I've watched it happen. I've seen the lights go out.'

'That's not the only reason Swan can't hand over the Savant,' said the Doctor. 'Is it?'

Luis shook his head. He went back to spooning his chocolate pudding around and around in its glass. I opened my mouth to ask a question, but the Doctor held up a hand to silence me. Luis muttered, 'What hatched out of that egg? What did it do to me?' He traced a circle in the air with his spoon, in front of his breastbone. 'Is this feeling going to stop?'

'Mr Perez,' said the Doctor, 'I promise you I'll do everything I can to help you –'

'That's not enough, man!' Luis slapped the spoon down on the table, knocking over the pudding. 'I have to get that thing back from her.'

'But that's exactly what we want you to do,' said the Doctor. Luis stared at him. We both did.

'Mr Perez, your contact with the Savant puts you in a unique position. You have already established a rapport with the creature. You should be able to approach and handle it safely. None of us could do that without risking a devastating psychological attack.'

'You mean it can't do anything worse to me,' said Luis dryly.

'That's one way of looking at it.'

'What if I can't let it go?' mumbled Luis. 'I feel like... if you tried to take it away from me again, I would kill you. I'd use it to kill you.'

'I think he could do that,' I muttered.

'We'll deal with that if and when the problem arises,' said the Doctor.

'You got to understand,' said Luis. 'I don't want that thing. I mean, I want it more than anything else in the world. I am not eating and I'm not sleeping because I can't think about anything except getting it back. I'm like a mother whose baby was kidnapped.' A few people were looking at us now. 'Except sometimes it's like I'm its baby. Like I'm a kitten mewing and mewing for its mama. This is worse than being in love.'

The Doctor brought Luis back to my flat. He made the man take a nap on the sofa while he explained the plan to us in the kitchen.

'In Luis's hands, the creature will be harmless.'

'Harmless to everyone except him,' said Peri. 'Won't it go on changing the structure of his brain?'

'I'm afraid he's already badly affected,' said the Doctor quietly. 'He can barely function as it is. If the Savant can re-establish contact with his central nervous system, there is a chance we can use it to return his brain patterns to their original state. We'll need the Eridani's help, of course, but I think I can convince them to do their bit.'

Peri said, 'Are you sure we can fix him?'

'No. I'm not,' said the Doctor flatly. 'I'm gambling what's left of Mr Perez's sanity that he can help us retrieve the Savant before anyone else can be harmed by it. If he can be cured, so can Swan and the people of Ritchie.'

'He's like a guinea pig,' said Peri, but she didn't protest further.

The Doctor made my bed. This was a strange thing to behold, especially when he plucked a sock from the sheets and flung it over his shoulder without a backward glance.

'Couldn't we just use the kitchen table?' I said.

'I want something with a little give,' said the Doctor, making a perfect hospital corner.

I sat down on the laundry hamper and watched as he smoothed out the covers. We had already lugged my TV into the bedroom – an ancient set donated to me by a fellow journalist who said it had been used to watch the Watergate scandal. My joke is that I prefer my television in black and white, like my newspapers. It was set up on the dresser, an inch or two sticking out perilously over the edge of the wood.

The Doctor placed the device in the exact centre of the bed, patting down the covers around the plastic ball. Then he fished in his jacket pocket and drew out an old-fashioned watch on a chain. He snapped it open. 'Just a moment now,' he said.

He switched the TV on and started twiddling the tuning dial up and down the channels. We stood, watching the dance of the static, the rise and fall of the ocean hiss. He flicked past the local TV channels without stopping, brief squirts of people and speech; then up and up into the higher frequencies.

'Ah,' he said at last. 'There we are.'

The roar and flicker resolved itself, and Mr Ghislain appeared on the screen. For someone supposedly transmitting from outer space, he looked remarkably crisp. He was still wearing his black suit and his hat – no sign of a spacesuit.

'– transmit to you,' he said. 'The Interrupt will neutralise the Savant's mental process. This will allow you to detach all undesirable connections. We are pursuing a reversal method for affected neurologies.'

'Hang on,' I said. 'Isn't everyone in the District also watching this show?'

'Not at all,' murmured the Doctor. 'The Eridani's' transmission is targeted to our co-ordinates.'

I wondered why they didn't just use the speakerphone again. Fear of phreaks eavesdropping on the conversation? Or did it just depend on which satellites they could hijack at any given time? I shook my head. I was starting to buy into the Doctor's cover story, imagining Ghislain and his exotic parrot lurking about somewhere between the moon and the sun. They were probably in a TV studio in downtown DC, and this transmission was being 'leaked' to eager Russian eyes.

'– affected neurologies,' said Ghislain, repeating his message. 'We will do all possible things to comply with your request to "leave the planet as we found it".' The message must have been recorded; the screen went blank for a few seconds, and then it started over. 'Within the prearranged time parameters we will transmit to you. The Interrupt will neutralise the Savant's mental process.'

'I don't think Peri will approve of that,' murmured the Doctor. 'A little adjustment may be in order.'

'What's the Interrupt he's talking about? A program? Something that will kill the Savant?'

'That's their plan. Simply destroy the component that happens to be running haywire. I'm sure we can do a little better than that. Shut it down and repair the damage it's done. All I need is a few moments with the Eridani's Interrupt device.'

There was a soft thump. We both turned. I swear the device had moved across the bedspread by several inches. The Doctor gave me an enigmatic smile and picked the thing up.

As good as his word, the Doctor sat down at the kitchen table and pried open the device with a set of jeweller's screwdrivers. He peered at its guts with an enormous Sherlock Holmes magnifying glass, 'hmming' and 'ah yesing' to himself. Half an hour later he announced that it would do what it was told now, and we could get going.

Swan had, all unknowing, emailed several pictures from each of her security cameras to Bob's computer. Bob set up the Apple to email those pictures to her at regular intervals – the same intervals as her minicomputer. Then he crawled across her kitchen floor, pulled the keyboard from the Eclipse down to a chair, and typed in commands to stop the real pictures being sent to her office. As far as Swan would be able to tell, her house was quiet and empty.

It would never have worked if Swan didn't have the willpower to leave the Savant behind. She was determined to stay at her office until she cracked the secrets of its program: she wanted to be able to take advantage of the Savant without it taking advantage of her. My bungled burglary must have convinced her that it really was safe to leave the Savant on its own.

The moment Bob gave us the all-clear, Luis was up the stairs like a raped ape. When the Doctor reached the bathroom doorway, he was already holding the Savant in his arms.

It was a kill or cure moment. If the Savant had lashed out at Luis the way it had lashed out at me, it might have been more than his already affected brain could handle.

But it snuggled comfortably into Luis's arms, playing with a TV remote which it had partly disassembled. There were individual buttons spread all over its sticky fur.

Luis didn't say anything. He just stepped out into the hallway, brushing past us, and sat down on the carpet with his back to the stair railing.

It took us a while to get Luis down the stairs. He wasn't interested in anything except the Savant. In the end Bob and I marched him out to the Travco while he cradled the thing against his chest, inside his sweater. It was hard to believe we were doing him any favours.

We sat him down on the bunk bed. Bob and I perched on the double bed in the back. Once again, Peri handled the maps and the Doctor did the driving.

'That thing freaks me out,' confessed Bob in a low voice.

I was sitting cross-legged on the bed, peeking out through the venetian blinds into the twilight. 'The Doctor reckons it's harmless.'

'I can't work out what it is,' he murmured. 'Is it a mammal? It's got fur. But it doesn't have a *body*. Just those three cylinders. Where are its eyes? How does Luis know which one is its head?'

'The one with the beak?'

'Yeah, but he doesn't hold it that way up.'

'Uh-oh. Doctor,' I called out. 'I think we're being followed.'

Bob peeked out through the blinds. A small, dark blue car was sitting right on our tail. 'Is that Swan back there?'

I staggered forward up the length of the Travco. 'Pull over,' I told the Doctor. 'I'll jump out and talk to her. As soon as she stops, you take off.'

'You're sure?' He was already slowing.

The car pulled over to the shoulder behind us. I jumped down from the Travco as it was still rolling to a stop, and then strode back down the gravel.

A moment later I was running back towards the departing campervan, waving my arms. 'Hold on! It's Mondy!'

The Doctor leaned out of the window. 'Find out what he wants.'

The phreak didn't get out of his car; he wound down the window. 'Hi Chick,' he said. He was doing odd things with his face, rolling his eyes and twitching his cheek, as if trying to point with his eyebrows.

'What's up? Are you following us?'

He grinned weakly, in between twitching. 'I guess I am. I guess I just want to see how all of this comes out.'

'How'd you find us, anyway?'

'Police radio,' said Mondy brightly. 'You just ask if anyone's seen the vehicle you want. They do all the work for you.' He quit twitching and gave me a 'you idiot' look. 'Wait, I have to blow my nose.' Mondy reached into his pocket and pulled out a wad of tissues. He extracted one of them and handed it to me. I uncrumpled it reluctantly to find three words written in thick black marker pen.

SWAN IN BACK, said the note.

Swan emerged from the back door carrying a shotgun. If I had thought fast enough, I could have slammed the door on her. But I didn't. Which meant I was on the business end of the gun a couple of seconds later. I'd been there just once before in my life, when I was fifteen years old and caught with a farmer's daughter. The same instinct possessed me then as it did now: I froze and shut up.

'You know what I want,' she told me.

I must have hesitated. Or maybe Mondy made a move she didn't like, I don't know. Swan turned and gave the Escort both barrels. The windscreen burst inwards, showering the front seats with glass. 'Holy crap!!!' announced Mondy. He shot out of the passenger side door and disappeared into the trees at the side of the road. His car rolled forward until it bumped into the Travco and idled there.

Swan cracked the gun to reload it. I grabbed the barrels, burned hell out of my fingers, and snatched them away. She flipped the shotgun closed as though she'd done it a thousand times, laughing as I blew on my fingers.

She gestured at the Travco, moving the gun in a small oval from me to the campervan and back. 'Open it up,' she said.

I did it, moving in slow motion, partly so she could see everything I was doing, partly to give the Doctor and co a chance to react. I had caught a glimpse of the Doctor watching in the rear view mirror, but I didn't dare look back there now in case Swan took it the wrong way.

Nobody, but nobody, stopped to see what was going on. I don't think anyone even slowed down.

I opened the narrow side door. Swan peered in at Luis sitting on the bunk bed, clutching the Savant like a dozing four-year-old.

'Hand that over or I'll blow your frigging head off,' she told him.

'*Que te jodan*,' he said, clutching the Savant so tightly I was worried it couldn't breathe.

'You know I'm not joking,' said Swan. 'You know just how I feel. You can either hold onto that thing and lose your skull, or you can give it to me right now.'

'You don't feel!' Luis was weeping. 'You're not attached to this thing as though it was your own arm or your own hand.'

I said, 'For God's sake, man, hand it over. It's not worth your life.'

'Maybe we can work together,' he begged her. 'I could come with you. I'll look after it for you.'

'You know that won't work,' said Swan.

'You'll kill it!' screamed Luis. He folded up around the Savant as though his own flesh and bones could save it from a shotgun blast.

That was when the Doctor hit the button.

The Savant didn't make a sound. It froze in position, one of its stubby hands still clutching half a Rubik's Cube.

Luis didn't make a sound. He was already half-slumped on the bunk bed. He just sank down further, like a child falling into sleep. The Savant slid from his lap like a living statue.

Swan screamed her head off.

The Doctor was out of the Travco with incredible speed. He slapped Swan's arms as she fired the shotgun, the pellets flying off wildly, the explosion turning the world silent for a long ringing second – punctuated by Peri screaming in the passenger seat.

The Doctor and I both grabbed for the gun, and found ourselves grabbing each other instead as the length of metal spun around in our grip. Swan had darted into the side of the Travco to grab the Savant. The Doctor pounced on the little yellow body. But she didn't even look at it. She grabbed Luis and dragged him onto the gravel like a side of meat.

And Luis had a gun. Swan fished it out of his jacket pocket and aimed it up at us, crouching over his limp body. She suggested strongly that we depart. The Doctor looked at them and decided to comply.

Luis sat in the passenger seat of Mondy's car, gazing evenly through the remains of the windscreen. Drops of rain were forming an intricate pattern on the surviving glass, glittering dots and spaces. Luis's shoulders had unknotted for the first time in days, his hands lying loose in his lap.

Swan said nothing. She drove through the gathering darkness, through rain that turned from spots to lines to a constant sizzling haze that dripped in through the broken windscreen. From time to time, when they were stopped at lights or when nothing much was happening on the road, she would glance at Luis. He watched the road with nothing to say.

It was hours later when the garage doors yawned for the Escort. Swan opened the passenger door and herded Luis into the house. Upstairs, she cleared all the junk out of the tub and ran a steaming hot bath for Luis. While he got undressed she laid the loaded shotgun across the little desk in the guest room.

She sat on the lid of the john while he soaked, both of them warming up after the long cold drive. When he was done she made up the guest bed and tucked him into it.

She sat on a wooden chair in the dark, turning a pen around and around in her hands, clicking the nib in and out. Luis sat quietly, propped up with three pillows. His eyes wouldn't close.

She brought him some of the Lego in an old plastic ice-cream container. She put it in his lap on top of the blankets.

Luis's hands dived into the container and started feeling the shapes with their fingertips, turning each one around and replacing it. Swan switched on a small lamp on the desk, dragged her chair to the edge of the bed and watched. In just a few minutes, those probing fingers had worked out how to stick two Lego pieces together. Soon Luis was building more and more complicated structures.

After half an hour Swan took the plastic container away. They were both going to need some rest. Tomorrow would be a big day for both of them.

100

The Doctor drove us to a gas station and pulled the Travco into the parking lot. Peri and I were both still vibrating with adrenaline. I was just starting to discover the little scrapes and bruises I had accumulated during those few dramatic seconds on the shoulder. A couple of police cars passed the station, heading back the way we'd come, sirens blazing.

'They'll get her,' said Peri. 'She must be driving the car with bullet holes in the windshield!'

'Unless she hijacked somebody,' I said.

'I doubt that.' The Doctor was perfectly calm. 'Swan will not want to involve anyone else if she can help it.' He wasn't even breathing fast, as though nothing unusual had happened at all. He climbed into the back of the Travco to examine the Savant.

Peri peered at it from the passenger seat. Its stiff, stretched-out shape reminded me of a cat I'd had as a kid, poisoned by a neighbour and found in frozen running position underneath a bush. We'd had to dig a very long grave for it.

'Is it OK?' said Peri. 'You didn't kill it, did you?'

'No I did not,' the Doctor replied. 'It has been thoroughly interrupted. In fact, it's quite comatose.'

'Now what do we do?' said Bob.

'I've arranged with its owners that they will collect it.'

Peri sat down on the bunk bed next to the solid Y. She tentatively stroked its fur. 'Maybe we should keep it,' she said. 'I don't trust those guys to look after it.'

'You don't establish an infraluminal interplanetary civilisation by being wasteful. I'm sure the Eridani will find some use for it, even though it's run off the rails of its original genetic program.' The Doctor didn't sound entirely convinced. But at least the little yellow bugger wasn't a threat to anyone any more.

I said, 'Didn't you say something about it being born pregnant?'

'Yes, well, it's best if they collect it sooner rather than later.'

'So we win,' said Bob. 'We've deactivated the Savant. We've stopped the threat to Earth. We, in short, rock.'

'What about Luis?' said Peri.

'Don't forget Mondy,' I added.

The Doctor said, 'I suspect Mr Mond is capable of effecting his own rescue. Luis Perez, on the other hand, will need more help than the police can give him, even assuming they can catch up with Swan.'

'She's crazy,' said Peri. 'I thought we were all dead. I thought she was going to shoot holes in the campervan until she got all of us. Like playing a video game.'

'There's method in her madness, rather than the other way around,' said the Doctor. 'Swan hasn't lost control. Her threats were very calculated, even though they're driven by her obsession with the Savant. No, she knew just what she was doing.'

'You mean she planned to kidnap Luis all along?'

'Now that is interesting...' The Doctor was staring off into the distance, as if watching a TV show only he could see. 'She switched targets almost the moment I activated the Interrupt. But she couldn't possibly have known I had the device, nor what it would do. So why the sudden change of plan?'

'Maybe she just wanted a hostage,' said Bob.

'That doesn't make sense,' said Peri. 'Why grab someone you'd have to carry? She could have got Chick, or the Doctor.'

'Something is going on here that we don't understand,' said the Doctor. 'And the reluctance of our friends the Eridani to be more specific is the root of our troubles. But there's not much we can do about them. What was that program that attacked the Apple II? What has she cooked up with alien help? Swan's our target.'

'Uh, excuse me,' said Bob, 'but she just tried to use *us* for target practice.'

'We have to know what's in her computer,' said the Doctor. 'All our sophisticated attacks have failed. I think it's time to try something a little cruder.'

Swan had two phone calls to make. Luis seemed happy to keep playing with the Meccano set she had given him, so she went downstairs, settled into the chair at the kitchen table, and picked up the receiver.

The first call was to my editor. 'There's someone I'd like to suggest you talk to,' she said. 'A former colleague of Mr Peters. Oh, of course, it's up to you. But let me give you the details.' She did, and then listened while my boss told her he had no intention of calling some guy long-distance and interrupting his Christmas break. 'Come on,' she said. 'Aren't your journalistic instincts itching? I just spoke to him myself. And do you know what he told me?'

She told him. My editor made that call.

Swan's second call was to Bob Salmon's boss. He didn't answer his work phone, so she tried his home number. After three rings he picked up.

'I'm afraid I have some bad news about one of your employees,' she told him. 'Robert Salmon was caught trespassing in my company's offices and in my company's computers. Now, I am willing not to go ahead with charges if you'll take action against him yourself.'

'I'm very shocked to hear this, Miss Swan. Bob has been an excellent worker. He's a bright young man. If the department decides to dismiss him, I'm going to be very sorry to lose him.'

'It's up to you, of course,' said Swan. 'I understand you may not be able to make a decision until the new year. Just call me back at this number when you do.'

Swan hung up and sat back in her chair. She was back in control, she was on top of the world. She had Luis and we had nothing. She had hurt us, and she could go on hurting us. She had been on the police radio on the way home, using a device which lowered her voice's pitch until it sounded like a man, confusing the reports until they would never know who the crazy lady with the shotgun was. She was untouchable.

Back at my flat, Mr Salmon was staring at the phone. 'I cannot believe I just made a prank phone call.'

'You didn't make a prank call, Dad!' said Bob. 'A prank call is when you phone a guy at the bowling alley and ask if he has ten-pound balls. Swan called us.'

Mr Salmon took out his handkerchief and dabbed his forehead. 'She sure was fooled,' he said. 'That's bought you a few more days, son. But she's going to be even madder when she realises she was tricked.'

The Doctor said, 'Miss Swan is going to have more important things to deal with. I guarantee it.'

Mr Salmon patted Bob on the head and went back to work.

Mondy emerged from the street after fifty-seven minutes, pushed the manhole lid back into place, and walked over to my car carrying his tapedeck and his trio of traffic cones. He sat down in the back and thumbed the 'play' switch. The tapedeck served up a bunch of beeping, roaring, and hissing. He was waiting for me to ask him what it was. But I already knew: it was the sound of a modem, the sound of someone dialling up a computer from a distance. Computers talk over the phone in what sounds like static or an angry cat, but is actually a firehose explosion of zeroes and ones blipping over the lines.

'You taped Swan calling up her work account from home,' I said. Mondy nodded. 'How does that help us? We don't speak computer.'

'Yeah, but other computers do. As soon as I play this back in my computer, we'll have Swan's password. It's a crude method, but I can usually get it to work. Then we just stroll into her account through the front door.'

And grab the Savant program. 'Perfect. Let's get to your mom's house.' I pulled out. The late-night traffic was quiet.

After a while, Mondy piped up from the back seat. 'Is it true?'

'Is what true?'

'What Swan said about you. I listened to her talking to your boss.'

'You tape that?'

'Nah,' said Mondy. 'No, seriously, I rewound the tape and recorded over it. The computer was all I was interested in.'

There was a long pause. 'Well, is it?'

'What do you think?'

'I think it's obvious bullshit. I think your boss will say it's obvious bullshit. I don't think you have anything to worry about, man.'

'Hope you're right,' I said.

Mondy played the recording again, as though he could fish Swan's password right out of the meaningless hiss with modem ears. 'The really simplest thing to do would be to play it back over the phone to her own computer. I've done that when I was in a hurry. It even worked a couple of times.'

'Mondy?'

'Yeah?'

'It is true.'

He slid down in the seat. 'Jeez Louise.'

My phone rang again. Peri said, 'Should we answer it?'

The Doctor shook his head. 'Mr Mond may not have restored the phone lines to their original state yet. Better to let it ring out.'

They all jumped when my answering machine picked up. Bob grabbed for the stop button, but the Doctor caught his hand. 'Too late,' he said.

'Chick?' It was my editor. He named the west-coast journalist he had just been talking to. 'Not to put too fine a point on it, he says you're, uh, a woman. The guy says, he, uh, saw it with his own eyes. Look, this is nuts. Will you call me back? Bye.'

Five minutes later a boggled Mondy and I walked into my apartment. The Doctor was working at the Apple. Peri and Bob were still staring at the answering machine.

Peri and Bob looked up at me, and I knew right away what had happened. I could see their eyes adjusting like the lens of a camera as they saw me for the first time. They both opened and closed their mouths like goldfish.

'Oh, spit it out,' I said, without taking the cigarette out of my mouth.

'You're a transvestite!!!' said Bob.

'Bullshit.' I could feel my hands curling into fists inside my jacket pockets. For God's sake, don't lose it. 'I'm a man. Same as you.'

Bob said, 'I think there's a *little* difference –' and then broke off, blushing. Peri actually laughed. The tension in the room broke a little. Mondy sat down next to the Doctor and loaded his cassette tape into the Apple's player.

I pulled my cigarettes out of my pocket. I really needed a smoke. 'You've got some funny ideas about what makes a man, boy.' I glanced at the Doctor. He was either too embarrassed to join in the conversation, or didn't give a toss. Or maybe he was just disgusted.

Stay cool. Don't give them anything. 'Where are we at?'

'We're in,' announced the Doctor. 'I'm looking at Swan's system right now.'

With relief, Bob shot over to his side. 'Look,' he said. 'She's uploading a TARred copy to another system. Maybe a backup? To keep it off her home machine in case the authorities take a look?'

The Doctor was shaking his head. 'No. Remember what it tried to do to our little computer?'

'Oh my God,' said Bob. 'It's uploading itself.'

'Once it copies itself to that new host, it will seize control. Send more copies of itself to more machines.' He sprang to his feet. 'There's nothing we can do from here. Quickly! We have to get to her minicomputer and stop it.'

'You want to break into her house again?' I said from the doorway as they ran into the hall.

Bob said, 'We've got nothing to lose.'

'We have the world to lose,' said the Doctor. They hurtled down the stairs.

I stood there alone for about two minutes. My hands shook a little as I lit a new smoke. It was all happening again, Sydney again, Los Angeles all over again. Every time I promised myself

I would never have to go through it again. It was like one of those bad dreams that come back just when you've forgotten the last time.

The phone rang. I snatched it up. 'Yeah?'

'I want you,' said Swan, 'to tell me everything the Doctor knows.'

My voice had turned into a growl. 'Lady, why the hell should I help you? You've already cost me my job.'

'Because I can do worse. Your old friend in Los Angeles is still pissed off with you. He's more than happy to tell anyone, any supermarket tabloid, about his encounter with the she-male freak from Aussie.' She pronounced it 'Awsss-ee'.

'Jesus, Swan,' I said. 'The Savant thing is dead. Or broken, or whatever. Its original owners have already taken it back. There's nothing left that I can give you.'

'All I want from you is information. The Doctor knows a lot more about all this than he's deigned to tell me. I want you to tell me everything you know. Or I make you a star. Take it or leave it.'

'All right,' I said. 'All right. Keep your hat on, we'll talk. Where are you right now?'

'At my house. You know where it is.'

'Not there,' I said. I named a diner in Rockville. 'I can be there in half an hour.'

'All right.'

'You can pay for the coffee.'

Swan was amused. She could afford to be. 'My pleasure.'

I chucked the phone into the kitchen, where it knocked a bunch of dirty coffee cups off the counter. It all landed on the floor in a satisfying explosion. When I saw Swan, so help me if I wasn't ready to hit a girl.

* * *

The Doctor broke a window, opened a door and pounced on the minicomputer. 'Where's it sending itself to?'

'The university's machine,' said Bob.

'It'll be all over the country in a couple of days. We'll never be able to stuff it back into the bottle.'

'Is there still enough time?!' said Bob.

'I think so,' said the Doctor. 'Look. It's only uploading itself at 300 baud.'

'My God,' said Bob sourly. 'We have only hours.'

'Let's not risk a nasty surprise,' said the Doctor. They bumped shoulders at the keyboard. The Doctor started hammering at the keys. 'It's useless! The system's ignoring input.'

'Uh, guys?' said Peri.

They both looked up at her. She was holding up the Eclipse's power cord, which she had unplugged from the wall. They both looked back down at the screen. 'It's still going!' said Bob.

'There must be an alternative power source,' said the Doctor.

'She's got a UPS,' said Bob.

'Guys?' said Peri.

They looked up again. Now she was holding the modem cord, which she had unplugged from the phone jack. They both looked back down at the screen. 'That's done it,' said Bob.

The Doctor shuffled through the papers and wires and takeout containers on Swan's table until he found a printout of the program. 'Bring a soft copy as well,' he told Bob.

'Already on it,' said the hacker, brandishing a floppy disk. 'You want me to trash Swan's hard drive? She'll have hidden copies all over.'

'If she's hidden copies in her computer, she'll have hidden them elsewhere as well. We'll never find them all.'

'Point,' said Bob. He stashed the floppy disk in his jacket.

'Now we've got a copy it won't take long to work out how it ticks.'

'The program should tell us something about the Savant as well,' said the Doctor. 'How it thinks, what its ultimate purpose is.'

'Isn't it obvious?' said Bob, as they took off. 'It's the ultimate hacker.'

I was surprised to see Luis sitting next to Swan, squeezed side by side into one of the diner's red vinyl booths. He didn't look up as I slid into the opposite seat, he just went on staring at the tabletop. 'What've you done to him?' I said.

'The Doctor did this,' snapped Swan. 'When he set off the device which fried the Savant's brain. It almost fried mine as well.'

I looked at Luis. His face was slack, his eyes unfocussed. To me he looked as though he ought to be slumped and drooling. But to the other folks in the diner, he just looked bored or tired.

'No,' said Swan. 'You can salve your conscience: the Doctor hasn't destroyed Luis's brain. Instead, he has transformed it.'

I had seen how badly screwed up Luis Perez had been by his contact with the Savant. It wasn't hard to believe he could be screwed up even worse.

A waitress ambled over. Swan put a hand on Luis's shoulder. 'Look at her,' she murmured. Luis stared at the girl's face while Swan said, 'We'll each have a black coffee and we'll each have a hundred dollars from the till. And I'll have a slice of Dutch apple pie. No ice cream with that.'

'Yes ma'am,' said the waitress. She drifted away again without writing our order down.

I was about to tell Swan that not everyone shared her sense of humour when the waitress returned, carrying a pot of coffee and a stack of small bills. She filled our cups and laid the money neatly out in front of us. 'I'll be back in a moment with your pie, ma'am.'

My mouth was hanging open, my cigarette dangling from my bottom lip. Swan and I scraped the money off the table into our laps. She neatly tucked hers into her handbag. I didn't know what to do with it, I just wanted to get it out of sight. In the end I stuffed it into my coat pocket.

'I can convince anyone to do anything,' Swan told me blissfully. 'I've tested it at the supermarket, and at the gas station, and at a toll booth.'

'It's a set-up,' I said weakly. But I had seen the people in Ritchie.

'I could *make* you tell me everything you know. Like, where are your tits, girl? What do you do, bind them?'

If you have ever felt totally helpless in your life – maybe if you've ever been mugged – you know how I felt at that moment. It was like the seat fell out from under me and nothing was holding me up any more. I was more scared than when Swan had the shotgun on me. I would rather have holes blasted in my gizzard than have something reach inside my skull and scramble my eggs. The smell of frying food made my stomach lurch and my bladder felt like a stone.

'Don't faint.' Swan was having way too much fun. 'I'm going to give you a chance to tell me of your own accord.'

'Yeah,' I mumbled.

'Yeah what?'

The back of my neck was burning. 'I bind them.'

Swan slapped her hand on the table. 'Not about that. Tell me about the little yellow guy.'

I took a deep breath. 'I'm gonna tell you what the Doctor told me. Don't blame me for it.'

'Go on,' said Swan. Sweat trickled down the back of my collar.

'He says the Savant, the original creature, was from outer space. I'm only telling you what they told me, I don't believe it myself. It was supposed to go to another planet, but it came here by mistake. It's part of a computer. So was the other device you found.'

Swan was nodding. 'What do you believe, Mr Peters?'

'There's been talk about biological computers for a long time,' I said quickly. 'I think it was stolen from a lab. Maybe in the States, maybe somewhere else.'

'You know what I think happened?' said Swan. 'I think the Doctor was just too late. I think the Savant was programming Luis's mind all along. To control a human brain, you need another human brain. You need the right hardware to run your program.'

I was trying not to look at Luis. Would that make any difference? 'What are you going to do?' I said.

Swan smiled. 'Anything I like.'

'Take over the Capitol?'

She looked at me blankly. 'I'm going to get myself some supercomputers,' she said. 'I've installed the Savant program across the network, so I'll always have access to whatever machines I choose. Access and power, that's what I'm all about.'

'But not political power?'

'I never read even the politics in the paper,' she said. 'I can't remember the last time I voted. Why are you so interested in politics?'

'I can't help it,' I said, in a voice like chalk. 'I'm a Washington reporter.'

'Oh... you mean, why don't Luis and I take over the world.'

'Uh, I didn't mean to give you ideas.'

'I will have to push the authorities around a little. I'm going to need total access to the phone system, for example.' She gave a loopy grin. A smile didn't belong on that face. 'Luis is a blue box,' she said. 'A blue box for the human mind. All you have to do is press the buttons, and you get access to the system. Open wide. And I've got it.'

My heart had just about jumped across the diner a moment ago. But Swan really couldn't see the potential of her mind-control device. Or, more likely, she really wasn't interested in world domination. Not the real world, anyway: her megalomania was confined to the world inside the computer.

The waitress returned with Swan's apple pie. Her eyes brushed over us, but her mind was far, far away. It was the look of Ritchie.

Swan was never going to stomp the world like Godzilla. Instead, she was going to leave a slow trail of collateral damage, like a man walking around with a radioactive rod in his pocket.

'You know,' I said, 'I miss summer in Sydney. I miss Avoca Beach. Maybe I'll put this hundred dollars towards a ticket home.'

'You do that,' said Swan. 'Go on home to your family, little lady. Buy yourself some pretty dresses and go for a walk on the beach.'

'Like you say,' I told her, standing up, waiting for her to make Luis stop me from going. But she didn't. She was enjoying the apple pie too much.

This would have been the moment to run. I had already crossed the line from observer to participant. Doing that had made me a target for the thing sitting in the diner.

I should have got on the road that instant. There was nothing left for me in Washington, not now the cat was out of the bag. There wasn't anything I could do to help the Doctor. It was time to do another of Charles Peters' vanishing acts, get on the road, drive until I couldn't stand the flash of the highway past my eyes any more.

I walked through the parking lot, crossed the road, and went into a phone booth. The traffic would hide me, and I was pretty sure Luis couldn't somehow detect me at a distance. One last call before I left. Luckily, by then the Doctor had returned from burglarising Swan's house.

I related her theory – that the Savant had been programming Luis as some sort of hypnotist, all along. 'No, no, no,' said the Doctor. 'It hadn't done anything to him except to create that intense bond. OF COURSE. When the interrupt pulse hit the Savant, it reacted by making a backup of itself. Right into poor Luis's mind.' His voice sagged. 'If he was aware of what was happening, he may even have welcomed it. The ultimate protection for the Savant – inside his own skull. It might have been better if I had simply let the Eridani kill the Savant. A sudden and painless death instead of this *infection*.'

'There's nothing we can do to make him normal again, is there?'

'It might be possible for the Eridani, but I doubt it. What is now inside Luis's head may not be human in any real sense.'

'Doctor, that's gross,' said Peri, in the background.

'Gross?' he said. 'Grotesque. But this is the Savant's whole purpose – find a network and copy itself throughout it. Was that the Eridani's real intent all along? Or is this just an unexpected branching of the program?'

'Are you saying it could happen again?' I said.

'If anything should happen to Luis,' said the Doctor, 'there's no reason the Savant couldn't repeat its little trick. Copy itself into a fresh brain.'

'Doctor,' I said. 'Could it happen even if something *didn't* happen to Luis?'

The Doctor froze. 'Yes,' he said. 'Yes, I think it could. If Swan realises that...' He wasn't talking to any of us, his eyes focussed on an awful vision: Swan and an army of Savants, increasing geometrically.

'Jesus!' I hissed. 'They're coming out of the diner!'

I started to scrunch down in the booth, then realised how much more conspicuous that would make me look, then realised that if I was scrunched down Swan wouldn't be able to see me through the traffic. The phone cord pulled tight as I crumpled into a hunched heap on the floor of the booth.

'Chick!' the Doctor yelled in my ear. 'What's going on!'

I caught a glimpse of Swan and Luis. Instead of going to Swan's car, they were heading across the parking lot.

'You'll love this,' I told the Doctor. 'Guess what's next door to the diner.'

And what could be simpler than walking into the bank together, filling out a withdrawal slip, walking together to the cashier's window, waiting while she fills a suitcase for you with hundred dollar bills, walking out of the bank, and driving off into the sunset? Why drive home, when you can go anywhere, have anything, do anything – if only you can think of it?

One

I didn't dare go back to my car in the diner's parking lot, not now. I didn't want to be there when Swan came out of that bank. She might have noticed that my car was still there – that would have made her suspicious for sure. Even if she hadn't she might just decide to do something to me, just because she could.

I called a taxi – not an easy thing to do when you're hunched down in a phone booth, trying to look inconspicuous (and failing mightily, judging by the stares of passers-by). I lurked in a shop doorway until my ride arrived. I hadn't seen Swan again, which hopefully meant she hadn't seen me.

Happily, the taxi driver wasn't a talkative one. I sat in the back with my eyes closed, leaning on the window, my face cupped in my hand. I felt as though I had run a marathon. It wasn't the cumulative sleeplessness and stress of the last few days; that was nothing new. It wasn't the abrupt end to my career in Washington. All of that fell away in comparison with that single encounter with Swan. I could not get the texture of the plastic tablecloth out of my mind. Its glossy red and white checks loomed in my vision for the whole journey back to my flat.

I had hoped for an undisturbed half an hour so I could pack my essentials. But the kids were there, fretting on the couch.

'You look terrible,' said Peri.

'Thanks,' I said. 'Where's the Doctor?'

'He's gone to stop her,' said Bob. 'He ordered us to stay here.

He said he could resist the Savant's effects on the brain, at least for a few moments. Long enough to use the Eridani device to switch Luis off. He said he could.'

I couldn't see why the Doctor would think his brain was any less vulnerable than any other human being's. It was probably just a bit of bullshit to keep his young friends out of harm's way.

'I had kind of hoped he had hooked up with you,' said Peri. Her arms were folded tight. 'He shouldn't be out there by himself.'

'He can handle himself,' I said.

'He does stupid things!' Peri almost shouted. 'He gets into the most terrible trouble. He always acts like he's invulnerable. He thinks he can shout his way out of anything.' She was miserable, scalp and stomach tight as nooses, looking like she was waiting for a loved one to come out of surgery. She paced the room, straightening up bits of my mess. 'When he said I should stay, this time I didn't even try and argue with him. I just sat down and let him go. Why am I here? I ought to be with him.'

Bob said, 'He knew what he was doing when he told us to stay.'

Peri didn't hear him. 'I want to be here. No, that's not right.' Something was dawning in her face. 'I don't want to be here. This is all wrong. I want to be wherever the Doctor is. Wherever he goes.'

'You know something?' said Bob. 'I *don't* want to be wherever he is right now.' He hunched his shoulders in shame. 'That sounds terrible.'

'Be fair on yourself,' said Peri. 'There are some things the Doctor can do that we just can't.' Bob gave her a pointed look.

Peri flopped down on the sofa. 'He still needs somebody to look after him. He doesn't have *anybody*. No family. Sometimes we visit friends of his, but we never stay long. But I *like* him.

And he likes me, and... I don't know. I just ought to be there.'

'I don't get it,' said Bob. 'You two fight all the time. Why do you even want to stay together?'

Peri's voice grew small. 'There was a time when he got really, really sick, and I had no idea what to do. I should have made him get help, but I just panicked. I guess in a way I'm still making that up to him.'

Bob said, 'Look at it this way. Look at it this way. If something does happen, you're safe here. You can stay. We'll call your folks.'

Peri gave him the look of death. Bob wilted, not sure what he'd said wrong. But he was right: she had not found herself stranded on a mountainside in a blizzard, or moneyless in a many-tongued city. If the Doctor didn't come back, the decision about whether or not to leave him had been taken away from her.

I sat in my bedroom next to two full suitcases, smoking and waiting. Waiting and smoking. There was half a sock hanging out of one of the cases. I flipped open the lid, stuffed it back inside, and slammed it shut again.

There was a bunch of stuff in the apartment. I'd give Trina a call, ask her to ship a few things to me wherever I ended up. She could have the rest, or give it to charity, or just let the landlord throw it all out, I didn't care. I had everything I needed in those two suitcases.

Hmm. Maybe Trina wasn't a good idea. I'd call Sally instead.

Peri, pacing the apartment, came in to see what I was doing. I snuck a peek at myself in the full-length mirror behind the door and combed my fingers through my hair. Now I looked dashing instead of just rumpled. Not that it mattered any more. 'I'm sorry you lost your job,' she said.

'Oh, I haven't lost it, exactly,' I said. 'If I talk to my editor, I can work this out. He's not real broadminded, but we get on well and he likes my work.'

'Well, that's good.'

'Except that he'll tell everyone in the whole office.' I stabbed the cigarette out viciously in the ashtray. 'He doesn't like secrets. He doesn't think it's fair to keep secrets. When he found out some guy in the mail room was a faggot, he made sure everyone from the janitor to the publisher knew about it.'

'That's really mean,' Peri said.

'I guess it saves him the trouble of having to fire people.' I said. 'I can't stand the thought of a lot of self-appointed experts trying to tell me I'm just a frustrated lesbian. Don't you worry about me, young miss. I'm going to write a book about all of this. It's about time I got my Pulitzer.'

'We were really worried about you,' Peri said. 'After you called from the diner. The Doctor said he wasn't sure if you'd be coming back.'

'That's sweet,' I said. (What she was actually saying was she still thought I was OK.) 'It was bloody creepy. Even as I was walking out of there, I was wondering if Swan had somehow given me a *command* to walk out. You know, I gave the waitress back the hundred bucks on my way out the door.' Peri gave me a pleased smile. 'Yeah, but was it really my idea? Or did Swan make Luis make me?' I took a long drag on a fresh cigarette and offered it to her, but she shook her head. 'Even now I feel hollow. There's no way to know if I'm me, or just acting like a robot.'

Peri said, 'Robots wouldn't – but if you had been affected, we'd know. You'd have that faraway look. All that confusion.'

'How do I even know we're having this conversation?' I blew out a cloud. 'I'll go nuts just wondering about it. I'm sure you're right.'

'Chick,' said Peri. 'Can I talk to you about, you know?'

I half wanted her to get out of there and half wanted to keep looking cool about the whole thing. 'Sure,' I said, fumbling for another smoke.

Peri gathered up her courage and said, 'When did you, uh, decide?'

'Found out for sure when I was fifteen,' I said. 'But I always knew. My mom and dad had been raising me wrong all those years.'

'But you, uh, you've got a girl's body, haven't you?'

'I'm a girl the same way you're a blonde,' I said. 'Only on the outside. Inside I have an X and a Y chromosome, same as any guy. But something went wrong, so my body doesn't respond to male hormones the way it should. My parents spent a small fortune on the tests, and then they wouldn't accept the results. They had brought me up as a girl.'

'You could have kept on being a girl,' said Peri.

'Yeah, but I'm *not*,' I snapped. 'Never was.' Now I'd hurt her feelings. I blew out a long cloud of smoke. 'What makes you a girl?' I asked.

Peri had to think about that one. The question isn't as simple as it sounds. 'I can have babies,' she said at last.

'I can't,' I said. 'No womb.'

'Oh... I guess I see. You know, it's funny. I'm sort of surrounded. The Doctor also –' she stopped short, colour jumping into her cheeks. 'Uh, never mind.'

'It's OK. You can tell me,' I said. I am a very wicked fellow; we were still on the record, until she told me that we weren't.

But Peri just shook her head, scrabbling around for a change of subject. 'What about your girlfriends?' she blurted.

'What about 'em?'

'Well, do they know?'

'I've never had any complaints.' She stared. I gave her my best dirty grin and took a long, slow drag on that ciggie.

'Uh,' said Peri.

'Relax,' I said. 'You're not my type.'

Two

The Doctor's entire plan could have been scuppered by his inability to imitate a decent American accent. Perhaps that's one reason he left Peri behind: from time to time he would tease her with an imitation of her voice, and she knew perfectly well what he sounded like.

When he called Swan, he spoke in his normal voice. She was returning to her car with her ill-gotten loot when she heard a phone ringing. It took her only a few moments to spot the one across the street. An empty payphone booth, ringing and ringing. It was practically calling her name.

She got in her car, carefully settling Luis into the passenger seat, and drove across the road to the other parking lot. The phone was still ringing when she reached the booth.

'Well?' she said.

'Swan,' said the Doctor. 'I have a device which will shut Luis down the same way it shut down your idiot savant. Indicate that you understand me.'

'You son of a bitch,' said Swan. 'If you come anywhere near either of us, I'll have Luis turn you into a frigging zombie. Do *you* understand *me*?'

'I'm already near you,' said the Doctor. 'Nearer than you realise. I only need a moment to operate the device. And then this spree of yours will be at an end.'

'You'll kill him,' said Swan. 'The way you killed the "idiot savant." Are you a murderer?'

'Listen very carefully,' said the Doctor. 'The Savant was programmed to reproduce itself. Its offspring would have known everything it had learnt. That program has been passed on to Luis.'

'And you're telling me this because...?'

'Luis will lay his eggs in the minds of other human beings,' said the Doctor. 'It's already begun. *Every* person you have manipulated now has a miniature copy of the Savant inside their skull, waiting to be activated. Every person who has come into contact with it in any way – there must be hundreds of people in the town of Ritchie alone. That's why they become so distant and confused – a large part of their mental activity is taken up by it, even in a dormant state. Just as the Savant was able to adapt itself to the network, it has adapted itself to human brains. Indicate –'

'– I understand,' said Swan. 'I understand you want to kill Luis. You know I can't let you do that.'

'Swan,' hissed the Doctor, 'this is no longer about your petty ambitions. It's about the safety and sanity of the entire human race. Each of those affected people will spread the infection to others. Within a few weeks, every person in the world could be affected. Billions of ticking time bombs. Just waiting for the Eridani to arrive and take advantage of them. I have no choice but to shut Luis down.'

'Screw you!' Swan screamed like a teenager. In the next moment her voice was back under control. 'I won't let you hurt him.'

'I won't have to hurt him if you'll only let me help you. We only need to isolate him. I may even be able to reverse some of the brain damage. The Eridani never intended to invade this world. They'll be keen to avoid an interplanetary incident.'

Behind the Doctor, Peri and Bob were wincing. But Swan took him at his word.

'Give me one good reason I should trust you,' she said.

'Good grief, woman,' shouted the Doctor, 'Haven't I made the picture clear enough for you? Do I have to describe in detail an entire world of zombies? A whole human race turned into dummy terminals for an alien power?'

'Just give me one reason why *I* should trust *you*,' said Swan desperately.

'I can't,' said the Doctor. 'That's a leap you're going to have to make yourself.'

Swan hung up.

This time, Washington's notorious traffic was on our side. As Swan was driving south to her home in Virginia, she became part of a queue of backed-up cars waiting to cross the Cabin John Bridge.[7] This was quite normal, but for a woman who's just robbed a bank, it was more than a little annoying. She didn't want any trouble, she just wanted to get home and get on with her new and satisfying life.

She switched on her police scanner, twiddling the dial up and down, hoping for news on the delay. And amongst the chatter, she heard her numberplate being read out.

She slammed on the brakes, causing the car behind her to kiss her bumper, and tuned back in.

There it was again. One officer telling another to keep an eye out for her vehicle, believed to be heading south on the Beltway. The other officer said they were stopping cars at the Cabin John Bridge.

She had slipped up somewhere. She had been so confident about her perfect crime that she had left some fingerprint behind, left some witness to tell the tale.

---

[7] Later renamed the American Legion Memorial Bridge

Chick Peters. That little faggot. Or bulldyke, or whatever it was. Swan had scared the man-woman thing so badly that she just about pissed in her pants. But she or he or it hadn't taken the hint. Peters had told the Doctor where Swan was and what she was doing, and one of them had told the police.

Swan would use Luis to kill both of them. Mash their brains between her fingers like a handful of mince.

That would have to keep. For now, she had two problems: the police, and the Doctor, who was out there somewhere in the traffic jam, looking for her. He was the real threat. She just needed a few minutes' peace, out of the pressure, to decide what to do.

Swan took exit 15 onto the George Washington Parkway, safely on the Maryland side of the bridge. The Parkway is divided, with no turnoffs, just exits. She already had a plan: take the ramp to Carderock, double back onto the parkway, heading south-east past the Beltway towards DC. She could get across the river on the Chain Bridge and be safely home in under an hour.

The Travco was waiting for her at the top of the Carderock ramp.

Her first urge was to ram it. Just aim the car at the side of the campervan and smash into it in a white blaze. She took a deep breath and let the station wagon roll to a stop on the side of the parkway, maybe fifty yards behind it.

'What's your range, Doctor?' she growled. She had the handgun in the pocket of her jacket and the shotgun in the back seat. And she had Luis. The Doctor must have expected her to fly past him on the parkway, giving him a few instants in which to activate his device and deactivate Luis. He had hoped to surprise her, because without that, he was hopelessly outweaponed.

254

He knew it. The Travco climbed out into the thin stream of traffic, running for it.

Swan had two choices at this point: she could stick to her original plan and head back to the south-east, or she could follow the Doctor and press her advantage.

It had to be now. As long as he was out there, she and Luis would never be safe. He was the only thing that could put a dent in her new life. The only obstacle left to overcome.

Swan pulled out and accelerated. She savoured the mental image of what would happen when they caught him up – the Travco suddenly losing control, careening off the road as its driver lost the mental capacity to steer.

Luis was infuriatingly calm and blank in his seat. She wanted to hit him. 'If you see the Doctor,' she growled, 'if you even *sense* him, I want you to drop him where he stands. Blow his brains out. Kill him. Any way you can. Do you understand?'

Luis just blinked slowly, but she knew her instruction had gone in. The Savant would be at least as determined to protect itself as she was.

The Doctor managed to keep ahead of her, driving wildly, weaving the dinosaur bulk of the campervan around the few cars on the road. Swan wanted to slam the accelerator to the floor, but something kept stopping her. It took her a few minutes to realise she didn't dare risk Luis's life: the urge to protect the Savant was too powerful. She swore and slapped the steering wheel. The Doctor had no such limitation, and he was getting away from them, even in that monstrosity.

The Parkway narrowed to two lanes, and then curved sharply. The Doctor turned hard left onto Macarthur Boulevard, without slowing down, almost side-swiping a VW Bug. He stayed on the road, accelerating away, Swan furiously trying to drive faster and failing. The Travco rounded a corner and was suddenly gone from sight. He was winning this video game. Swan wove down the hairpin turns as fast as she dared. She was aware they were heading back towards the water. But the Doctor had no plan that she could see: he was just frantically trying to put distance between them.

She rounded another sharp turn and slammed on the brakes. The Travco was stopped right across the road. There was a car backed up behind it, the driver already out and pulling open the Travco's doors. There was nobody inside.

Where was he? Hiding amongst the trees? She looked around, frantically. But the trees were naked, standing like narrow arms with a thousand fingers, nothing but open space between them. He'd stand out like a crow on snow if he was there.

She had to find him and kill him, right now, right this minute. The question was, what range was safe? And how far could the Doctor's device reach – less than fifty yards, but how much less?

'Luis,' she said, 'that man in the green shirt standing beside the campervan. I want him to come here.'

Luis turned his attention to the man, who was pacing up and down beside the open door of the Travco. The man's irritated walk didn't change. He slapped his hand against the wall of the vehicle.

Then Luis had a very short range indeed. Swan let the car roll forwards until she was within shouting distance of the man. 'Did you see the driver?' she called out.

The man pointed down the road, past the Travco. 'He took off like a rabbit out of a box,' he said. 'The law must be after him, that's all I can say.'

Swan backed up, aimed her car at the trees, and roared around the Travco, her tyres spitting half-frozen mud. She shot past a guard in a little white tollbooth, leaving him gaping.

'Up ahead,' said Luis.

Swan nearly crashed into a tree. She swung the wheel and screeched to a halt in an empty parking lot.

'What did you say?'

Luis's voice was low and gravely, as though he hadn't used it for years. 'Up ahead,' he murmured.

He *could* sense the Doctor. Not close enough to kill, or he would have done it instantly. Oh – perhaps Luis was sensing the Doctor's lethal device. One piece of technology picking up vibrations from its kin.

They were in Great Falls Park, and they had run out of road. 'Get out,' she told Luis, shutting off the engine. She grabbed the shotgun out of the back seat. The parking lot was next to a visitor's centre in an old tavern, and a canal that ran parallel to the Potomac River. 'In the house? Luis, is he in the house?'

Luis shook his head. He pointed vaguely across the canal, towards the river.

Swan took Luis by the hand and led him over the wooden bridge to the towpath on the other side. Water roared through the lock beneath their feet. 'He's trying to lead us away from other people,' she muttered. Their boots made a plasticky crunch on snow and red gravel. 'Very heroic. Remember, the moment you can do it, kill him.'

Her head swung from side to side, waiting for the Doctor to spring out from somewhere – even from the sluggish water of the canal. A pair of geese ran out of their way. UNSAFE ICE, warned a sign. A guy riding a bike glanced at them and sped away in panic.

Now Luis was leading her, his cool fingers still intertwined with hers. She understood now that there was nothing left of her friend; she was being pulled along by an alien, not a human. A machine built out of the ruins of Luis's brain, using his neurons for scrap. There were so many things she needed to think about. What the Doctor had told her, about the eggs. About whoever had come up with this technology in the first place. About what Luis was doing to her mind, to her brain. But she couldn't think about any of it now. They had to get rid of the Doctor. And then they would go somewhere quiet, and she would be able to sort it all out.

A side path split away from the towpath. Luis didn't hesitate, turning onto a wooden bridge that crossed the first gush of the Potomac. He stopped partway across, turning his head slowly, like someone moving the aerial on top of a TV. Maybe the rocks were getting in the way: everything here was stone, slashed and sliced and shattered by the water. It seethed beneath the bridge in patterns as complex as the static on a screen, forming miniature whirlpools, little channels, swirling backwaters.

Suddenly Luis was moving again. The bridge became a raised walkway across an island of grey rocks and grey trees. There was no-one here. Swan wanted to stand still for a moment, to sit down and rest. Everything was lit up with winter sunshine, fresh and cold and clear, as though frozen in crystal. A single raptor drifted overhead, black wings spread wide. It folded itself into a tree as they ran by.

There was a second bridge, this time over a rocky gully where only a trickle ran through. 'Stop,' said Swan quietly. Luis stopped in his tracks, staring intently up ahead.

'Wait here for one minute,' she murmured. 'Then follow me.'

She went forward. How far did the wooden trail lead? She could hear furious white noise ahead, the sound of the Great Falls. The Doctor was running out of dry land.

The trail ran out, suddenly, turning into a wide wooden platform on the edge of a cliff. There was a huge rock in the centre. Swan edged forward in case the Doctor might be crouching behind it, keeping the shotgun at the ready. But there was no-one here. Swan barely glanced at the Falls themselves, a gorge a hundred feet wide, a great flat expanse of rock being demolished by violent water.

He must have left the trail. The only cover was the boardwalk; everything else was raw trees and rocks tumbled like dice. But if he was down there, hidden by the wood, he couldn't see her. Come out, come out, wherever you are.

Luis was crossing the bridge behind her. She decided to move things along. She pointed the shotgun down at the planks and pulled the trigger.

Wooden shrapnel and smoke exploded up around her. She dodged back, cursing, blinded for a moment by a rain of splinters. She batted them out of her face with her gloves.

The Doctor appeared from beneath the platform on the far side. *He held a ball of plastic in his hand.* He stared at her: where was Luis? Why weren't they together? In that split-second, Swan knew she had the drop on him. Behind her, Luis stepped up onto the platform.

Look Ma – top of the food chain!

'*Do it,*' screamed Swan, but Luis already was.

It was like sticking your thumb into the torn wires at the back of an electric kettle. It was like jamming your head inside a bell and then striking it as hard as you could. It was like putting on headphones and pressing 'play' without realising the volume is turned all the way up. It was the feeling of the circuitry printed inside your head getting ready to shift and change.

There was a crucial instant, like the moment of unbalance on a tightrope, when the Doctor was about to fall. Mentally flailing for anything to grab onto, *anything* to focus on, anything to deflect the process that was taking root inside his skull. The more he tried to focus, to remember what he was supposed to do, the more it seemed to feed energy to that process. The roar of the falls and the winter sunlight grew into a blur like gravel in the eyes and ears.

He had fallen to his knees on the rocks, and in front of him were the contents of his pockets: coins and trinkets, transistors and toys. On a piece of paper there was a design drawn, its lines and curves carefully marked out in a pattern of geometric relationships and symbols. It was Bob's occult sigil, the diagram he had given the Doctor to protect him from whatever cosmic forces Swan might be able to yield.

And bless you, Bob, bless you, it didn't mean a thing.

In that split-second of distracting nonsense, the Doctor's thumb pressed into the trigger of the device.

120

We waited for hours. Bob and Peri waited to see what was going to become of their lives. I waited to see how my book was going to end.

And then the door opened. The Doctor came through. His black suit was dusty and damp and one of the knees was torn. Otherwise, he looked entirely undamaged.

'Doctor!' shouted Bob. The Doctor gave a little bow.

'You could have called!' said Peri, trying hard not to burst into tears.

'How do we know it's him?' I said.

The Doctor raised an eyebrow at me. 'Do I strike you as the somnambulistic victim of neural reprogramming?'

Peri hugged him. 'You are OK, aren't you?'

The Doctor nodded. He looked tired, but satisfied, like someone returning from a long day's good work.

Bob said, 'What about Swan? And Luis? What about the Savant? Is the Earth safe? What happened?'

'Well,' said the Doctor, 'I'll tell you.'

Mondy had continued monitoring Swan's calls the whole time. He had overheard me setting up the meeting in the diner, and passed it on to the Doctor. The moment the Doctor was finished at Swan's house, he put the pedal to the metal to try to catch us up. He knew the number of the payphone across the street because he'd been there five minutes ago. When he called me and then Swan at the payphone, he was just around the corner.

The police radio we had 'borrowed' let him broadcast a phony message about the roadblock on the bridge. (In fact, the slow traffic was quite normal.) He had hoped to channel Swan's movements until she was as isolated as possible – it hadn't been his plan to end up in a tourist attraction. But at least, in the depths of winter, there hadn't been that many people around.

The Doctor admitted, with a mixture of humility and grouch, that he had overestimated his own ability to withstand the Savant's mental onslaught. 'I deal with brainwashing and other such nonsense all the time,' he said, with a dismissive wave of his hand. 'This was different. It was far more invasive, far more physical. The more I fought, the more I *thought*, the more it was able to turn my own mind against me. Bob's diagram bought me a moment of grace. For just an instant, I wasn't thinking at all.' Bob looked equal parts chuffed and puzzled, but he was happy to accept his role in saving the day.

Peri kept giving the Doctor hugs. She even made a cup of tea and brought it to him, while they both joked about it. She looked more relaxed than she had since I had first met her, and not only because the crisis was over: she had made up her mind about where she wanted to be.

We saw Mr Ghislain once more. The Doctor pulled some strings to get us access to the rest home where Swan and Luis had been placed for observation, and perhaps a few more so that I could come along for the visit. I don't know what strings he pulled to allow Mr Ghislain to bring his parrot.

I don't know for sure who Ghislain or the Eridani really were. I prefer my initial guess: Russian agents whose technology – a supercomputer with organic components, possibly intended for space exploration – had got loose, perhaps after a deal with a double agent went sour.

Swan and Luis had been moved to a little patients' lounge for our visit. They sat side by side on a faded brown sofa, next to a shelf full of tattered paperbacks and National Geographics. They were a pair: both quite relaxed – none of the stiffness of a victim of catatonia – both staring at nothing. Waiting for input, for instructions.

Mr Ghislain sat before them for a long time, consulting a device he held in his lap. His parrot perched inside its cage on top of the bookcase.

At last he said, 'Events have repeated themselves. At the moment you sent the interrupt signal to the Savant structures inside Mr Perez, it acted in self-defence by creating another copy of itself.'

'I should have realised that would happen,' said the Doctor. 'Luis copied himself – copied the Savant – into Swan.'

Ghislain said, 'However, the interrupt signal then shut down the new Savant as well. Evidently it was unable to copy itself to your mind.'

The Doctor admitted, 'If I hadn't been distracted at the crucial moment by Bob's bit of scribble, I'd be sitting on that sofa beside them.'

'Is there hope for them?' I asked.

'We may be able to reverse some of the changes to their neural pathways,' said Ghislain. 'But I regret neither one will be restored to their original state. I propose you permit me to take them to our ship.'

'No,' said the Doctor.

'They can no longer function in this society. We offer to care for them.'

'And do a little experimentation at the same time? No,

Ghislain. Do what you can for them, but they're not leaving Earth.'

'The Eridani regret this outcome.'

'Regret it? A successful test of your new weapon?' snapped the Doctor. Ghislain looked at him placidly. 'The "supercomputer" these devices combined to create. It was a cuckoo's egg all along – designed to infiltrate a society, no matter what technological level it might have achieved. It could adapt itself to any network, from a highly advanced computerised net to organic brain structures. Create a version of itself for any environment, and then spread itself like so much viral payload.'

'It is truthful that the slow package was unintended for Earth,' said Ghislain. His face was blank as ever, but his grammar was breaking down in the face of the Doctor's onslaught. I thought of Operation Sea-Spray, a biological warfare experiment in the early fifties. The Army sent aloft a bunch of balloons carrying a supposedly harmless bacterium, *Serratia*, then burst them over the Bay Area. That harmless little bug lodged itself in lungs throughout the city, causing a steep rise in pneumonia.

'Intended for a rebellious colony? Or any medium-tech civilisation that would gratefully accept your "gift"?' The Doctor planted his hands on his hips and loomed over Ghislain. 'I expect you not only to do your best to restore the minds of these people, but of all the people touched by your technology. Do you understand?'

I don't know what power the Doctor had over the 'Eridani': presumably he had threatened to expose them. But they seemed happy enough to do as they were told. And why not? Each victim they examined would render more valuable data on their trial.

The Doctor arranged for Ghislain (and his parrot) to visit

Ritchie, and went along with them to keep an eye on things. Ghislain brought yet another device, one that could unpick the mental knots left behind in the unknowing victims, snipping out the time bomb of hundreds of Savant programs nestled in nervous tissue, waiting to hatch.

They walked the streets for a day and a half, letting the device pick out men and women and children who had been affected, getting close enough to them to let it do the rest of its work. Ritchie's zombies knew no more about the cure than they did about falling ill. It wasn't perfect; the Doctor suspected a lot of people would be left with small, odd gaps in their memories, perhaps even occasional, minor speech or concentration difficulties. 'The small but noticeable scars of neurosurgery at a distance,' he said, with a mixture of sadness and sourness. But the job was done; in the end, there were only two people Ghislain couldn't restore to pretty much normal.

Once upon a time there was a young princess who lived by the seashore. And God, her life was dull. She couldn't strap on armour and ride a chariot into battle, like her brothers the princes. She would never be a great king or a master sailor, just a prize to be fought over. She had nothing to do but sit in a field near the ocean, picking flowers with her ladies-in-waiting. Until one day they were approached by a huge white bull. The young women were badly frightened, but the princess knew she had found her ship, her chariot. She climbed on the back of that bull, ready to ride.

Maybe that's how the story goes.

So where are they now?

Bob's out there riding the new frontier. 'Power,' he explains, 'is something you can borrow. The alchemists knew it. The first cavemen who stuck horns on their heads were trying to borrow the power of the animals.' He knows from first-hand experience as sysop that the law isn't interested in people breaking into computers; that's fantasy land. They want real break-ins to investigate. All that computing power is there for the taking.

So Bob skips from system to system inside the growing network. There's a chart on the wall of his office; every few weeks he finds a new computer that's been caught in that giant fisherman's net. He's still his dad's good little boy, kind of: he never breaks anything and he never takes anything. He just travels, late at night when no-one's using the machines, following the route traced out by the blinking cursor, mapping the human race's brave new world. Like Dean Moriarty, he only steals cars to take joyrides. To him, the network is like a single, huge computer.

Somewhere in safekeeping – he wouldn't tell me where – he has the Eridani's remote control device. The Doctor handed it over to him, he said, in case the Eridani ever decide to visit Earth again. One day Bob hopes to be a sysop for NASA.

Mondy is now working somewhere in the telco. Heaven help us.

You know where Swan eventually ended up. She vanished from the rest home about a month after the Doctor and I paid our visit. The contacts I now have at the theme restaurant helped me track her down at the Bainbridge Hospital. I've been officially denied permission to visit her three times. Luis managed to escape the CIA's attentions and is being cared for by his family in Puebla. I'm told they both have lucid periods, as though waking up out of a long sleep; they can speak and write and seem quite normal, if a little slow and distant. On the anniversary of our last meeting, I ordered some flowers for both of them, over the net.

* * *

Peri had been ready to give up the ride and wade back to shore. But somewhere along the way, she changed her mind. Maybe it happened all at once when she paced my apartment, knowing she ought to be by his side; maybe she got there in a lot of little steps. In any case, I reckon she's going to keep holding on loosely.

The day she and the Doctor left, I visited them at the hotel. For the first time, I got to see the Doctor in his 'ordinary' clothes. The black suit was gone. Instead, he was wearing the coat I had glimpsed in the hotel closet – an old-fashioned coat that came down to the tops of his calves, big lapels, big pockets. One lapel was orange and the other was pink, with a Bill the Cat badge pinned to it. All those patches – tartan, red, big blue and white checks – made it look as though it had been repaired over centuries by a dynasty of blind seamstresses.

Somehow I could imagine him trekking through the dust of Nepal or Morocco or even striding up Tottenham Court Road, looking utterly unselfconscious even as the natives stared. Customs officers and government ministers would take him seriously. No-one else could have got away with it. 'What seems extraordinary in one place seems utterly ordinary in another,' he pronounced. 'What's fashionable in one era seems ludicrous in another.'

'Yeah, and disco's gonna make a comeback,' I said. He just raised an eyebrow at me.

I waited with him and Peri in the lobby, while the concierge ordered them a taxi to take them back to their boat. They looked comfortable together, standing closer than friends but not as close as a couple. When a bellhop stared at the Doctor's coat, Peri first looked down in embarrassment, then stared back until the bellhop hurried on his way.

They were both vague about where they were going next. 'So

are you gonna write a book about us?' said Peri, changing the subject.

'Oh, yeah,' I said. 'I'm not getting much out of east-coast journalism. I think I'll write me a bestseller and then hang up my typewriter for a while.'

'Will you put *everything* in it?' she said.

'Everything.' Peri looked at the Doctor, a little panicked. 'Don't worry. Names will be changed to protect the innocent.'

'Very well,' said the Doctor.

Peri touched my elbow, shyly. 'You're gonna be OK?'

'Thanks for your concern, little lady.' I pecked her on the forehead, making her blush. The taxi was pulling up in front of us. 'I'm more worried about where your life is going to lead you. You take care of each other, now.'

I looked at the Doctor over the roof of the taxi. 'You're never gonna tell me *everything*, are you?' He just shook his head, with a wicked smile. 'Oh well. Can't blame a guy for trying.'

And me?

Once the final draft of this manuscript is in the hands of my publishers[8], I'm heading back to the city of Angels. Maybe, from there, it'll be a plane back to Sydney. I'll make up my mind as I go. Maybe I'll even find somewhere I like between one side of America and the other, and stop there for a while. I've bought a little Citröen, in honour of the one I destroyed on my way out of California, all those years ago. I put my typewriter in the trunk, but then thought better of it. By the time I feel like writing again, I'll probably be using a computer to do it.

Will computers of the future have biological components,

---

[8] An Australian, writing an American story for British readers. I pity the poor copy editor who has to cope with my spelling.

maybe modified human brains? It's a nightmarish concept, and yet there must come a point at which the computer can't get any faster without also speeding up the lump of cold porridge that's trying to interface with it. And that, ladies and gentlemen, is us.

Maybe the story goes like this:

The princess cried out as the bull plunged into the ocean, his skin the colour of the foaming surf that surged around him. She was terrified he would drag her beneath the waves. But instead the bull swam in powerful strokes, further and further from the shore, deeper and deeper into the ocean. Soon the shore behind was just a shape, then a line, and then it was lost to her.

The sea was rough, but the bull's strong swimming kept them safely afloat. Slowly the princess let go of her frightened grip on the bull's neck. She eased herself up until she was sitting, her knees holding his muscular back in an easy grasp. Soon she was riding the bull without difficulty, her eyes fixed on the blue curve of the horizon, eager to see what would emerge from the waves.

'Well, what do you know,' said the princess. 'I was a cowboy all along.'

Acknowledgements

CHICK PETERS would like to thank his interview subjects, especially Peri, the Doctor, and Ian Mond, for giving so much of their time to talk to him.

KATE ORMAN would like to thank Nicola Bryant, Mark Bernay and Evan Doorbell, the denizens of alt.folklore.computers, Kyla Ward, Lloyd Rose, Lance Parkin, Greg McElhatton, the Infinitas writers' group, Alryssa and Tom Kelly, Mum and Dad for the loan of the loft, and Geoff Wessel for FLEX YOUR HEAD. And, as always, her busy bee Jon, without whose help this book simply could not have been written. Forgive me, all of you, for all the good advice you gave which I didn't take.

About the Author

CHICK PETERS lives in Tiburon with his wife Sally, three kids, and two cats.

KATE ORMAN is the granddaughter of Jack Warren Orman (1916–2001), from whom she ultimately inherited a great part of her sense of humour and turn of phrase. She has written or co-written eleven *Doctor Who* novels; her short stories have appeared in *Interzone* and *Realms of Fantasy*. Kate lives in Sydney, Australia, with her husband and co-author Jonathan Blum. You can visit their home on the Internet at http://www.zip.com.au/~korman/.

BBC DOCTOR WHO BOOKS

'EIGHTH DOCTOR' RANGE

THE CITY OF THE DEAD by Lloyd Rose
ISBN 0 563 53839 2
GRIMM REALITY by Simon Bucher-Jones and Kelly Hale
ISBN 0 563 53841 4
THE ADVENTURESS OF HENRIETTA STREET
by Lawrence Miles
ISBN 0 563 53842 2
MAD DOGS AND ENGLISHMEN by Paul Magrs
ISBN 0 563 53845 7
HOPE by Mark Clapham
ISBN 0 563 53846 5
ANACHROPHOBIA by Jonathan Morris
ISBN 0 563 53847 3
TRADING FUTURES by Lance Parkin
ISBN 0 563 53848 1
THE BOOK OF THE STILL by Paul Ebbs
ISBN 0 563 53851 1
THE CROOKED WORLD by Steve Lyons
ISBN 0 563 53856 2
HISTORY 101 by Mags L Halliday
ISBN 0 563 53854 6
CAMERA OBSCURA by Lloyd Rose
ISBN 0 563 53857 0
TIME ZERO by Justin Richards
ISBN 0 563 53866 X
THE INFINITY RACE by Simon Messingham
ISBN 0 563 53863 5
THE DOMINO EFFECT by David Bishop
ISBN 0 563 53869 4

'PAST DOCTOR' RANGE

THE DEVIL GOBLINS FROM NEPTUNE
by Keith Topping and Martin Day
ISBN 0 563 40564 3
THE MURDER GAME by Steve Lyons
ISBN 0 563 40565 1
THE ULTIMATE TREASURE by Christopher Bulis
ISBN 0 563 40571 6
BUSINESS UNUSUAL by Gary Russell
ISBN 0 563 40575 9
ILLEGAL ALIEN by Mike Tucker and Robert Perry
ISBN 0 563 40570 8
THE ROUNDHEADS by Mark Gatiss
ISBN 0 563 40576 7
THE FACE OF THE ENEMY by David A. McIntee
ISBN 0 563 40580 5
EYE OF HEAVEN by Jim Mortimore
ISBN 0 563 40567 8
THE WITCH HUNTERS by Steve Lyons
ISBN 0 563 40579 1
THE HOLLOW MEN by Keith Topping and Martin Day
ISBN 0 563 40582 1
CATASTROPHEA by Terrance Dicks
ISBN 0 563 40584 8
MISSION: IMPRACTICAL by David A. McIntee
ISBN 0 563 40592 9
ZETA MAJOR by Simon Messingham
ISBN 0 563 40597 X
DREAMS OF EMPIRE by Justin Richards
ISBN 0 563 40598 8
LAST MAN RUNNING by Chris Boucher
ISBN 0 563 40594 5
MATRIX by Robert Perry and Mike Tucker
ISBN 0 563 40596 1

THE INFINITY DOCTORS by Lance Parkin
ISBN 0 563 40591 0
SALVATION by Steve Lyons
ISBN 0 563 55566 1

THE WAGES OF SIN by David A. McIntee
ISBN 0 563 55567 X
DEEP BLUE by Mark Morris
ISBN 0 563 55571 8
PLAYERS by Terrance Dicks
ISBN 0 563 55573 4
MILLENNIUM SHOCK by Justin Richards
ISBN 0 563 55586 6
STORM HARVEST by Robert Perry and Mike Tucker
ISBN 0 563 55577 7
THE FINAL SANCTION by Steve Lyons
ISBN 0 563 55584 X
CITY AT WORLD'S END by Christopher Bulis
ISBN 0 563 55579 3
DIVIDED LOYALTIES by Gary Russell
ISBN 0 563 55578 5
CORPSE MARKER by Chris Boucher
ISBN 0 563 55575 0
LAST OF THE GADERENE by Mark Gatiss
ISBN 0 563 55587 4
TOMB OF VALDEMAR by Simon Messingham
ISBN 0 563 55591 2
VERDIGRIS by Paul Magrs
ISBN 0 563 55592 0
GRAVE MATTER by Justin Richards
ISBN 0 563 55598 X
HEART OF TARDIS by Dave Stone
ISBN 0 563 55596 3
PRIME TIME by Mike Tucker
ISBN 0 563 55597 1

IMPERIAL MOON by Christopher Bulis
ISBN 0 563 53801 5
FESTIVAL OF DEATH by Jonathan Morris
ISBN 0 563 53803 1
INDEPENDENCE DAY by Peter Darvill-Evans
ISBN 0 563 53804 X
KING OF TERROR by Keith Topping
ISBN 0 563 53802 3
QUANTUM ARCHANGEL by Craig Hinton
ISBN 0 563 53824 4
BUNKER SOLDIERS by Martin Day
ISBN 0 563 53819 8
RAGS by Mick Lewis
ISBN 0 563 53826 0
THE SHADOW IN THE GLASS
by Justin Richards and Stephen Cole
ISBN 0 563 53838 4
ASYLUM by Peter Darvill-Evans
ISBN 0 563 53833 3
SUPERIOR BEINGS by Nick Walters
ISBN 0 563 53830 9
BYZANTIUM! by Keith Topping
ISBN 0 563 53836 8
BULLET TIME by David A McIntee
ISBN 0 563 53834 1
PSI-ENCE FICTION by Chris Boucher
ISBN 0 563 53814 7
DYING IN THE SUN by Jon de Burgh Miller
ISBN 0 563 53840 6
INSTRUMENTS OF DARKNESS by Gary Russell
ISBN 0 563 53828 7
RELATIVE DEMENTIAS by Mark Michalowski
ISBN 0 563 53844 9
DRIFT by Simon A Forward
ISBN 0 563 53843 0

PALACE OF THE RED SUN by Christopher Bulis
ISBN 0 563 53849 X
AMORALITY TALE by David Bishop
ISBN 0 563 53850 3
WARMONGER by Terrance Dicks
ISBN 0 563 53852 X
TEN LITTLE ALIENS by Stephen Cole
ISBN 0 563 53853 8
COMBAT ROCK by Mick Lewis
ISBN 0 563 53855 4
THE SUNS OF CARESH by Paul Saint
ISBN 0 563 53858 9
HERITAGE by Dale Smith
ISBN 0 563 53864 3
FEAR OF THE DARK by Trevor Baxendale
ISBN 0 563 53865 1

SHORT STORY COLLECTIONS

SHORT TRIPS ed. Stephen Cole ISBN 0 563 40560 0
MORE SHORT TRIPS ed. Stephen Cole ISBN 0 563 55565 3
SHORT TRIPS AND SIDE STEPS
ed. Stephen Cole and Jacqueline Rayner
ISBN 0 563 55599 8

The Worlds of Doctor Who

March 2003 – Also this month

From BBC Video:
Meglos
by John Flanagan and Andrew McCulloch
Featuring the Fourth Doctor, Romana and K9

From Big Finish Productions:
The Dark Flame
by Trevor Baxendale
Featuring the Seventh Doctor, Ace and Benny

Doctor Who Books Telepress
covers, reviews, news & interviews
http://www.bbc.co.uk/cult/doctorwho/books/
telepress

Coming soon from
BBC *Doctor Who* books:

Reckless Engineering

By Nick Walters
Published April 7th 2003
ISBN 0 563 48603 1
Featuring the Eighth Doctor

'What right do you have to wipe out a whole reality?'

The history of the planet Earth has been splintered, each splinter vying to be the prime reality. But there can only be one true history.

The Doctor has a plan to ensure that the correct version of history prevails – a plan that means breaking every law of Time. But with the Vortex itself on the brink of total collapse, what do mere laws matter?

From the Bristol Riots of 1831 to the ruins of the city in 2003, from a chance encounter between a frustrated poet and Isambard Kingdom Brunel, to a plan to save the human race, the stakes are raised ever higher until reality itself is threatened.